THE FEMALE BREEDERS

MELANIE BOKSTAD HOREV

ALSO BY MELANIE BOKSTAD HOREV

The Female Saga

The Female Breeders

The Female Uprising

The Desert Shadows Saga

Twilight Divide

Desert Shadows

Shifting Sands

The Skies Series

Skyhaven

Grounded (coming soon, 2025)

The Anger Series

Blaze of Anger

Dance of Anger

Bolt of Anger

The Deep Blue Colony Series (young adult)

Deep

Emergence

Revelation

Breaking the Code Series (young adult)

The Architect

In loving memory of Rina Horev and Larry Bokstad. I miss you both terribly.

THE FEMALE BREEDERS

CHAPTER 1

NEEN

NEEN SALVEK WAS tired of waiting. It was insufferable.

It had been weeks since she'd finished her degree, and still the council hadn't notified her about her work assignment.

The sun outside was setting, its tired beams marking the end of another day. Neen looked out across the skyline of High City. The pinkish light from the sunset caught the reflection of the city's central district's gleaming white towers and glass windows. Off in the distance, the Arena Dome shimmered. Its exterior was all glass — a special kind that allowed only those from outside to look in.

Neen's residence was too far away for her to see inside the Dome now, but there were times when she'd walked about the city and wandered by it to see what the males were doing.

She never got too close, of course. Even though none of the males could see out of the one-way glass, she felt uncomfortable getting near. Neen knew her history well. The males were not to be trusted.

Since it was twilight now, the glass of the Dome would

be shifting soon. It was almost time for the evening report. When that time came, the glass would switch to a giant LED screen, and all the screens across the city would broadcast the news.

Three times a day, High City officials would broadcast these reports: sunrise, midday, and sunset. They were never particularly interesting — what news could there be in a city with no real crime, no social ills, no suffering? — but the council insisted on the thrice-daily routine.

Sisterhood. Community. A reminder of how far the world of EVE had come since the dark days before the revolution.

The women of High City, it was believed, needed these reminders. Despite the security of the Dome, women still needed males to breed with. Every month, there would still be intimate contact between them. The citizens of EVE needed to remember the horrors of male dominance; there was no letting one's guard down, even during breeding sessions. As repetitive as these reports were, they were necessary. The survival of the sisterhood depended on it.

Neen didn't need to worry about becoming too attached to a male breeding partner. She was classified at fertility level D, the lowest. Even if she was interested in breeding, she would never be selected. The doctors who ran the breeding program only wanted the women with the most chance for successful insemination and full-term, healthy pregnancy.

Like Ems.

Neen's best friend would be arriving soon from her clan lands. After all, it was almost time for the breeding trials, and Ems would need to watch the males compete in order to make an informed selection.

Neen wasn't sure how she felt about Ems getting designated a breeder. As children, they'd both laughed when their teachers explained the breeding process. It was still quite comical to Neen even now, but she understood the necessity. The genetic processes necessary to develop the clans' specialized traits meant breeding the old-fashioned way.

Scientists had tried to replicate the process in the lab, but the experiments always delivered inferior results. If they wanted to keep the genetic enhancements of each clan intact, then for better or for worse, they needed to breed with the males.

Still, Neen thought the whole thing sounded awkward. She respected the women who had the courage to breed with the males, but she had decided a long time ago that she could never go through with it herself. It wasn't like she had a choice anyways, low breeding class and all.

Ems had been of a similar mind, but perhaps that had changed now. This was the first time Ems had been classified as fertility level A.

Neen missed her. They hadn't seen each other since Ems finished her training early and was assigned to the leadership circle in her clan lands. That was over a year ago. Ems had risen fast since getting her assignment. She had recently been selected clan leader and won the vote by a large majority.

Seeing her friend's success made Neen even more restless. Her classes at the university never really challenged her, her internship work had been monotonous, and now that she had graduated, all this waiting for an assignment was driving her crazy.

It insulted her too. Hadn't she been at the top of her class as a Triverser? Hadn't she finished her training faster than anyone except her Sixter friend Ems?

It was ridiculous that the high council hadn't chosen an assignment for her yet.

Wandering around the city, reading books alone in her residence, chatting with Ems every other day via their networked screens — it was just too much sameness, day after day, no change.

Neen needed a challenge. All her life she had felt this restlessness. Nothing seemed to be enough.

And yet she felt guilty at the same time. Was she ungrateful for the world her foremothers had created, a world free from want and needless suffering? A world in which women could finally — after centuries of oppression — flourish?

But her mind was never still. Everywhere Neen looked, she analyzed and contemplated and wondered how things could be made better. Their society was nearly flawless, but it wasn't perfect. There were still things that could be improved. Neen was hoping the high council would give her a position within city planning or even the breeding labs. Perhaps there was a way to revisit the old experiments of breeding without intercourse, of ensuring the genetic enhancements for each clan were successful without having to mate with the males.

Or perhaps there was a way to change the males. To make them less dangerous.

Neen knew she shouldn't be entertaining such thoughts, but they had crossed her mind more than once before. With all their scientific breakthroughs in genetic technology, wouldn't it be possible to breed males who were not like their ancestors, who weren't violent or deceitful or hardwired to desire the subjugation of women?

These were dangerous thoughts. The idea that males could be reformed, that they could be fundamentally changed, was not the kind of thing a woman said openly.

She heard a familiar shrill whistle from the kitchen, the antique kettle ringing loudly in the quiet apartment.

She got up to make her tea, choosing an herbal mix from her tidy cupboard and breathing in the bright smell of camomile and mint. She scooped the loose leaves into her brew basket, placed it over her teacup, and then lifted the ancient cast iron kettle from the stove. She admired the sturdy kettle as its hot contents poured over the tea leaves.

Neen had found the kettle in an antique market years ago, and while Ems had found it annoying, Neen adored the ancient relic. A calmness came over her as she breathed in the scent of steeping tea. It was a calmness she had longed for all day. Neen yawned and rubbed her eyes. She hadn't slept well last night, tossing and turning with uncertainty.

Neen sighed, waiting for the evening report to begin. It was the last thing she wanted to see, but there was simply no choice. Even if she tried to block out the images and sounds, the evening report couldn't be turned off.

Just as the Dome glass outside and the networked screen on her lap both shimmered and went black, there was a knock at her door.

Both the knock and the voice announcer from the evening report startled Neen. She could hear the familiar, too-happy voice of councilwoman Sienax echoing from her tablet screen, but she blocked it out and went to the door.

Standing there was high council member Nekka, the representative of Clan Triverser.

Neen stepped back and looked at her with wide eyes. The council members didn't usually make personal visits to new graduates awaiting assignment, councilwoman Nekka least of all.

Nekka had sometimes observed Neen in her classes and

even given the younger Triverser a few half-hearted kudos on occasion, but she wasn't exactly a warm or friendly presence to the students in the Institute, or even the clerks in government.

Nekka was distant and somewhat unapproachable. Perhaps it was her Triverser nature — many of Neen's clan were cerebral, more focused on solving an equation than on being bosom buddies — but Nekka was perhaps the most inscrutable of all the high council members. She was certainly the least amiable. To have her standing in Neen's doorway right now, her gray hair tied back tightly in a neat bun, was a bit intimidating.

"Councilwoman Nekka," Neen said, stepping aside so the older woman could enter, "what an unexpected honor." She held out her hands so that Nekka could greet her in the formal manner.

"Hm?" Nekka looked at Neen's outstretched hands, palms facing up, waiting to be clasped. But Nekka waved them away. "Never mind all that," she said. "There's no one watching."

Without being asked, Nekka took a seat on Neen's sofa. The two women were dressed almost identically, each wearing a jumpsuit with the light brown Triverser colors on the top and the circular EVE insignia just under the collarbone on the left side.

Nekka looked Neen up and down. "You're much prettier than I remember," said the councilwoman. "Not very typical."

Neen squirmed under the gaze of the older woman. Her physical appearance had been a slight source of embarrassment when Neen was a child; Triversers were valued for their intelligence, not their looks. Only the males cared about such things; it was another way they had dehumanized women in ancient times.

"It can't be helped," Neen replied, ignoring her discomfort. "I don't let it get in the way, though."

"No, you don't."

They both had to speak loudly, ignoring the prattling of Sienax and the other voices coming from Neen's tablet. Despite the banality and repetitiveness of the evening broadcast, there was no way to turn it off.

"Congratulations, by the way," Nekka continued. "Graduating early. Youngest in your cohort. Impressive." The way she said it, though, didn't sound particularly complimentary. Something in Nekka's matter-of-fact manner was off-putting.

Still, Neen knew the councilwoman was incredibly intelligent and well-respected. A true matriarch of society. A compliment from Nekka — even a perfunctory one — was something to be proud of.

"Thank you, councilwoman," Neen replied. "I must admit I'm anxious to get my work assignment."

Nekka nodded and a thin smile spread across her lips. "I bet you are."

Neen waited for her to say more, but the droning of the report was all that passed between them. Not knowing what else to do, Neen glanced at her tablet.

The broadcast was showing its usual ode to the glories of EVE, a montage of the ways different women in High City had helped each other throughout the day. There were shots of Triverser doctors chatting with their patients, images of Evox actors performing for an amphitheater of patrons, scenes of smiling Trabador construction workers building a new public library. The voice-over reveled in the achievements of this woman-centered society, all while lovely, harmonious melodies flowed from the soundtrack.

Then the bucolic images faded and darkness covered the

screen. The glass panels of the far-off arena dome turned dark as well. Every screen in the city was showing the same thing: darkness.

Sienax's voice grew lower, more ominous. "We cannot forget, my sisters. We can never let it happen again. The beauty of EVE must never be tarnished."

Then a flurry of images. Burning torches marching through ancient streets, women screaming, bodies being trampled by soldiers, gunshots and teargas everywhere. Then sporadic, grainy footage of men speaking to audiences from centuries ago, defending their draconian laws, fear-mongering about the breakdown of society, justifying the subjugation of women as the only way to restore law and order.

The images were disturbing, even after seeing them night after night for nearly her entire life. What men had done to women in those ancient times was awful.

Neen picked up the tablet and flipped it over so that the images couldn't be seen. Only the sound was still audible, just more muted.

"The males are too dangerous to be trusted," Sienax's voice continued." Never forget the ringing of the bells and the birth of EVE. Together, as women, we are stronger than any male. Together, as women, we will flourish. Together, as women, we will see a new tomorrow. Together."

The music was now that beautiful and sentimental strain again, a final crescendo just before the end of the broadcast.

Nekka stared at Neen. "Don't like what you've seen?"

"No," said Neen. "It's an important message. Necessary, even. It's just— we're trying to talk. I'd appreciate having an off switch sometimes."

As soon as she said it, Neen wished she hadn't. It wasn't

acceptable to question such things, especially in front of a high council member.

But Nekka didn't react. She simply observed Neen with that thin smile on her lips.

Neen decided to sit down across from her. She felt less on display if she was sitting down.

"The males are too dangerous to be trusted," Nekka repeated, almost to herself. "Isn't that right, Neen Salvek?"

At first, Neen thought Nekka was speaking rhetorically. Of course the males were dangerous. What could be more obvious? But when Nekka sat patiently waiting for an answer, Neen realized the councilwoman's question wasn't rhetorical.

"Yes, of course," Neen answered. "We all know what they did centuries ago. No male can ever be trusted."

"And yet, each month, for days at a time, we place ourselves in the same rooms as the males, allow them to mate with us, and surrender some part of our safety to their trust."

"The women who choose to breed are brave indeed," Neen repeated the slogan she'd heard a million times before. It wasn't that Neen didn't believe it, it was more that she was tired of having to repeat these trite bromides. As a Triverser, it was hard to shut one's brain off sometimes and just go with the flow. Neen especially bristled at the constraints.

"A bit of a mixed message wouldn't you agree?" said Nekka. "We can't trust the males, and yet every month..." Nekka's eyes peered intently at Neen.

As a matter of fact, Neen could agree. She had wondered the same thing herself. It was a bit of a shock to hear a councilwoman so openly questioning the policies and messaging of their world, but Neen had to admit, she'd contemplated the same.

Perhaps Nekka was hinting that Neen would be placed

with a bio lab to study ways to make breeding obsolete. Perhaps she would get assigned to design a new security system in the breeding suites. Neen's mind whirled with possibilities.

Finally, she might get to do something. Neen had waited long enough.

"The competitions will be starting soon," Nekka continued in that off-hand, impersonal way of hers. "I believe the first shipment of males arrives tomorrow morning." Nekka wasn't looking at Neen anymore; her eyes had drifted to the large window overlooking the city.

"As you may know," she continued, "lately we've seen an increase of women rejecting their breeding partners once they were alone in the breeding suite. Most women cited incompatibility, but a few reported extreme discomfort and a sense that their male partners were not willing to abide by our consent rules. Of course, those males were quickly removed from the program—"

Neen noticed Nekka's eyelashes flicker ever-so-slightly. It had been a gift from Neen's earliest years — the ability to notice these slight shifts in body language — something unusual for a Triverser. Ems had always joked that Neen was part Sixter somewhere in her ancestry.

But when Neen noticed this slight eye movement from Nekka, it made her wonder. It wasn't that Nekka's tone of voice changed; she was as matter-of-fact as ever. But something else had changed in the councilwoman.

Did Nekka disapprove of removing males from the breeding pool? After all, if a male couldn't breed, then it was best for him to be put to useful work instead. Without the males' efforts in the mines, they wouldn't have enough raw material to power the communications network.

Perhaps Neen misunderstood.

"What I'm proposing is a new procedure for screening the males," Nekka continued as if nothing had changed. "Psychological profiling before they even begin their trials. If a male is deemed unstable or not fit for breeding because of some mental defect, then he can be removed from the program earlier. Women will feel more comfortable knowing their males have been thoroughly screened ahead of time."

It made perfect sense to Neen. She was surprised something like this hadn't been instituted before.

"I can see the question forming in your mind," said Nekka, without taking her eyes off the view of the city skyline. "Why haven't we done this before? Frankly, in earlier eras, we were content with lower birth rates. Our population was bigger then. Not as much urgency. But now, members of the high council are concerned. We can't sustain these rates. Something needs to be done."

"Let me guess. You're one of those concerned council members," Neen replied. She didn't see the need to beat around the bush. Neen hardly ever did.

"I am," Nekka replied, finally turning to look at Neen.

Neen could see that Nekka was pleased.

"I must admit the program is controversial. Talking with the males, treating them as more than pieces of flesh. Some within the government don't see the point. Even women classified to breed often don't see these males as anything more than objects meant to further the species and create gloriously enhanced female progeny. The idea that men would have real—" Nekka stopped suddenly.

Neen could see color rising to the old woman's cheeks. It was surprising to see Nekka lose any composure, even something as innocuous as this. But it was clear that the councilwoman had said more than she intended. Neen wondered what to make of it.

Nekka turned to the window again. "I'm proposing a beta version of a new program," she continued, her voice resuming its measured and dispassionate quality. "Psychological profiling for all males designated breeding class three or higher. To be done here in High City before the commencement of the breeding trials. Profilers have the authority to designate males as unfit for breeding based on several mental and emotional factors. This will help us avoid so many rejections during actual breeding." She moved from the window back to the door of Neen's sterile, bleached apartment. "I've selected you to take the lead on this project. A complete dossier has been uploaded to your tablet with all the necessary data."

Neen was surprised. Her academic work wasn't focused on psychology. Planning, infrastructure, systems engineering, biochemistry: these were the things she had studied. She expected an assignment in government or science, something that would challenge her intellect. But talking to the males? Getting to know them and making judgments about them? Why her?

"Hesitant?" Nekka asked, that thin smile curling the corners of her lips again.

"No, it's just—"

"You'll be alone in the room with them," Nekka continued, not waiting for Neen to finish. "It's the only way we can get a true read on their psychological state."

Nekka waited for Neen's objections, but the younger woman said nothing.

"Most Triversers wouldn't take on this assignment. Too dangerous." Nekka let the implications of her statement hang in the air.

Neen jutted her chin. "I'm not *most Triversers*."

Nekka let out a little bark of a laugh. "I didn't think so."

Neen didn't let Nekka see her hands start to quiver. Being alone in a room with a male was something only breeding women did.

But still, Neen had to admit her fascination. Her mind drifted back to her younger days as a child, when she would often steal glimpses of the pre-pubescent males in Young Dome. They didn't look particularly happy, but then, why should they? They were de facto prisoners, kept under constant surveillance, intended only for breeding purposes. Did they accept their lot in life? Did they have any feelings beyond their rudimentary biological needs?

Neen had wanted a challenge. Perhaps this was it.

"Well?" Nekka said, standing in the doorway.

Neen took a deep breath. "I accept."

"Good." Nekka nodded. Neen caught a glimmer of satisfaction in the councilwoman's eyes. "Very good. I look forward to your first report." This time, Nekka held out her palms for the customary salutation.

Neen clasped them.

"Together," both women said in unison.

The door slid closed, and Neen went to the couch to sit down. Her networked screen was still facedown on the table.

"I wanted a challenge," she said to herself, sighing. But she didn't pick up the screen. She probably should've started studying for this new assignment — after all, the males were arriving tomorrow from the clan lands — but something held her back. She kept replaying the conversation with Nekka in her mind.

The males were dangerous. Everyone knew that. But if the demographic data was confirmed, if they were struggling to get women to mate with the males, then something needed to be done. Neen liked the idea that she could help, that by doing this work she could make things better for the women who were able to breed. Women like Ems.

Neen was just about to pick up her screen when another knock came on the door. Perhaps Nekka forgot something. She glanced around the room, but all she could see was her cold herbal tea on the sofa table. Neen went to answer the door.

"Herria!" Neen blurted out. "I mean, councilwoman Herria, welcome." Neen stepped aside to let the Sixter high council member enter.

Two council women in one night? Looks like the tea would stay where it was.

Herria Skalon swept into the room, all energy and enthusiasm. She smiled warmly at Neen and offered her hands for the customary greeting.

"Congratulations!" Herria said, taking Neen into a friendly embrace after they finished clasping hands. "I just heard about your new assignment. I'm excited to see what comes of this. You're more than ready for the challenge, that much is assured."

Herria made herself at home in Neen's sitting room. She glanced at the facedown screen and almost reached for it, but then she looked back at Neen.

"Nekka tried to keep things under wraps, just for security's sake, but I managed to needle it out of one of her clerks. Tell me, tell me, what do you think of this whole program? Any possibility of success?" Herria's charm was contagious, like children's laughter on a warm summer day. Her broad, blinding smile and easy nature were designed to put people at ease. Despite her rather shocking head of ice-blonde hair, closely cropped, she exuded both strength and compassion. She patted the sofa for Neen to sit down.

"Well," Neen began, unsure how to proceed. Even

though Herria seemed enthusiastic, Neen thought she noticed a slight twitch in the other woman's lips. "I haven't gone over the dossier yet, but I do think it makes sense to screen the males more thoroughly before their competition and eventual breeding."

"Indeed it does!" added Herria, widening her smile more.

The slight twitch was still there. A crack in the facade.

"So," Neen continued, "I should probably get to work." She picked up her networked screen.

"But I wonder," Herria continued, her face looking overly thoughtful, like someone who had just entertained a disturbing idea. "If the beta program works out, then we'll most likely increase the program, assign more women to profile these males, invest more resources into it. More and more women sitting in rooms with males and talking to them. Not for breeding, just for... talking. Seems an awful effort, don't you think?"

"I suppose, but if it makes women feel safer with their breeding partners, then isn't that a good thing?"

"Only if you think we can continue forever with this breeding nonsense." Herria said it with a twinkle in her eye, as if she were sharing a private joke with Neen.

Neen could feel the pull of Herria's personality. There was something intriguing about the way the councilwoman made her feel as if she were part of an inner circle, part of something intimate.

"We'd all be better off without these troublesome males!" Herria added, shaking her head but ruefully smiling.

"Yes, breeding does present its challenges," Neen tried to agree. She wasn't sure what Herria was implying. "It would be a benefit if we could figure out how to keep developing our genetic enhancements without all the fuss of intercourse with the males."

"Not just intercourse, my dear," Herria replied. "It's the males themselves, don't you think? Storing them, guarding them, raising them in Young Dome. We need to feed them, clothe them, keep them alive, and for what? So they can breed with us and advance the female race. Hardly an efficient system."

Neen couldn't argue about the inefficiencies, but what was Herria suggesting? The competitions and breeding sessions were a hassle, it was true, but even if they could figure out how to keep their genetic enhancements without old-fashioned breeding, they would still need to do something with the males, they couldn't just—

Could they?

Neen felt her skin prickle. No, she thought, that's impossible. That's not what councilwoman Herria means. It couldn't be.

"Would you mind keeping me abreast of how your assignment goes?" Herria said, leaning in toward Neen in that conspiratorial, ingratiating way of hers. She put her hand on Neen's and squeezed it with affection. "I'm just concerned all that contact with the males might have a negative effect on your well-being," Herria continued. "I don't want to see anything happen to you."

Neen tried to smile, but Herria's words from earlier still rang in her head. *It's the males themselves, don't you think? We'd all be better off without them.*

"Yes, definitely," Neen said suddenly, trying to appear calm. "I'll let you know how it goes."

"Keep me informed," Herria said again.

"Yes. I will."

"Good."

Herria was gone almost as quickly as she came. That was typical of the Sixter high councilwoman, Neen thought.

Everyone knew Herria was a ball of energy, a dynamic presence. Such a contrast to tight-lipped, buttoned-up, deliberative Nekka.

Neen slumped on her couch feeling exhausted. She looked at the darkness falling over High City like a blanket. She wasn't sure why she'd just lied to the councilwoman, but she had.

When it came to her new assignment with the males, Neen had no intention of telling Herria anything.

CHAPTER 2

NEEN

"YOU'RE GOING TO NEED THIS."

The guard handed Neen the pistol. It felt quite heavy in her hand. Thanks to her ballistics studies at the Institute, Neen could probably take it apart and reassemble it in only a few minutes, but still, she had never actually held a firearm before. Triversers were meant only to study these things, not use them. That was for Benglions.

The Benglion guard looked Neen up and down. "Still don't see the point," she said. The guard towered over Neen, looking down at her skeptically. She sighed. "But the high council makes these decisions, not me."

Neen didn't put the pistol into its holster right away. "Couldn't one of them just take this from me?" she asked the guard.

The Benglion laughed. "I thought you Triversers were supposed to know everything!"

"Well—"

"The security chip in their arms," the guard continued, cutting Neen off. "If they even brush their grubby fingers across that thing, the chip will release a toxin into their bloodstream." The guard smiled, seeming to relish the thought. "Instant death."

Neen was kicking herself for forgetting this. Of course, she had studied the chip implants —every male had them so they could be tracked and monitored — but she had forgotten the detail about contact with firearms and the toxin.

"Right, yes," Neen said, brushing off her forgetfulness with her best nonchalant face. "Let's go." She put the pistol in the holster around her waist and pushed a strand of her honey-brown hair behind her ear. She felt particularly small next to the Benglion guard, though she wasn't short by Triverser standards.

The guard led her out of the security room into a tunnel-like hallway. There was no obvious source of illumination, but the hallway glowed with a faint bluish light. The right wall was made of steel, but the left wall was all mirrored glass.

Neen stared at her reflection as she followed the guard. It was strange to see herself in the mirror when she knew that from the outside, women walking around the Dome could see through the glass and look right at her. Neen started to understand what it was like for the males. Their every movement could be seen by the eyes of the world, but all they ever saw was their own dim reflection.

Neen stopped looking at the mirror. She didn't want to see herself anymore.

"Use your tablet to communicate with us. We've got you hooked up to our network," the guard instructed. "If you need anything, just send us a message." The guard's voice sounded both bored and annoyed.

"Remember," she continued, "don't make any physical

contact with the males. Better to use the pistol too early than too late, if you feel threatened. Males are not allowed to leave until you say so. No one will be monitoring your sessions—" the guard stopped and shook her head, "— damned if I know why. But I'd advise you to record the sessions on your end, just so we have a record in case of an incident."

"Do you think there will be an incident?" Neen asked. As they trudged down the endless hallway, she started to imagine several worst-case scenarios, each one more horrible than the next. The guard's annoyance didn't help.

The guard didn't turn around; she just kept leading Neen down the hall. "Who's to say."

The list of dos and don'ts continued until they reached a secured metal doorway on the right. Next to the door was a dark glass touch panel.

The guard reached out her hand and pressed her palm into the panel. The glass glowed red, illuminating the outline of the guard's hand, then Neen heard a soft ping and the glass glowed green.

"In you go," the guard said as the steel door slide open. "And remember, they've been off their meds for the competition training. Could see some aggression. Benglions especially." The guard cast a leering smile at Neen and then practically shoved her into the room. "Have fun!"

The door slid closed as soon as Neen was inside. The room was sparse, just two steel chairs and a perfunctory table. There was a pitcher of water and one glass on the table.

"Comfy," Neen said, wondering if her back was going to give out after sitting in that chair for eight hours a day. Maybe I can get them to bring in some couches, she wondered. Or some pillows at least.

Neen knew it was pointless. They would never approve

any comforts for the males, and even if she requested them for herself, they'd make some excuses about budgeting. Neen could tell from Nekka's dossier and the memos she had gotten from the high council offices that this assignment was not exactly a popular one within the government.

She sat down in the cold chair and started reviewing her notes. She flicked her tablet screen with her forefinger, scrolling through the questions Nekka had prepared for her. They were all so straightforward. Neen worried these questions wouldn't elicit any answers worth hearing. If she was to get a sense of the males' states of mind, of their feelings and desires, she'd have to ask questions that went a lot deeper than these.

She'd tried to think of things to ask last night, but no matter how hard she'd tried, nothing really came to her. Neen seriously wondered why Nekka had selected her for this assignment. She wasn't a people person. She wasn't an Evox or a Sixter. What did she know about probing the minds of a bunch of males?

With a sigh of resignation, she pressed the button on her screen to signal for the first male to be brought in.

Within a few seconds, the secured door slid open and a different guard from before led in a Benglion male.

He was a hulking mass of muscles. Even taller than the female guard who led him in, the male looked like a colossus. His long blonde hair was tied back in a ponytail; his face was chiseled rock.

But what made Neen's eyes widen was the size of his biceps. They were huge. Like granite boulders the size of her head.

The guard sat the male down in the chair opposite Neen and the table. With a smirk, she patted the giant on his shoulder and then left without a word.

Neen gulped. "You should have no problem winning your cohort," she blurted out. It was all she could think to say. Neen silently cursed herself for being so blunt.

The male sat quietly in the chair. He looked straight at her, his eyes never leaving her face. His muscles looked like stone, and his face did too.

Neen was surprised. Males were required to respond whenever a woman spoke to them, but this one just sat there staring at her. Did she detect the hint of a smirk on his lips?

Neen made a note on her screen. She looked over the questions again. No, she thought, these won't do.

She decided to go off-script. "Listen," she started, "I know you probably don't want to talk to me, but nothing will happen. I promise. I'm just here to learn more about you."

The male's eyes smoldered with loathing. There was no mistaking it now. Even though he didn't move or react, Neen could feel this male's antipathy toward her.

Neen looked at her notes again. "Lekko, right? Okay, let's try this. I have the power to reject you right now from the trials, is that what you want? You won't even get a chance to compete, let alone breed."

The male, Lekko, made a harsh grunt in the back of his throat. But he was stone-faced.

"You don't want to breed?" The idea surprised Neen. She had been taught that almost all males, no matter the clan, had the overwhelming desire to copulate with women. Those that didn't were usually classified Type IV and rejected from the breeding pool. She made another note on her screen.

As she made note of things, Neen noticed Lekko's eyes watching her. She detected a slight relaxing of his facial muscles.

"My body is made for breeding," he said at last, his tone gently mocking her but compliant enough to avoid reprimand. "It serves the sisterhood of EVE." He put emphasis on that last word, and Neen thought he made it sound like a curse.

Neen nodded. He was no fool. "Clever," she said. "You know what you're doing."

At least he's not just a block of stone, she thought. She could tell this male had antagonism toward the society he was forced to participate in, but he also knew how to survive.

"You could probably snap my neck right now and take this pistol." Neen indicated the firearm at her side. "You wouldn't get far, perhaps, but you'd have the satisfaction of doing it. Is that what you want?"

Now Lekko reacted. He laughed. "I'm no fool, woman. I'd be dead the second my hand touched the grip."

Neen reviewed her notes. "You've bred before." It wasn't a question.

Lekko gave the slightest of nods.

"No problems?"

"You said it already. I know what I'm doing."

"Your body is made for breeding?" Neen tried to give back a mocking smile.

Lekko just shrugged a shoulder. He was done glowering at her. His expression went blank again.

Neen could tell that Lekko wasn't happy with his lot in life, but he wasn't about to risk it either. She tapped a few things on her screen, then slid her finger across the green approval button.

Was she doing the right thing? Was approving Lekko a good idea?

When they had finished, a guard came in to take Lekko away. As he stood up to leave, he bowed to Neen in mock formality.

"Thank you for letting me serve the sisterhood of EVE," he said, grinning. There was no mirth in it.

The guard pulled him up and shoved him out the door.

Neen sat alone with her thoughts. Maybe it wasn't wise to pass Lekko. Perhaps the fertile women would be put off by his arrogant demeanor. He was certainly physically impressive, though.

Neen wondered if she would allow him to mate with her. The question was one she had never seriously considered before. She thought about Lekko's arms wrapped around her in an embrace.

No, she thought, not him. But other women might find that attractive. There was something to be said for his stature, his strength, the way he seemed to command the room even without speaking. Some women might enjoy having his powerful frame at their disposal. He had bred before, after all.

Neen decided to stick with passing him. For now. She could always revisit her judgments later tonight, after some thought.

She pressed the signal on her screen to let another male in.

The male who walked in this time was different from Lekko. Leaner, but still muscular. His brown hair fell across his forehead, a bit sticky with sweat. He smelled musky, but Neen was surprised to find the scent was not unpleasant. Like oiled leather and sandalwood.

Neen could feel her face getting flushed. She wasn't sure why she was having this reaction. Embarrassed, she looked down quickly at her screen. *Tem MI-1338, age twenty-five, breeding class II*.

"Tem," she said not looking up. "This is your first trial, yes?"

"Yes."

I'm being ridiculous, she thought. He's just a male.

Taking a deep breath, Neen gathered her composure and looked up at him.

Tem hadn't been looking at her, but when she lifted her head, he glanced her way and gave the briefest of smiles. Neen felt her face redden again.

"I guess we've both just graduated," she said, trying to sound jocular, hoping to hide her flushed expression

"Graduated?" Tem looked confused.

Neen squirmed. Her attempt at humor had fallen flat. "I just meant— Anyway. How do you feel about the trials? Ready? Excited? Nervous?"

Tem's face flinched a bit when she said "nervous."

"It's okay to be nervous," Neen continued. "The trials aren't easy."

"I'll be fine. My body is made for breeding."

"Sure, but I wasn't talking about the breeding." Neen tried to smile. Lighten the mood. It wasn't going to be easy getting into these males' heads if all they did was repeat the government's slogans. "The trials. The competition. I've seen that Lekko guy! Winning won't be easy."

"I just have to pass my trial." Tem wasn't looking at her. His head hung down.

Neen felt the sudden urge to reach out and brush the sweaty hair from his forehead.

Stop it, she told herself. Focus.

"Yes, that's true," she continued. "But don't you want to win your cohort? You'll get to breed if you do."

Tem didn't react. "Yeah. Sure."

Tem was holding something back. Neen could tell. She hadn't expected the males to be so moody, so sullen. She thought they all lived for these competitions, for a chance to prove themselves. Males were competitive by nature, after all.

"Were you working out? Before I called you down for this —" Neen wasn't sure what to call these sessions. Interviews? Interrogations sounded wrong. But — Neen realized with a pang of guilt — that's exactly what they were.

"I was working out. Yes," Tem answered.

"What do you like doing when you work out?"

Tem's eyes shifted toward Neen. She could tell he was trying to figure out the best way to answer.

"I'm a fast runner," he said at last.

"That's great. What about combat? I know they train you in different styles, do you have a favorite?"

Tem's eyes cast downward again. "No."

Neen waited for more, for some kind of additional comment, but Tem was silent. He shifted in his chair.

"Okay... well..." Neen was getting frustrated. At least Lekko was arrogant, somewhat mocking. She could tell what he was thinking. But this Tem was just too closed off. She didn't care if his hair flopped down over his forehead in an appealing way, she was going to fail her assignment if he kept blocking her out.

"So running, you're good. What about swimming? Climbing? There's a part of the trials where you have to scale a wall and rush into a burning building. I've seen bigger Benglions than you freak out when they see those flames. Think you can handle that?"

"I hope so." Tem was now staring at the wall to his right.

"Right. So no favorite fighting style. What's your record in training? How many fights have you won?"

Tem's eyes flashed. He scowled at her. "Doesn't your screen have all that information? Why ask me?"

Neen straightened. That was something, she thought.

Some anger at least. "I was just making conversation," she said.

"Is that what you call it?" There was no mistaking the bite in his voice.

Neen glanced at her screen. "To be honest, there's no record of your training fights in my data."

Tem squirmed again, rubbing the back of his neck.

"It's almost like you haven't done any training fights," Neen continued, almost to herself. "That can't be right." She scrolled through Tem's data again.

"It's not wrong," he said at last. "I—" He stopped himself.

"You've never had a training fight?" Neen was incredulous. This couldn't be possible. He's Benglion. They're bred to be like warriors.

"I've— I've never fought," Tem replied.

Neen could see his body almost shrink down. Ashamed.

"All my bouts were forfeits."

Neen was shocked. This male was going to fail his trial if he couldn't fight. "But how?" she asked. "You're Benglion!"

"Yes, I suppose I am. Bred for superior strength. Bred to take risks. But when I have to fight—"

Tem's eyes started to get red-rimmed. He bit his lip and looked away.

"Tem," Neen said softly, "I'm here to listen. You can tell me what's bothering you."

As she sat watching him, Neen wondered if she should be taking notes on his emotional state. He was clearly upset. What if he wasn't stable enough for the trials? Or what if he made it through but couldn't handle breeding?

Tem's voice shook her out of her thoughts.

"I can see their faces," he said in a low voice. "Nothing behind the eyes."

Tem wasn't looking at Neen or anything in the room. He was lost in a memory.

"They enjoy pain," he continued. "Giving it. Watching it in others."

"The other males?" Neen wasn't sure what he was talking about.

Tem shook his head and squeezed his eyes shut. "The matrons. They let it happen. They watched. They didn't stop it." He covered his face with his hands.

"Stop what?" The words seemed to catch in Neen's throat.

Slowly, Tem slid his hands down his face and looked up at her. He stared right into her eyes. The anguish was still there on his face, but something else appeared too.

Neen tried to find the word to describe it, but her mind grasped at straws. That look... it was so...

Human.

"I know you've probably read all about Young Dome," Tem began, his voice shaking a bit. "You've probably studied its history — your history as a woman and mine as a male — you've done a lot of studying in your Triverser universities, and I'm sure you think you know what it's like, but I can promise you, you have no idea. The matrons, they didn't care about us. They wanted us to fight, to tear each other apart, to torment the weak ones and hurt the vulnerable ones. And they stood there and watched. And when they didn't watch, they whipped. They beat. There was nothing there of warmth or kindness. Only the rules we had to follow and a reminder that we were males, good for nothing but competition and breeding!"

Tem was breathing heavily now. Finally, his eyes flashed that anger again, but it wasn't the arrogance of Lekko or the aggression Neen had been taught to expect from the males. It was a kind of righteousness, a fury at the suffering he'd had to endure.

Neen knew the males in Young Dome were educated and raised by women in preparation for their integration into the adult domes in the clan lands. The Young Dome wasn't really a home for these young males, just a place to raise them until they were useful.

But they were males. They didn't need a home or affection or anything like that. Everyone knew that males only needed their basic physical needs met. They weren't as emotionally sophisticated as women.

Neen watched Tem's expression, the mix of resentment, pain, and sorrow that crossed his face. She was still trying to process what he'd told her of his childhood.

"So you're telling me that the Young Dome matrons let you and the other young males hurt each other?" Neen asked. "And they didn't stop it?"

Tem scoffed.

"Listen, I'm trying to understand you," Neen continued. "What exactly happened in Young Dome?"

"I was skinny. Weak. Smarter than the other Benglions. Little males don't like it when someone's different."

"So they picked on you?"

Tem shook his head. "They pulverized me. Day after day after day. And after a while, I just kept my head down. Let them beat me, didn't fight back. I had to survive. And your kind—" his eyes flashed — "Your kind just watched. Never helped."

Neen was appalled. How could the matrons have let this happen? Not tried to stop it? No child deserved to be beaten day after day, not even a male child.

"Whenever I'm in the fighting ring now..." Tem's voice

trailed off. Neen saw his eyes start to glisten, filling with tears. His face turned red with shame.

"I'm sorry." It was all Neen could say. What else could she do? Feeling powerless, she reached out for the pitcher of water and poured a glass.

"Here," she said. Standing up, she walked to the other side of the table and handed the glass to Tem.

At first, he didn't react. He was trying so hard to hold everything in. Then, slowly, he reached up with his hand.

Neen was close to him, much closer than she had ever been to any male before. His smell was stronger here, the sweetness of his perspiration and the faint scent of sandalwood...

For a split second, their fingers touched. Tem took the glass and drank a long, deep sip. He didn't hand the glass back.

Neen stood there watching him, suddenly feeling foolish.

"So yeah," Tem said at last. He stood up without Neen's permission and put the glass back on the table. He faced her. "This is my first competition. And I'll probably fail. Thanks for asking."

* * *

WHEN NEEN LEFT the Arena Dome, she was exhausted. Who knew sitting all day could make her muscles ache?

But it wasn't the sitting. It was the tension of having to wrestle something other than canned responses from the males. Of struggling to get them to open up. To speak the truth.

Most of the males were unremarkable. They were ready for the trials, ready to win and get on with breeding.

Some had to be dismissed right away. They immediately

gave Neen a bad feeling. Some seemed too eager for breeding. Some were almost somnolent, like sleepwalkers amid a dream. These Neen rejected too; they hid too much behind a mask. No discernible personality. Not worth the risk.

But then there were others — like that Tem — who were not at all what Neen was expecting. Tem had been so... vulnerable. Even though he'd tried to hide it, Neen had seen the tears forming in his eyes. What he'd told her about Young Dome was disturbing, to say the least. She couldn't stop thinking about it.

She also couldn't stop thinking about that touch. It had been so brief — barely anything — and yet why did she still have butterflies in her stomach even now, hours later, when she thought of it? His fingers had been smoother, smoother than she expected. That touch was like a little jolt of electricity.

Neen quickened her pace through the plaza. This district of High City had a beautiful greenway where small groups of children ran and laughed together at their games. Tanned and flushed faces ran past Neen; she watched as the wind rushed through their pigtailed hair.

Neen realized she probably should have known that growing up in Young Dome wouldn't have been very comforting. She watched the young girls play tag.

Nearby, a couple of caregivers were watching the children at their games. The two women leaned in close to each other and shared an intimate conversation as they kept their eyes on the laughing girls.

These women — the caregivers — worked at raising the female children of EVE. Neen remembered her own caregivers, those warm and loving women who hugged her freely and without condition, who taught her how to be patient and kind and look at the sunset with awe every evening. She and Ems had loved their caregivers, had felt so safe and valued under their protection.

Even now, Neen could see those memories in her mind's eye, memories of running through the parks of Sunset City with Ems, looking for grasshoppers and trying to catch them, of listening to their caregivers teach them how to identify the difference between grasshoppers and crickets, between oak leaves and maple, between planets and stars.

The two caregivers stood up. Neen was shaken out of her revelry. She heard the caregivers shouting at the laughing girls and calling them in.

The children came scampering over, gathering around these older women, bobbing up and down with excitement to tell them how the game had transpired.

Neen couldn't help but smile. She remembered those feelings of unbridled merriment, warmth, laughter, and joy. She and Ems had been so happy then. Such simpler days.

With a jolt, Neen realized that none of the males had ever felt that feeling. None of them had ever known the affection of a caregiver.

Before this assignment, Neen wouldn't have cared. She had always figured the males had what they needed in Young Dome: food, clothing, shelter. Males were different. Affection was unnecessary for them.

But that wasn't true. Neen had seen for herself with Tem. He was hurt. Suffering. Scared.

Neen turned to look back at the Arena Dome. It wasn't too far away. She could see through the one-way glass, watching the Benglion males as they ran around the track, lifted weights, sparred in the combat circles.

She couldn't see Tem, but she wondered what he was

doing. She wondered suddenly if he'd ever — even just once in his life — had someone care about him.

Neen sucked in her breath sharply. She realized she already knew the answer. Tem did have someone who cared about him.

Her.

CHAPTER 3

NEEN

"WHY DO you think you'll fail, Naal?" Neen tried to sound supportive. The male across the table was scowling again. His arms were crossed. Closed off.

But just moments before he had confessed his anxieties to her.

Neen couldn't get a read on him. Despite being an older Benglion, Naal was still muscular, but his hair was graying around the temples, and his hairline was receding. Neen could see from her intel that he was a borderline case. Almost classified as Breeding Class III. Not good. But then why was he so hostile? she wondered. She was trying to help him.

"You don't really care," Naal replied. "You tricked me just now. Should've kept my mouth shut."

"I didn't trick you, Naal. I'm just trying to learn more about you."

"So you can judge me. That's all this is. Another competition."

Neen hadn't considered it before, but he was right. She was judging him. That was her job. Judgment, evaluation, decision.

Neen squirmed a bit in her seat. Did she like having this much power?

It was the second day of interviews, and she was still making her way through the Benglion males. Naal was her third of the day. A tough one.

"Listen, Naal, I'm just trying to make sure you can handle everything. Emotionally, I mean. The trials, the competition, selection, breeding. I'm here to help."

Neen was stretching the truth. She wasn't doing this for him but for the breeding women, her sisters. They needed to feel secure in the breeding sessions with these males. If she could get males like Naal to open up, maybe she could weed out the unstable ones...

Neen thought suddenly of Tem. Was he unstable?

No. He was just traumatized. He had suffered in Young Dome. He needed help, but he wasn't unstable...

Okay, Neen thought, maybe I don't know why I'm doing all this. She knew what Nekka had told her, but this assignment wasn't what she expected.

"I've been selected to breed many times before," Naal said, interrupting Neen's thoughts. "I don't need your help."

Neen noticed his knee was twitching. Again. Ever since he sat down, Naal had been shaking that left knee up and down. A nervous tick.

Fear. That's what it was. With each new interview, Neen noticed these males were afraid. They wouldn't admit it, but they always had a tell. For this one — Naal — it was the knee twitch.

But what are they afraid of? Neen thought. Is it really about qualifying at the trials and winning their cohort? Are they afraid they won't get to breed?

"It's okay to be scared," Neen said.

"You don't know what you're talking about." Naal's voice

was raised. His knee jumped faster. Neen could see his ears go red.

"I only know what you've told me," she replied. "You think you might fail. Those were your words. You're worried."

"You really don't know," Naal said, grimacing. He looked like he was ready to be sick. "You really don't." His eyes darted around the room for an escape.

"Tell me, then," Neen continued. "What don't I know?"

Naal looked pale. Neen really thought he might retch. Instead, words burst out of him, spittle and anger flying.

"I'm going to be erased!" Naal's eyes were wild. "Too old. Class Three. I'll be nothing!"

Erased? Neen didn't understand. Naal was raving.

"Going to a Work Dome isn't the worst fate in the world, Naal," Neen replied, trying to stay calm. His outburst was unnerving. She didn't touch the pistol at her side, but she was glad it was there. "You'll be helping us build infrastructure. It's good work for a male who is too weak for breeding. You'll be helping women and males alike."

Even as she said the words, Neen knew they were a bit ridiculous. Who would ever want to spend their twilight years doing monotonous laboring work? Perhaps the Trabador males didn't mind, but the rest of the clans? Neen knew it was a kind of punishment. But still, not something to get so worked up about.

Naal was shaking his head and almost talking to himself. "You don't know anything. You don't know. I'm done for. Erased."

"Why do you keep saying that? Erased how?" It wasn't a word Neen had ever heard before in this context. In all her studies, in all her training, she'd never encountered the term 'erased' when it came to the males.

"It's not a Work Dome," Naal answered, starting to rock back and forth. "That's not what it is. The mines... the mines are hell. The mines are death. Pits of toxic metal and fumes. And just before they send you, they erase you. You become nothing." He looked up at her, wild-eyed. "Erased."

After this speech, life seemed to drain out of Naal. He slumped in his chair, unmoving.

"How do they erase you?" Neen asked. She didn't mean to, but her words came out like a whisper.

Naal didn't answer. His head still hanging low, Neen heard soft sobs coming from his throat.

"Naal, how do they erase you?"

Slowly, Naal looked up. Bleary-eyed and quivering, he spoke. "No good for breeding, so there's no need for what does the breeding." He made a snip-snip motion with his fingers.

"Wait—" Neen tried to process what he was implying. "That can't be. I've never heard anything about that."

Naal started to laugh at her ignorance, but the laughter mixed with sobs until he started shaking again, almost convulsing. "Erased... erased... erased..." He kept repeating it, laughing and choking back angry tears.

Neen didn't feel like doing any more interviews that morning.

* * *

WHEN SHE PASSED her wrist across the scanner, she was still shaking.

The scanner beeped. ONE MEAL. The machine sensor glowed green, letting Neen know she'd been approved.

The dining hall was quiet. The lunch hour rush hadn't yet arrived.

Ems was already waiting. With a beaming smile, she waved Neen to her table.

Upon seeing Ems, Neen felt her body relax. A flood of good memories, good feelings, calmness, and joy radiated through her from head to toe.

"It's been too long, sister," she said, pulling Ems into an embrace. Neen was careful not to squeeze her too tightly or too long, however. No need to overwhelm Ems's senses.

While Neen wasn't a particularly tall person, she was practically Benglion-sized compared to Ems. Ems was the very definition of petite: small, thin frame, elfin-like features.

Neen ran her fingers gently through Ems's hair, feeling the soft, bouncy curls glide through her hand. Ems's hair was so soft and blonde that it almost looked like downy feathers.

"Neen, you're shaking."

It was true. Despite feeling much calmer now, a slight shiver still prickled her skin.

Neen couldn't forget about that last interview with Naal. She told her best friend what had happened.

"I've never heard of such a thing!" Ems said. "I'm clan leader of Sunset City, I would've been told about something like that, if such a program existed. It sounds like this male was manipulating you."

"But it would be possible to keep hidden," Neen replied. "Males who fail their trials are taken from High City right to the Work Domes. They don't pass back through the clan land Domes."

"I suppose it's *possible.*" Ems was trying to be supportive, Neen could tell. But her friend was still skeptical. "I don't see the point, though," Ems continued. "Why torture them like that? And I'm sure he's exaggerating the conditions of the Work Domes. How would he know anyway? He's spent his entire life either in Young Dome, Benglion Dome, or here at the Arena."

Neen couldn't argue with that. There was simply no way a male like Naal could have the kind of information he'd claimed to know.

"Mmm," Ems said, trying to change the subject. "Squash soup."

As a Sixter, Ems could smell food from the kitchen even before it had been fully prepared.

Neen tried to catch a whiff of something in the far-off kitchen, but all she could smell was the faint odor of whatever cleaning solution had been used to wipe their table.

"Speaking of the Arena..." Neen said, raising her eyebrows. "You're going through with it then? First timer?" She grinned playfully.

"Don't start with me, Neen Salvek!" Ems said, laughing. "I know I've been bumped up the fertility ladder, but that doesn't mean I'm for sure going through with it!"

"This may be your best chance," Neen answered. "You know how fickle our fertility can be."

"I suppose. But it could be too overwhelming. All that touching, the contact. I worry it'll be too much."

Like all Sixters, Ems had enhanced sensory powers. Her sight, taste, touch, hearing, and smell were all far more advanced than those of other clans. Ems's sensory perception, in particular, was even stronger than most. Her concerns about overstimulation weren't unfounded.

"I get it," Neen said. "But maybe for you it would be unbelievably amazing. You never know until you try. It may turn out to be even better than you expect!" Taking a sip of water, Neen gave her friend a knowing look.

"Neen, dear," Ems replied, "we don't need a male for that particular pleasure!"

Both women tried to maintain their composure, but it was no use. They burst out laughing. Neen felt the water in her mouth almost squirt out her nose.

"You're right," Neen said, managing to swallow her sip without choking. She was still in a fit of laughter. "Despite our best efforts to educate them, I've heard the males are still on a steep learning curse when it comes to that."

Ems snorted too. Both women laughed again.

"Neen, you're too much!" Ems said, wiping laughing tears from her eyes.

"I'm just saying," Neen said, grinning. It felt good to laugh and let all that tension from earlier be released.

After the giggles subsided, Ems's face grew more serious. "You know why I'm really here, don't you? It's not just the Arena competitions."

"You didn't tell me. I thought that was all. The competitions, breeding season."

"No. That's not all." Ems blushed a little. "Herria's invited me to be her personal secretary."

"What?"

Ems nodded. "I can hear your heart beating faster. Is that excitement for me and this opportunity, or something else?"

"I mean— You're clan leader in Sunset City. Why would you leave that?"

Ems shifted a little in her seat. Her eyes glanced sideways. Was Ems getting uncomfortable talking openly? Neen wasn't used to her friend being defensive.

"Personal secretary to a high councilor," Ems said, a bit of an edge to her voice. "It would put me next in line to fill Herria's shoes when she retires."

"That woman is never going to retire." Neen didn't mean to sound so biting, but it was no use hiding her feelings from

Ems. Neen couldn't remember a time Herria hadn't been a council member for the Sixters.

Ems shrugged. "I didn't say I would take the assignment. Just here to check it out."

Now even Neen could smell the savory aroma of lunch. Their soup arrived, brought to them by a diligent Trabador server.

Once the bowls were set in front of them, Ems was almost overcome by the scent. She closed her eyes and began to breathe slowly.

Neen had seen Ems do this many times before. All Sixters have calming exercises they do to keep their sensory powers from overwhelming them.

Finally, after several seconds, Ems opened her eyes and took the tiniest of sips. Neen watched as her friend luxuriated in the tastes and smells of the soup.

"It is good, isn't it?" Neen said, not realizing until her first bite just how hungry she was.

They ate in silence so that Ems could concentrate on not letting her sense of taste get overwhelmed.

As the luncheon wore on, more and more patrons started to file into the dining hall. The sun broke through the overcast morning clouds and filtered into the huge windows all around the room. Everyone kept their voices pretty low. With Sixters working as chefs in the kitchen, women were respectful of their need for quiet and calmness.

"Herria is brilliant, though," Ems said as she took her last sip of the soup."I can hear that sigh, Neen, even though you're trying to hide it."

"Brilliant, maybe. But she's too— I don't know how to explain it. She's just too... too..."

"I've never known you to be at a loss for words."

"Maybe I'm not. Maybe I just don't want to say the word out loud."

Neen glanced quickly at the half-dozen screens mounted around the room, all of them showing beautiful footage of the five clan capitals on a continuous loop. All the images were innocuous, but Neen knew these screens were also tightly controlled and could even monitor what was going on in front of them.

"You're heart rate is quickening again."

"I know."

"Neen, what's bothering you? Is it still that male from earlier? I told you, he's completely ignorant. Forget his delusions."

"Is he the one who's ignorant? I do wonder..."

"Neen." Ems looked hard at her friend.

Neen felt a little bit like a child being scolded by a caregiver. "You don't know what these males are like, Ems," she protested. "What they tell me. Their fears. What life was like in Young Dome."

Neen didn't even mean to bring up Young Dome, but the words just popped out. And suddenly an image of Tem jumped into her head: Tem as a young, brown-haired little boy, skinnier than the rest. Tem, getting taunted and teased and beaten up by sneering bullies.

"Neen, my sister," Ems said, "please don't let these males manipulate you. Honestly, I don't know why Nekka didn't give this assignment to a Sixter. We can tell when we're being lied to. One of us would have no trouble telling if a male was deceitful."

Neen hadn't finished her soup, but suddenly she wasn't hungry anymore. She tried to breathe calmly, to not let her body betray her to Ems.

We can tell when we're being lied to.

Sixters could sense the subtlest change in a person's breathing or heart rate or pupil dilation. How could Neen have forgotten this? Ems was her best friend. She had intimate knowledge of what a Sixter could do. Couldn't Ems almost read her mind at times? Couldn't she sense when something was wrong or when Neen was holding back?

And if Ems could do it, then Herria certainly could too.

And Neen had lied to Herria just the other day. What was Herria thinking, even now, about Neen and her assignment with the males? Did she know that Neen had lied to her?

"I forgot," Neen said, wiping her lips with her napkin. "I have a meeting with Nekka soon. Going to have to cut this short."

"Oh, okay." Ems looked disappointed.

"I'm so sorry."

"No, that's okay." Ems flashed a reassuring smile. "We'll catch up later. I'll swing by your place in the evening."

Neen got up.

"Please, though," Ems said, reaching out to squeeze Neen's hand, "don't let those males manipulate you. We all know they love nothing more than to control women, to make them feel powerless. I know you can resist."

Neen tried to match her friend's smile, but it was a feeble attempt. She knew Ems could probably tell she was faking it, but what could she do? Whether Ems could sense it or not, Neen couldn't change how she felt.

* * *

THE HIGH-SPEED LIFT took Neen up to the top floor of the high council building.

She didn't really have a meeting scheduled with Nekka,

but when she contacted the councilwoman after leaving Ems in the dining hall, Nekka said to come right away. Security didn't even ask any questions, just scanned Neen's wrist chip when she entered the building and led her to the lift.

"Didn't expect a personal report so soon," Nekka said when Neen entered her office. "Sit."

Nekka didn't get up or give Neen the greeting. Again the high councilwoman had ignored custom. Instead, she kept her eyes on a large desk screen, barely glancing Neen's way.

"Thank you for seeing me, councilwoman."

"*Nekka* is fine. Don't feign politeness. I'm immune to it."

"Okay. Nekka. I really am sorry to barge in here without a formal appointment, but I'm having trouble with my new assignment—"

"Really? Should I get someone else to take over?"

"No, that's not what I meant—"

Nekka still looked at her screen intently. It was like Neen wasn't really in the room, just speaking through a telelink or something. "Maybe I should have assigned a Sixter. Better suited perhaps. Ah well!" Nekka spoke almost to herself. "You know how we are. Stick with our clans and those we know best."

"I'm *not* handing in my resignation." Neen didn't mean to say it so sharply, but she also didn't like having her abilities questioned. Nekka was treating her like some kind of petty bureaucrat, or worse, like a male.

"That's good to know." Nekka still kept on reading something on her screen, then touched it a few times, then kept on reading.

Neen was getting frustrated. She felt the sudden urge to throw something, but when she glanced around the room, she saw practically nothing besides the desk, Nekka's chair, and Nekka. Maybe I can throw that stupid screen, Neen thought.

The room's spartan furnishings, its cold, gray walls, even the window behind the councilwoman — with its curtain closed — made the office decidedly unwelcoming.

Still, Neen wouldn't be put off, even if Nekka seemed to be giving her the cold shoulder. It didn't make sense for the councilwoman to accept her request for a meeting and then practically ignore her.

"What I'm trying to say," Neen began, trying to soften her voice, "is that the males have told me some disturbing things. Awful things. And I'm looking for answers."

"Hm." Nekka leaned in closer to her screen as if caught up in some particularly interesting grain reports.

"Councilwoman?" Neen said, exasperation creeping back into her voice. "Nekka?"

"What have they told you?" Nekka's face was as still as glass. She still didn't look Neen in the eye but only watched her screen.

"One mentioned today something about being... erased."

Neen waited for Nekka to say or do something, but there was only silence.

"He heavily implied," Neen continued, "that we forcibly castrate the males who don't pass their trials. And that the Work Domes are essentially death camps. I know it sounds ludicrous, but he was terrified of it all. He really believed it."

At last, Nekka looked at Neen. "Why shouldn't he? It's true."

"What?" Neen couldn't believe the calmness in Nekka's voice.

"It's true. When a male isn't fit for breeding, he's gelded."

"What? That's barbaric! And pointless! It's not like he has any choice whether to breed or not. We decide those things.

Why not just send him back to his clan dome and be done with it?"

"Why not, indeed. But then how would we guarantee our control? How would we make sure he was eliminated from our society?"

"Eliminated? You mean the Work Domes?"

"Your male interviewee was not wrong there either, I'm afraid. To call them domes implies they provide some measure of shelter, some protection. But the males who are sent there get nothing but a brief respite from the cobalt and lithium mines. The toxic fumes eventually destroy their lungs, or if they're lucky, a cave-in ends things quickly. The Work Domes are, simply put, factories of death."

Nekka lifted a smaller, handheld screen off her desk and flourished it. "But they give us these beautiful tools, don't they?" Her face was grim.

"How can this be acceptable? Males may not be equal to the rest of us, but they don't deserve to be tortured and then poisoned to death!" Neen was yelling now and not ashamed of it.

"Does this prick your conscious, Neen Salvek?"

Nekka's face was as still as glass, but Neen saw her fingers clench around the handheld screen.

"It does." Neen refused to lie.

"Talking with the males has gotten to you, I see. Softened you up."

"No, but—"

"As it should be." Nekka put down the tablet and folded her hands. For the first time since Neen walked in, she looked at Neen's face with kindness. "When you start to see these men as humans, you start to see the world differently."

Men? Yes, Nekka had said men. Neen ran her mind back

through their previous meeting a few days ago in her apartment. Yes, Nekka had said men then too.

"Is this what you wanted?" she asked the older woman.

"What I wanted?"

"To make me see the males as human? To know the truth about what we do to them?"

Nekka sighed heavily. She shrugged. "I wanted an ally, I suppose." She didn't elaborate.

Reaching into a drawer in her desk, Nekka took out a thin silver necklace with a half-moon, bluish-gray pendant on its chain. It was delicate and glimmered a little as it spun on the chain. Nekka held it out to Neen. "For luck," she said. "And to remember that we're in this together."

Neen took the necklace, surprised that Nekka was offering her such a lovely token of friendship.

"Why do we do this to the males?" Neen said quietly, feeling the pendant rest softly against her chest. "Why the cruelty? We don't need to."

"No, we don't. But the cruelty is the point. We must 'never forget' what the men of the past did to us, or haven't you heard? So we must make sure they pay, even their descendants fifteen generations later."

"But we're ashamed to admit it!" Neen felt her face flush with anger. "The high council keeps these details from the public. If this vengeance was so righteous, then shouldn't we celebrate every time we mutilate one of these males? Why the secrecy?"

"I knew I made the right choice," Nekka says. "There's no stopping you from getting right to the heart of the matter. The question is, now that you know the truth, what are you going to do about it?"

The question hung in the air like a sword over Neen's head.

* * *

NEEN HOPED Ems would understand that she had to cancel their get-together. She also hoped Ems couldn't detect the lie about having a headache. But all the things Nekka had said to her earlier were making her thoughts swirl, and she needed time to think.

The teapot whistled on the heating unit. Neen poured the boiling water over her tea leaves and waited for them to steep.

The lights in her apartment were dimmed. The world outside her window was dark too, the only light coming from the glorious towers and high rises of the city. Those lights looked like soft blue stars hanging low in the sky.

Neen rubbed her temples. Maybe she did have a headache after all.

What are you going to do about it?

Nekka's words echoed in her head.

She closed her eyes and tried to think, tried to make a plan. But all she could see was the face of Tem: his shame, his anger, his pain. And her own part in it. Whether they knew it or not, the women of EVE were complicit.

She saw Tem's eyes, the fear hidden behind them, and the way he tried to hide his shame, and she couldn't help but remember his smell, the tang of his sweat, and the muskiness she found strangely pleasant when she stood next to him. She remembered the jolt of electricity that coursed through her when their fingers had touched.

She had dampened those feelings at the time, had tried to remember her assignment and her responsibilities, but now something had changed. Something welled up inside her. A different responsibility.

If Tem couldn't pass his trial, he'd be erased.

What are you going to do about it?

Neen stared out her window and watched the lights of the buildings sparkle. All of this technological wonder, all of this accomplishment, but for what?

She saw Tem again, remembered his voice, remembered the sorrow that haunted it when he spoke of the trauma of Young Dome.

What are you going to do about it?

Neen had forgotten about her tea. She had made up her mind.

She wouldn't let it happen. Not to Tem. Somehow, someway, she was going to help him pass his trial.

She wasn't going to let him be erased.

CHAPTER 4

EMS

EMS TOOK three deep breaths and then followed Herria into the meeting room.

Unlike other buildings and rooms in EVE, the high council meeting room was a feast of stimulation: plush, old-fashioned chairs, upholstered with velvet green cushions; antique chandeliers of glimmering crystal; a long mahogany table atop an intricately patterned rug from the desert regions of the old world.

Ems couldn't believe that Herria or any other Sixter could concentrate in such a room. It took Ems several seconds to get her bearings, and even then, she found her eyes were overwhelmed by all the colors, shapes, and patterns.

When she glanced at Herria, though, the high councilwoman seemed unperturbed. How does she do it? Ems thought.

Ems herself felt awkward. Herria already had an assistant. Grex, the Evox, trailed the councilwoman like a lost puppy, all the while giving Ems the nastiest of looks.

Why does she need me when she has Grex? Ems

thought. She watched Grex's eyes and the fawning expression on her face whenever she looked at Herria. Herria barely noticed Grex's pleading need for attention. It was like the other woman wasn't even there.

"Have a seat here, Ems, dear," Herria said, motioning to a row of chairs along the east wall. "Though, I hope soon you'll take your place at the table." Herria winked in that ingratiating, conspiratorial way of hers.

Grex, nose in the air and disdain plainly evident, sidled her way to the chair next to Herria's at the long table. Ems couldn't miss the sneer directed her way by Grex.

Ems just shrugged. She was beginning to wonder if this was all a mistake. All the politicking and maneuvering that came with a position in the high council offices was exhausting. Just being in that room with all the councilors, their assistants, and the garish ancient furnishings was giving Ems a slight headache. She closed her eyes and tried to focus on one sense at a time, letting her ears take over.

"Shall we call to order?" Ems heard Herria say. The other high councilors agreed, speaking "Aye" in one voice.

Ems took a deep breath and slowly opened her eyes. Each of the councilwomen was seated around the large table, and at Herria's cue, they stood. Starting with Herria and continuing to each of the five high councilors, they did the customary greeting.

"Together." Herria and Nekka clasped hands first, speaking the words in unison. But Ems could see the tightness on Nekka's face and hear a slight strain in her voice. There was something off about the greeting, though Herria seemed perfectly amiable. Nekka, however, was not. Ems wondered if Herria could sense the tension in the other woman's voice.

They went around the table, each councilor greeting the

next. Nekka to Reslan of Clan Trabador. Reslan to Sienax of Clan Evox. Sienax to Forta of Clan Benglion. Then Forta back to Herria.

When the greeting was finished, Herria sat down and the others followed suit.

Each of the councilwomen was older, some with graying hair, like Nekka, some with the lines and wrinkles of wisdom and age, but all of them still looked sharp and focused. Seeing them all around the table, Ems noticed that Herria — despite her ice-blonde hair — actually looked the youngest of all. Her skin was taut and somewhat pale, barely a wrinkle in sight.

Strange, Ems thought. She had always thought Herria was one of the older councilwomen, close to Nekka's age. She looked amazing sitting near Nekka, whose face was lined with creases and whose gray hair was tied back in a tight bun. Compared to the Triverser councilwoman, Herria looked to be in the prime of fertility.

As the women sat, Ems concentrated on listening to their pulses and breathing. Nekka was unbelievably calm, while Forta and Sienax were normal. Reslan's heart raced faster than the others.

Nervous?

Ems wondered about that. Perhaps as the youngest high councilor, Reslan was insecure.

Herria's heart rate was impossible to detect. Ems couldn't get a read on her at all. That was strange. Herria must be a master of self-control.

Nekka started to speak, naming the first item on the agenda when Herria interrupted her.

"Before we get to that, dear Nekka, I'd like to press an issue that's been weighing on me."

"Weighing on you?" Nekka repeated, raising an eyebrow.

Now Ems could feel Nekka's pulse quicken.

"Heavily, I'm afraid," Herria continued. "We've discussed it before, but now I fear the matter is getting more urgent. Last meeting, you yourself have brought up our dwindling birthrates, and I've been ruminating on that, wracking my brain for some better solution."

"I thought we had a plan," Nekka said. "My Triverser prodigy, Neen Salvek. She's begun interviewing and profiling the males. If all goes well, we can roll out the program more fully."

"Ah, yes. Neen and the profiling of males." Herria smiled, cat-like. Ems could tell there was a bit of mockery in the way Herria said it.

Ems felt her cheeks flush. She shifted in her seat. Herria might be on the high council, but nobody dared mock Neen in Ems' presence. She started to stand up, to speak out in Neen's defense.

But then Nekka glanced quickly at Ems. A warning look.

Ems settled, sighing perhaps a bit too loudly. She knew Nekka was right. A visitor to the meeting couldn't possibly speak. Breaking protocol could mean punishment. Ems bit her tongue.

"As I said before, Nekka," Herria replied, "I think this plan is intriguing. But frankly, it's slow-going. Even if we had dozens of interviewers like Neen working on it, the process takes a long time. I think we should explore other options."

"Ah yes, 'other options,'" Nekka said.

Herria beamed. "You know me well, Nekka. I've said it before and it's worth repeating. There's no reason why we can't devote more resources to laboratory breeding."

"I agree," Forta spoke up. "It would make things much easier with the males. The competitions and breeding sessions are always a security challenge."

"I'm inclined to agree too," Sienax said. "It's worth another look."

Ems saw Nekka's eyes shift ever-so-slightly toward Reslan.

The Trabador councilwoman spoke up. "Yes, uh, it could be. But we've tried lab breeding before with less-than-ideal results. Might we be throwing good resources after bad?"

"We tried it over twenty-five years ago, Reslan," Forta replied. "You weren't even on the council then. It's high time we tried again."

Ems watched Nekka scan the others. She could feel the councilwoman's heart quicken and then heard her take several deep breaths to calm down.

"There's certainly nothing wrong with exploring all options," Nekka said slowly. "But resources are not infinite. If we put more scientists and technicians into this, then something else will have to be cut. If anything, I see a need for our Triversers to be working with the Trabadors to improve infrastructure, farming techniques, sustainability. We've spoken before, haven't we, Reslan, about the climate issues related to our agriculture?"

"Yes, that's true," said Reslan, her eyes darting from Nekka to Herria to Forta. Ems thought she looked a bit like a cornered rabbit hoping for an escape.

"Important, necessary things, I'm sure," Herria interrupted. "But even agriculture and infrastructure pale in comparison to our declining birth rates. If we can't sustain the population, we can't sustain our way of life. Too many women are rejecting their breeding males. Our numbers of suitable Class A fertile women are dwindling. I dare say, the breeding process is obsolete anyway. It's a black mark against progress that we haven't figured out how to breed our genetic enhancements in the lab."

"Hear, hear!" Sienax said.

Ems winced. She wasn't expecting Sienax's cheer. It was a bit too loud, and Ems hadn't been concentrating on controlling her hearing.

Herria, however, remained calm. "Sienax, you've said before that many women face emotional dangers in the breeding suites."

"Indeed," Sienax replied. "All that physical contact with the males, the time alone. It wreaks havoc on a woman's emotional state. My Evoxes struggle sometimes."

"Not just Evoxes," Forta chimed in. "Some Benglion women too find it difficult to detach."

"And if we're going to speak of human capital, of needing to put resources where they'll best be used," Herria continued, looking pointedly at Reslan, "then how can we ignore the time it takes for pre-and post-natal care? Women who are carrying fetuses are not exactly the most productive members of society."

"Yes," Reslan said, looking sheepishly from Herria to Nekka, "that's true, I'm afraid."

"It's settled then?" Herria said. "Or shall we enter a formal vote?"

All the councilwomen besides Nekka looked satisfied.

"No need for a vote," Nekka said, her voice sounding tired.

"Then it's settled," Herria said. "We'll begin putting more resources into laboratory breeding immediately. I have high hopes. By this time next year, who knows what we'll have accomplished!"

The other three councilwomen nodded, but Ems heard Nekka's breathing quicken.

Why was Nekka so opposed? Ems couldn't figure it out. Having to breed in such an antiquated way was to no one's benefit. Developing the enhancements in the lab would make things so much simpler.

Ems thought about her own upcoming participation in the breeding cycle. She had been hoping her fertility demarcation would be like Neen's, Class C or D. But to be Class A? To go through the process of choosing a breeding partner and being intimate with him for days in a row? And then, most likely, to carry the expected fetus to term?

Ems wanted to serve her clan, to do the work she was bred to do. She was a Sixter, a woman whose senses could help her pilot an aircraft at supersonic speeds, or notice the slightest change in taste when seasoning food, or perceive alterations in the environment that would help maintain EVE's systems and controls.

Yes, producing a baby would serve her society, would help further the population, but if she was being truly honest, participating in the breeding process never appealed to her. Hadn't she and Neen snickered about the awkwardness of it all? What could a male know about pleasing a woman anyway? The resources, the dangers, the risks.

If only I could skip it altogether, she thought.

Ems sighed. There was no way. If a woman was Class A, she had a duty to breed. Yes, the leaders of the breeding program gave lip service to women having a choice — "You can always say no to your breeding partner if you don't want to consent," was the party line — but Ems knew the reality. Women who rejected their breeding partners in the suite were taking a risk. The high council reviewed all these cases and women who rejected their partners often saw their work assignments altered — demoted, really — and their living credits were reduced, sometimes severely.

The fact that lately so many women were rejecting their

partners spoke to how bad the breeding process must be. To risk work demotion and reduction of credits rather than mate with a male spoke volumes to Ems.

But deferments were rare. Only a member of the high council could grant them.

Ems watched Herria seamlessly — effortlessly — bring up another item not on the council's official agenda. She had to admit, Herria was a powerful influencer. The kind who got what she wanted.

"I'm speaking of a general feeling among the women," Herria said, referring to those women classed C and D fertility who felt inferior to the women of higher classes. "I've been on an informal listening tour around High City and some of the clan lands too, and what these women tell me is so heartbreaking. They feel like second-class citizens. They feel 'lesser' because of their inability to conceive. I know we're committed to messaging that speaks of the glories of breeding — of furthering our enhancements and growing the female population of EVE — and I know how important it is to keep high-fertility women in good spirits as they must consent to breed with the males, but don't you see how wrong it is that by encouraging these women of high fertility, we are thereby denigrating those women who aren't?"

There was quite a murmur of consent from all the women at the table. Even Nekka nodded along with Herria's speech.

Ems thought of Neen. Did her best friend feel "lesser" because of her low fertility? Was she jealous of Ems? Ems never got that impression, but was it possible that Neen was hiding it from her?

It would be hard for Neen to hide something like that, but the thought of Neen feeling inferior made Ems want to skip the breeding process even more.

"I agree wholeheartedly with you, Herria," Sienax proclaimed. "In our push to extol the virtues of furthering the population, we've communicated a false ideology. Our class C and D women are just as worthy, just as important to the progress of EVE as our higher classes."

"Hear, hear!" Forta said, oblivious to the volume of her voice.

Herria barely flinched at the loudness of the councilwoman's voice. Ems was in awe of her self-control.

"I agree as well," said Nekka, her voice quiet and steady. "Perhaps a messaging campaign to reinforce the value of all citizens of EVE."

"My communications office will begin right away," replied Sienax. "We can roll something out within a fortnight."

"Perfect!" Herria beamed. "I know our sisters who struggle in this will be comforted by whatever you cook up."

"But may we return our attention to the items on the agenda—" Nekka began.

"Certainly," Herria said.

Nekka's pinched, thin lips were the only sign of displeasure at the table. "I know you are all well aware of the reports submitted from my Dome oversight committee," Nekka continued. "We've spoken of Dome conditions before but still haven't settled on what to do about them. I'm thinking of Young Dome in particular, but there are new reports that suggest disturbing things are happening in the clan Domes as well, and in our Arena Dome."

Ems leaned in. She remembered what Neen had said the other day about the males being "erased." Was this what Nekka was talking about?

"Disturbing things?" Herria said, incredulity flashing across her face.

"Reports of rumors swirling around the Domes, frightening the males," Nekka explained.

Herria laughed. "Shouldn't the males be a little bit frightened? I mean, it's a small price to pay for all that they did to women over the centuries. A little discomfort? Anxiety? Forgive me, Nekka, but I'm having trouble sympathizing with the males. What did they once call us? The 'weaker sex.' I suppose the irony is lost on them now."

Others around the table laughed with Herria.

Nekka did not.

"Males have been told what happens when they fail their trials," Nekka said, speaking over the laughter. "They know what happens," she repeated.

The laughter started to die down.

"They are being tortured with this knowledge," Nekka continued, looking straight at Herria. "My sources have told me that as punishment for disorderly conduct, the males are subjected to witnessing the process."

The room had turned utterly silent.

"Careful, Nekka," Herria said through gritted teeth. For the first time since the meeting started, Ems could sense Herria's heart beating faster. "This is *not* something we should discuss at an open council meeting." The clip on the word "not" landed in the room like a heavy stone.

All the assistants — except Grex, Ems noted — looked around the room at each other, confused. Ems could feel pulses quickening, breathing getting shallower, sweat glands starting to react. Grex sat perfectly still and utterly calm, looking up at Herria with what seemed to Ems's eyes almost like adoration.

Was it true, then? Ems wondered. Was this "erasing" real? The thought was disturbing, to say the least. It was one thing to punish the males, but to mutilate them like this? Ems didn't want to think about it.

Forta leaned forward toward Nekka but kept one eye on Herria too. "I'll have my captains look into it. Find out if anything unauthorized is happening. I certainly agree that any and all punitive actions taken against the males should follow standard protocol. Nothing else is acceptable." Here Forta looked directly at Herria.

Herria met the other woman's gaze with a serene placidity.

Ems didn't like that look. Why did Herria suddenly seem pleased when just moments before Ems could tell she was getting upset?

"Good, good," Herria replied. "Nothing unauthorized should ever occur. We all agree on that."

There was a pause as all in the room exhaled in relief.

"But," Herria continued, speaking as if an idea were just popping into her head, "perhaps it's something to consider."

"Consider?" Forta asked.

"Perhaps it's a good thing for the males to know what's in store for them if they fail their trials," Herria answered.

The room went deadly silent again.

"Do you really think...?" Reslan began, but her voice faded.

Ems watched Forta and Sienax share a glance, then their eyes moved fleetingly toward Herria's.

"It might make them behave better in breeding sessions," Herria continued musing. "Something to consider." She said it like it was the simplest of suggestions.

Nekka stood up. Her face was flushed. "It's psychological torture, Herria, and you know it!"

Herria just chuckled. "Stop being so dramatic, Nekka

dear. 'Psychological torture'? They're males. Meant for breeding. There's no need to start coddling them."

"Not abusing them isn't the same as coddling. We shouldn't debase ourselves. It's unbecoming of us to treat the males as subhuman."

"They may be genetically human," Herria replied, lips curling up to reveal her teeth, like a cat ready to swallow a sparrow, "but let's not get too sentimental. They're still males. Still dangerous."

Murmurs of agreement passed around the room. Even Ems couldn't help but concur. Every day of their lives, from childhood onward, all women of EVE were reminded of the dangers of males. They were a necessary evil, but an evil nonetheless. Nekka was acting as if the males were somehow equal to women.

I hope Neen isn't getting any ideas from her, Ems thought.

Ems also didn't like the tension between the two councilwomen. It was obvious to anyone — not just a Sixter — that Nekka and Herria did not agree on much. Too much conflict. And conflict between women was dangerous. It led to dissent, and dissent was forbidden.

Women were meant to work together, to solve problems amicably. Hostility and conflict were male traits. How could the high council function properly if Nekka and Herria were so opposed?

The meeting soon adjourned, though that final debate was never properly settled. Ems wasn't sure how she felt about it.

Herria got up to leave, with Grex close on her heels.

A pathetic puppy, Ems thought, as she watched Grex.

Herria handed Grex a small handheld tablet and told her to go send a report. Ems tried to get a quick look at the screen, but couldn't. Grex stuffed it under her arm and turned to leave, scowling at Ems as she went.

"Come, Ems," Herria said, "let's chat in my office."

Ems was surprised by Herria's office decor. It reminded her a bit of Neen's apartment, with a flare for old technology, but Herria's antiques put Neen's teapot and saucers to shame. Everywhere she looked there were items from centuries ago: halogen lamps with painted shades, paper books bound with leather, floor rugs with ornate patterns like the one in the high council meeting room. It was a feast for the senses in much the same way as the meeting room, and Ems took several slow, deep breaths before she could take it all in.

"It's to remind me of the dark days," Herria said, answering Ems's unasked question. "So I never forget the world we came from, before the founding of EVE."

Ems went up to one of the lamps and felt the fabric of the shade, letting the heat of the lightbulb radiate near her skin. It was nothing like the cool, efficient lights they used now. Ems drank in the warm glow.

"What did you think of our meeting?" Herria said, crossing the room and sitting on a plush leather couch. She smirked in a self-satisfied way. "That lamp isn't the only thing giving off heat."

"I was surprised by the tension," Ems admitted. "You and councilwoman Nekka don't see eye-to-eye."

"That's putting it mildly."

"I don't want to speak out of turn, but it troubles me."

"Does it?" Herria waved a hand, dismissing Ems's concerns. "You needn't worry. A reckoning is coming and rabble-rousers like Nekka will need to make their choice."

"Make their choice?" Ems pulled her hand away from the lampshade. She felt a strange shiver run down her spine.

"Big news is coming, Ems. Nekka's way of doing things will soon be... obsolete."

The way Herria said that last word made Ems think of Neen and her budding relationship with Nekka. Neen was becoming a kind of protege of hers. What could all this mean?

Herria leaned back into the couch cushions and put her feet up on the cherry wood tea table. "Are you excited for the competition in a few weeks?" She winked at Ems. "To watch the males go on display?"

Ems felt her face flush. "The competitions are always exciting," she said. It was true. Ems loved the contests, particularly the one where Sixter males had to tell if their opponents were lying.

"Yes, they're thrilling," Herria concurred. "The lying challenge is one of my favorites. But, of course, I can always figure it out before the males do."

"Me too," Ems said, smiling despite herself. Although the competitions were exciting to watch, she knew if she herself was competing, she'd easily dominate. Perhaps that was by design. The males could never equal the women even if they too were bred for superior traits.

"Still," Herria continued, "it would benefit us all if we could figure out a way around this old-fashioned breeding business. I can sense that you aren't too keen about it yourself."

Ems couldn't lie. "I'm not. I've never been."

"Why don't you skip it this month?"

Ems's eyes widened. Was a member of the high council seriously suggesting she skip the breeding process?

"You shouldn't ever be forced to breed with a male," Herria said. "None of us should. That's the kind of thing males did to us in the old days. And yet, here we are, perpetuating the whole system. Honestly, there's no rush to have offspring."

"What about the low fertility numbers?"

"Oh, that?" Herria waved a hand again, dismissing the notion. "Nekka is a drama queen. Over-reacting. I'll get you a deferment for this cycle. Let my office handle it."

Herria stood up and took Ems's hands into her own, squeezing them tightly. Ems almost winced from it. She tried to smile. Herria was just doing the faux-intimacy thing that Ems had observed so well, but there was something about the strength of her grip that felt vaguely threatening too.

"I need you with me," Herria said, her eyes gleaming at Ems. "Not off in some prenatal center."

"I—" Ems began. She didn't know what to say. "I'll let you know, Herria."

Herria leaned in and spoke softly in Ems's ear. "Don't wait too long. We'll have some big news to announce in the coming weeks. I want you to be with me when we make the announcement."

"And I'm guessing," Ems replied, "you aren't going to tell me what it is until I agree to be your personal assistant." She almost asked about Grex and what would happen to her position if Ems accepted, but the thought went unsaid.

"That would be spoiling the fun, don't you think?" Herria continued. "You really should say yes. I can sense your pulse quickening. Don't deny it!" She gave one last little squeeze of Ems's hands then let go.

"I won't," said Ems. "But I can sense your pulse too. You're awfully eager to get me on board."

"Why shouldn't I? I have an eye for talent."

Ems smiled demurely. "I'll think about it. But I need some time."

"That's wise. Don't jump into anything too quickly. But

don't be so cautious that you miss a great opportunity either." Herria winked again.

Suddenly Ems felt a strange compulsion to say yes, to agree to Herria's offer.

Why am I thinking this way? she wondered. These new thoughts were shouting their way into her head and she didn't like it.

Ems pushed back, focusing as hard as she could on calming her mind and rejecting the intrusion.

"Oh," Herria said, under her breath, "that's interesting. Very interesting."

Ems, at last, had pushed the thoughts away. Her head was clear, even though she was breathing heavily like she had just run a mile. She looked at Herria who was staring at her with a strange hunger in her eyes. "What's so interesting?" she asked, still breathless.

"Ems, my dear," the councilwoman replied, "I knew before that you had potential, but it wasn't until just now that I realized how much potential there really is." Herria cupped her hand under Ems's chin. "Don't wait too long deciding. I think there's a lot I can teach you."

"Teach me?"

"I won't pressure you anymore," Herria said, taking her hand away and patting Ems on the arm. "Think about it. Take your time. Let's talk again around competition time. And don't forget what I said about that deferment."

Ems hadn't forgotten. The upcoming breeding cycle was still foremost in her mind. All she had to do now was figure out whether to become personal assistant to the most powerful woman in the world or do her duty to society and breed with a male.

The choice — to Ems's surprise — wasn't as easy as she had anticipated.

CHAPTER 5
NEEN

"NEEN, WAKE UP!" the voice was a hoarse whisper.

"Huh?" Neen felt her sweaty cheek peel off the tablet screen. She had fallen asleep at the desk. "Right," she said, still groggy. "Sorry."

Pelon stood above her, nervously checking the mounted screens around the lab. She bit her bottom lip. "Classes are starting soon," she said, still urgently whispering.

"Don't worry," Neen answered, now more alert. "They can't see us, remember? I've twinned them to the feed in the next lab over."

Neen couldn't help but smile to herself. It was an old trick she'd maneuvered as a student to get more practicum time in the lab. Neen had figured out how to reroute the visual feed of the laboratory security screens so that they picked up the feed of the lab rooms nearby. It wouldn't work for any network outside the lab rooms, but if the screens were wired to the same central link, Neen could "twin" the screens so they shared one feed.

Gave her an edge in exams, being able to work after hours on her experiments.

Now she hoped all those extra hours in the bio labs would serve her well.

"Did you make it?" Pelon asked. She was a Triverser like Neen, but still in the Institute studying. They had shared some classes together, but Neen was able to graduate early. Students and teachers around campus still called Neen "prodigy," but she tried to ignore the somewhat sarcastic tone that came with it.

"I think so," Neen replied.

"That's good," said Pelon. "Because you gotta go. Now."

Neen didn't need to be told twice. She gathered her things, handling a small insulated nylon case carefully.

"Did you get it done?" Pelon asked, excitement in her eyes. Pelon had always admired Neen.

"I think so. Luckily I fell asleep after I finished the last test."

"Here's to more good luck."

"Thanks, Pelon. I'll need it."

"What exactly is this all for?" her old classmate asked.

"If I told you, you'd probably never see me again." Neen smiled, trying to make it seem like a joke. If only Pelon knew the risk she was taking, she'd never have let Neen use the lab.

"No need for that!" Pelon laughed. "I'm looking forward to you being on the high council someday."

"If I don't get caught now!"

Neen rushed out, hoping Pelon remembered to restart the lab screen's feed before anyone noticed the twinned images.

Just as the first rays of sun crested over the horizon, Neen emerged into the open air and headed toward the Arena Dome.

* * *

"HE'S HERE ALREADY?" the guard said, surprised to see Tem waiting in the room. "Spending a lot of time with this one, aren't you?" The guard raised her eyebrows at Neen.

Neen detected a sharpness in the other woman's voice. She realized she wouldn't be able to plan too many sessions with this male or else security might suspect something amiss.

"He's an edge case," Neen said, improvising. "One or two more sessions should probably do it."

One or two more sessions? Neen felt her stomach lurch. Why had she boxed herself in like that? Two more sessions weren't enough.

She clung to hope that her experiment would work.

"Hello, Tem." Neen and he were alone at last.

"Hello." He looked at her pistol. Neen could see the puzzlement on his face. She also couldn't help but notice that he was cleaner this time, not as sweaty. His dark brown hair was combed back, out of his eyes.

They were dark eyes, almost black, and the way they stared at her made Neen turn away.

"I thought we should meet again," she said, pretending to read something on her handheld screen. "I thought—"

Now that it came to it, Neen was nervous to tell him why she had scheduled this follow-up. He had no idea how much had changed for her these past few days, how much Naal's story had haunted her, how Nekka's words had spurred her to do something.

"Am I in trouble or something?" Tem asked.

"What? No! Definitely not."

"Then why—"

"I thought of a way to help you."

Tem couldn't have looked more disbelieving. Neen

watched his face register feelings of suspicion, confusion, and doubt all in a matter of seconds.

"Really," Neen continued. "After what you told me, and... after learning more about what goes on here, I decided I could help you pass your trial. Maybe even win your competition."

"What if I don't want your help?"

"That would be pretty stupid of you." She'd blurted it out without thinking. As soon as the words left her mouth she cursed herself for saying them. Why was she always so blunt? Why did she have to insult him like that?

"Just a dumb Benglion, is that it?" Tem said. "What if you speak slowly? Then maybe I'll understand why a woman is trying to help me."

"Can we please not do this? We don't have to be enemies."

"Don't we?"

"Listen, Tem. I know what happens to males who don't pass their trials. I know." Neen tried to hold his gaze, tried to help him see she could be trusted. "Please."

Tem looked at her, searching her face for the truth.

Neen didn't know what else she could do to reach him. Almost unconsciously, she let her fingers slide over the necklace Nekka had given her, feeling the smooth face of the half-moon pendant.

Tem watched her. His face was inscrutable, but as he studied her, Neen could see him softening.

"You know what happens to us?" he said, at last.

Neen nodded.

"And you don't want that to happen to me?"

"I don't." Neen realized how that sounded. "Not to any male," she added quickly.

A half-smile crept over Tem's lips. "Not to any male," he repeated. "But I'm the one you've got."

"You're the one I can help."

"How?"

"I think I've found a way to suppress your trauma." Neen opened the nylon case from the lab. Inside was a vial of clear liquid and a syringe.

Tem shifted uncomfortably.

"It's nothing bad," Neen said, trying to sound as calm as possible. "Just a neural blocker serum. Should reduce the fear response in your brain. As a Benglion, you already have fewer inhibitions and can handle fear well, but this formula should intensify that response to stimuli. It'll block the anxiety you feel when confronted with physical violence."

"Did you test this beforehand?"

Neen bit her lip. "No. There wasn't time. But it's safe, trust me."

"Safe, fine," Tem said, "but effective?"

Neen hesitated. She believed in her skills — she knew this would work — but how could she make Tem believe?

"I know what I'm doing," she answered. "This kind of thing is one of my specialties."

"Like the pills they give us to subdue all the males?" Once again, Tem managed to land his hit.

Neen wasn't involved in manufacturing those pills — she wasn't even born when they were created — but she was a woman of EVE, and her tacit participation in this society meant tacit approval of its policies. Thinking about those pills now, how they drugged the males and rendered them docile and compliant, renewed her guilt about the things being done to them in her name.

"It's a similar process, but my serum won't cloud your mind so much as free you from your fears."

"But what if it doesn't work?"

"It will."

Tem didn't say anything, so Neen filled the syringe.

"Are you okay with needles?" she asked.

"Does it matter if I'm not?" Tem grinned.

Neen couldn't help but smile. "No, I guess it doesn't."

"I'll be brave," he said, teasingly.

Tem pulled back his sleeve. He didn't flinch, didn't even move when Neen injected the serum.

Standing that close to him, Neen could see how muscular he really was. He may not have the height or bulging biceps of someone like Lekko, but Tem was unmistakably Benglion.

She couldn't help but catch a whiff of his scent. The clean smell of soap was evident, but there was that other smell, that pleasant woodsy smell she had noticed the first time. Neen could see his face up close now, the softness of his brown eyes, the trim cut of his beard that showed off the fullness of his lips. When she took the syringe out of his arm, she tried not to drop it.

"All set," she said, trying to regain her composure. She put the syringe and vial back in their case.

"When will it start working?"

"Any second now."

"I don't feel anything."

"How about now?"

Neen aimed the pistol right at his head. She didn't flinch as she held it inches from his skull.

Tem didn't move. "Am I supposed to be scared?"

"I could kill you."

"But I know you won't."

"Do you?"

Tem just laughed. "Neen, didn't you say you wanted me to survive? You're not fooling anyone with that gun!"

Neen lowered the pistol. She realized now how silly her little ruse was. Of course the pistol wouldn't scare him! There was no possible way they could test his fear response, just the two of them, here in this room. They would have to wait until something happened to him in the Dome. A confrontation.

"Can I tell you something?" Tem said. "I should've said something earlier."

"Something?" Neen didn't like this. It sounded like a confession, and not the good kind. "What?"

"The pills," Tem said, "they don't work on me."

"They don't work on you?" Neen was sure she misunderstood him. "That's not possible."

"It is for me. Listen, I don't understand it, but the pills have never had much effect on me. At first, I felt a kind of brain fog, but it went away after a couple of hours, and then after that, every time I took the pills, the fog was thinner and thinner until it was nothing at all."

"You mean you feel no difference between now and when you take the pills?"

"None."

Neen's brain whirled. How could this be? EVE's scientists would have controlled for all circumstances, made sure whatever pharmaceuticals were manufactured would be one hundred percent effective. It just didn't seem possible that the pill wouldn't work on Tem.

Were there others? What if this wasn't uncommon, and when the males were taken to the breeding suites the mood-influencing drugs they'd ingested didn't work? Is this why women were rejecting so many breeding partners?

Neen worried that she would have to report this to the council, but something made her hesitate. If she said anything, then what would that mean for Tem? Would he be erased immediately?

"Maybe—" she struggled to find an explanation. "Maybe my serum will be different. The neural effect is more straightforward, not nearly as complicated as the pills you take for breeding or living in the clan Domes."

"But what if it's not different? What happens if this serum doesn't work?"

Neen could tell Tem was trying to keep his voice steady, but there was the slightest of breaks when he spoke that last question. She tried smiling, tried being the confident, unflappable prodigy everyone believed her to be.

"It will," she answered. "I know it will.

"And if it doesn't?"

"If it doesn't, we'll find a different way."

We.

When she said the word, Neen felt her stomach flutter, the kind of flutter that came from wanting something so badly that it became a physical need.

Was there really a "we"? She and Tem had just met.

Neen did her best to dampen these feelings. If the serum didn't work, she wasn't sure what to try next. How could they find a way when everything seemed stacked against them? Together or alone, Neen worried this problem was too complicated for her to solve.

She hated that feeling. She had always found answers for everything when she was a student. No problem was unsolvable. But this one was different. How could she possibly fix something this big?

* * *

"YOU'RE LATE." Sona Lohen looked Neen up and down, surveying her like a drill sergeant.

"Lost track of time," Neen answered, breathless. "The interviews with the males can be intense."

"I bet." Sona barely disguised her dislike of the situation. She motioned for Neen to come with her as she walked along the interior perimeter of the Arena stadium. Sona was making notes on her tablet. "We'll have to talk while I run some security checks," she said.

Neen didn't mind. Hopefully, Sona would be more interested in the security than in Neen's work with the males. She still didn't understand why Nekka had instructed her to meet with Sona in the first place.

The captain of the Benglion special forces strode across the palisades with determined focus, tapping quickly on her screen, barking out stray orders to her officers working at the various checkpoints in the stadium, and otherwise being the consummate professional and commander of all Dome security within High City.

"What can you report?" Sona asked Neen.

"Uh—" Neen wasn't sure what to say.

"Security risks? Borderline cases? Males we need to keep a special eye on?" Sona spoke at a clipped pace, barely looking at Neen but monitoring everything else around her.

She reminded Neen of a hawk, like the kind who sometimes perched on the highest towers of the city, their bodies erect, their eyes scanning everything, looking for a mouse to squeeze in their sharp talons. Sona's body was all pent-up strength and speed, her chiseled muscles encased in the close-fitting jumpsuit of her clan's highest-level police force. Neen was somewhat in awe of her. Sona reminded her of one of those depictions from ancient times of warrior women. She half expected the captain to wield a sword and shield instead of a gun.

"Didn't Nekka brief you?" Sona asked, slight exasperation in her voice.

"She said we needed to meet," Neen replied.

Sona smirked. "Typical Nekka." She stopped for a moment and turned to face Neen. "Is there anything you can tell me that might help my security forces? Any males that are still in the running that we might need to watch?"

"Well," Neen trod carefully, "I suppose there are a few." She was reluctant to paint the males badly, but she did mention what she'd learned about Lekko, Naal, and a few others. "I don't think they're security risks," Neen added.

"The big one, he seemed hostile?" Sona asked.

"Lekko seemed resentful. About his situation. But I don't think he'd be hostile."

"You didn't reject him outright?" Sona raised an eyebrow.

"He's bred before."

"Hm." Sona looked down at the stadium floor where Trabador males were setting up equipment for the trials. They were all under heavy guard. Sona's guards.

"I guess keep an eye on him," Neen offered. "But I don't think he's dangerous."

"Good. Because if he is, you'll face quite an inquiry from the high council for your blunder."

Sona started walking again, tapping more messages into her tablet. "Anyone else?"

Neen thought of Tem. He was no security risk, that was for sure. But what would happen to him in the fighting ring? It's not like Sona would want to help out there. She probably had no qualms about watching the males lose their fights. Not breeding material, after all.

"Have you ever bred before?" Neen found herself blurting out.

Sona stopped in her tracks.

"I'm sorry, I shouldn't have—" Neen began.

"No, it's alright," said Sona. She faced Neen again. "We shouldn't be ashamed to discuss such things. It's our duty to serve the sisterhood, breeding included."

Neen waited for her to say more.

Sona sighed. "I was in the program. Once. Class B. But I didn't conceive. They quickly removed me after that."

Neen thought she saw a look of relief on Sona's face. "You weren't disappointed?" she asked the captain.

Sona smirked again. "Hardly."

"So you didn't form any kind of attachment with your breeding partner? I've heard that sometimes happens."

This time Sona laughed. "Definitely not." She shook her head and looked at Neen as if the younger woman were a child.

"I just wondered—"

"I did my duty," Sona continued, not unkindly. "But I'd much prefer the bed of my lover."

Neen understood. "Apologies, Sona."

"No need."

"Is she Benglion as well?" Neen knew it was common for women to have romantic partners of the same clan, but not unheard of for women in High City to sleep with those from other clans.

"She is," Sona replied. "Li is her name. She's a guard back in Bells, in the clan Dome."

Sona's face was wistful as she spoke of Li, and Neen wondered what it must be like to live and work so far away from the one you loved.

Suddenly Sona's tablet pinged. A message.

"Excuse me," she said, moving away from Neen for some privacy.

While Sona read her message, Neen looked down over the railings to watch the workers below. The males looked almost like robots, their bodies moving without emotion or even a hint of joy as they labored. Neen had never seen the Arena Dome before the trials. The thrill of watching the males compete was less thrilling now that she had seen behind the veil. The grim reality of their situation was no longer fodder for her entertainment.

"Neen." Sona's voice was sharp.

Neen thought they had gotten on better footing with each other, but Sona's face did not look pleased.

"Were you given permission to access the breeding suite feeds?" Sona said, striding over.

"What?" At first Neen thought about her little trick with twinning the lab screens, but that's not what Sona meant. "I didn't."

"Someone did," Sona continued, looking strained.

"Breeding sessions aren't scheduled until after the competitions," Neen said. "That's three weeks away."

"I know. But it's standard protocol for my office to check the networks several times both before and after the competitions. Make sure everything is secure for breeding. But just now I got a report that someone outside my department accessed the feeds. They used authorized codes to get in, but I don't recognize the source."

"It wasn't me." Neen couldn't hide her annoyance. Wasn't Sona supposed to be an ally of Nekka's? Why was she so suspicious of Neen's activities?

"Nekka didn't authorize something like this?" Sona asked.

"Ask her yourself. Don't drag me into it."

Sona rubbed the bridge of her nose. She was clearly stressed. Sighing, she shook her head. "You're right, Neen. I shouldn't have jumped to conclusions. It's frustrating trying to make sure everything is ready when so much seems to be going wrong."

Sona didn't elaborate, and as much as Neen wanted to ask her what else was going "wrong," she bit her tongue.

"It's okay," Neen said. "You have a lot to worry about. I don't envy your job."

"Nor I you," Sona said, a slight smile coming back to her face. "Day after day with those males. I can't imagine a more unpleasant task."

"It's not so bad for me."

Sona raised an eyebrow.

"Really," Neen insisted. "I guess Nekka knew what she was doing when she picked me."

"Nekka always knows what she's doing." Sona sighed again and looked back down at the alert from earlier.

"So who could have accessed those screens?" Neen asked. "And for what?"

"That's what I want to know. Someone with high-level clearance needed to authorize this. I thought perhaps Nekka might have given you permission. But I suppose that doesn't really make sense," Sona said, almost talking to herself. "Who would want to check those feeds? For what purpose?"

"Are you sure it wasn't someone from your department?"

"I'm sure."

"Then it was someone else from the high council?"

Sona didn't answer. Both she and Neen knew that it wasn't wise to question the actions of the high council. Even here, at the heights of the Arena Dome, with barely anyone around, they knew that screens could be monitoring their every word. Even their handheld tablets could be used to spy, if necessary. It wasn't likely — Sona was head of the security special forces after all — but it wasn't impossible.

"Speculation is unnecessary, Neen. Let my office handle it."

Neen understood. "Are we done here?"

"Yes. For now."

Neen turned to go, but Sona called her back.

"Neen," she said, speaking in a low voice and leaning in. "Good luck in there with the males. Keep your pistol close. And if you ever need some target practice..."

Neen thought of her earlier attempt to frighten Tem with the gun. Would she have been willing to pull the trigger if he *was* a threat? Neen couldn't imagine Tem being dangerous. Even though he was Benglion — trained to fight, stronger and quicker than the other clans — Neen couldn't bring herself to see Tem hurting her.

"... I can show you how to use it," Sona finished. "Just say the word." She put a hand on her own gun, holstered at her waist.

Neen gave a faint smile. Sona's offer was meant kindly, but Neen wasn't quite sure how to respond. Could she shoot a male if she had to?

As she left the platform and descended back down into the bowels of the Dome, Neen wondered what would happen if the males attacked. How would Triversers like herself respond?

She glanced at a security screen on the wall. She felt safer knowing the males were monitored at all times. And the guards were armed. And if any male tried to escape, the chip in his arm would release its deadly toxin.

But in the breeding suites... It would only take a few seconds for something to happen... and if the pills didn't work... even one male with immunity could wreak havoc...

Neen thought of Ems: small, delicate, wonderful Ems. What would happen to her in the breeding suite with a male who was immune to the mood drugs?

Neen knew she should tell someone. Nekka, at least, should know. But if she spoke up, if she exposed Tem, what chance did he have? He'd be sent to the Work Dome without a second thought. Erased. Doomed. Even Nekka, who seemed to hate what was happening to the males, couldn't save Tem if his secret got out.

Neen couldn't understand it, but as much as she worried about Ems, as much as she loved her, she couldn't bring herself to betray Tem.

Maybe this is what they meant about the dangers of men. How could she be so conflicted? What was happening to her? Why did she care so much about him? They had only met a few times.

But there was something in the way he looked at her, in the way he spoke of his pain and revealed his vulnerability. Neen couldn't get the image of a young Tem out of her head. A boy with no one to care for him.

Things were only going to get more complicated. Neen knew it. She had to trust that somehow Tem was the only one with immunity to the drugs. That had to be it. No other males were immune. And somehow Neen's serum would still work. It had to, or else Neen didn't know what to do.

It was a faint hope. Every minute that passed made her doubt more. Doom encroached on all sides. It was going to explode in a few weeks when the competitions started and the breeding selection began.

And what about those security screens in the breeding suites? Neen couldn't stop thinking about what Sona said.

Someone had gained access to them. Someone wanted to circumvent the normal security. Someone with connections to the high council.

Someone who didn't want to be discovered.

CHAPTER 6
TEM

HE HADN'T SEEN her in over a week. Tem wasn't sure why, but he found himself getting upset by her absence. Hadn't she promised him?

But a week had gone by and no word.

Then today, the summons.

"No practice for you, MI-1338," the guards had said. "You've been requested elsewhere."

They shoved him into the interrogation room. It was empty, except for the table and two chairs. The pitcher of water was gone.

When Neen walked in, Tem tried not to react. He was going to stay calm. He wouldn't let her see anything beyond the mask of his face.

"The guards have started commenting," he said before she could sit down. He definitely noticed her eyes glancing at him as she walked past.

"Commenting?"

Did that get her attention? Tem could tell how proud she was, how much she hated anyone questioning her motives or her intelligence.

"Yes, they whisper and stare. A lot. I suppose it's a good thing we haven't seen each other in a while. Might quiet down the rumors."

"I admit," Neen said, "I thought it best to limit our time as much as possible. The guards aren't the only ones who might wonder what's going on."

"And what *is* going on?"

Her eyes were bright, expectant. "Has the serum worked?"

Tem wasn't sure why, but he felt bad disappointing her. He shifted in his chair. "I wish I could give you better news."

Neen's face dropped. "Are you sure?"

"I think so," Tem answered.

Neen swore under her breath.

"I'm sorry," he said.

"You don't have anything to apologize for," Neen said. "I'm the one who screwed up. Are you really sure it didn't work?"

"I went into the fighting ring. But I could barely focus. If I hadn't been sparring with my friend Dron, I probably would've had a panic attack."

"Your friend?" Neen sounded surprised.

"Yeah, I'm pretty horrible, aren't I?" Tem said. "Who would want to be friends with me?" He he rolled his eyes to let her know he was joking, but still, he couldn't believe her ignorance. As if all the males in the Domes were just isolated automatons, no feelings, no need for friendship.

Her face blushed. "That's not what I meant," she said quickly. "I just—"

"I know." Tem smiled genuinely this time. "But is it really so hard to believe that we males have friendships in the Dome?"

"Have you known this Dron a long time?"

"A few years. We were assigned to the same training sessions and kinda hit it off. He's funny. You'd like him." Tem realized how stupid that sounded. When would Neen ever meet some random male in the Dome? Unless she was a breeder. But didn't she say she was disqualified? Tem didn't like the idea of Neen breeding with Dron. An impossibility anyway. They were different clans.

"I'm sorry," Neen said. "I shouldn't have assumed anything about your life. But if you got into the ring and didn't have a panic attack, that might indicate the serum is working."

Tem shook his head. "I wasn't 'fighting' Dron. It wasn't real. I couldn't get into the ring with anyone else."

"But still. You got into the ring."

Tem appreciated Neen's optimism, but he knew his body. He knew what it felt like to have that fear welling up inside him, and he knew that the serum hadn't suppressed that fear.

"You don't have to win, Tem. Just pass your trial. Fight to a draw."

"I don't think I can. I wish I could, but there's something different about me. The pills don't work. Your serum either. Nothing."

He tried to hold himself together. It wasn't that Tem couldn't face fear or hold strong in the face of danger. He had the fastest time in rescue drills. He would run through fire to save his friends. But when the time for fighting came, all he saw were those jeering, hateful female faces, those women who should have helped him but didn't. They swam around his vision like sharks, waiting to devour.

Tem looked at Neen's face. Hers was so different from those grinning sharks. When he looked into her eyes, he felt for the first time in his life that maybe he could fight back. He wanted to believe. But even against Dron, he couldn't shake the nauseating fear. He hated himself for being unable to put aside that part of his childhood.

"Maybe we can just talk." Neen tucked a lock of her honey-brown hair behind her ear. "About your youth. I know I'm not a specialist or anything. I'm no Evox. But maybe if we just talk, maybe you can let go of the shame that's holding you back."

Talk? Tem didn't see what good that would do. He could try explaining it again, try to help her see what it was like, but how could that help him overcome anything?

The old nagging thought about why Neen was helping him came back. Sure, she'd said it was because of the Work Domes, because of what they did to males who failed. He had heard those rumors too. Naal had been having nightmares about it for months. But Tem still wasn't sure he could trust Neen, even after what she'd risked.

Hadn't Naal said not to trust the females? Neen might think she wanted to help him, but she was still part of the system, part of the oppression. She wanted to help Tem, but she didn't give a damn about the males as a whole.

He couldn't help frowning and retreating into himself.

"What if I start?" Neen said, undeterred. "You know, I used to sneak off to catch a glimpse of the youths in Young Dome. I was always so curious. I know what it's like to be different from others. We women aren't allowed to be different either. Taking an interest in Young Dome was not normal behavior."

Tem scoffed. "That's what made you different? Catching peaks at the boys in the Dome?"

"It's more than that!" Neen continued, blushing again. "I've always wanted more. Our lives in the clans are stifling. I'm not a Trabador, so I'm not expected to work in the fields or forests, and I'm not a Sixter, so I'm not supposed to pilot aircraft or ships, but I've always dreamed of them. I've always wanted to hike into the open wilderness and explore and soar above the clouds."

"You don't like being a brilliant Triverser?"

"I do like engineering and planning and biochemistry. It's not that." Neen looked wistfully at some unseen vision behind Tem's head. "But my heart wishes it could do more."

Tem didn't hide the bitterness on his face when she looked at him again.

"Oh," she said. "Oh no. I'm sorry, Tem. I didn't realize—"

Of course she didn't. Female privilege. "I'm sorry you don't get to do all the things you want," he said, his voice trying to contain its anger.

"I shouldn't have complained," Neen continued. "You're right. I'm not a prisoner trapped behind these impenetrable walls."

"Walls that if we even so much as try to breach them will kill us," Tem reminded her. "Walls we can't even see out of. Did you know I've only felt the outside air three times in my life? Once when I was born, once when leaving Young Dome, and once when leaving the Clan Dome to come here. Three times. Do you know how often I see the digital images your high council broadcasts and wish I could really touch those blades of grass, those mountains, those waters? To feel the wind across my face?"

His heart was beating faster. He thought Neen would be mad, but instead, her eyes glistened.

"I'm sorry," she said, eyes now downcast. "Most of us are ignorant of what it's really like in here. I had never thought—"

"Yeah," Tem replied. "Just because my world is a prison doesn't mean you don't feel shackled in some way too. It's a rotten world, that's all."

Sparks of fire flickered suddenly in Neen's eyes. He had gone too far. "It was even more rotten when males ran things," she challenged.

Tem found his own voice rising. "It wasn't rotten because it was run by males," he answered. "It was rotten because it was run by rotten people. Male or female, it doesn't matter. There's no monopoly on wickedness."

"Except right now in our world there is no hunger or crime or war," Neen countered. "Women did that."

"And put males in Domes."

Neen's lips grew thin. He could see the struggle happening within her between indoctrination and compassion.

"I'm just saying," Tem continued, his voice calmer, "it's wrong to judge people based on something they didn't do. I didn't subjugate you, Neen. None of us alive in this Dome did."

"I know," Neen said. "But males are dangerous. They can't help it. We know that your brain chemistry makes you more violent. Hostile. Look at us now, arguing when I'm trying to help you! We can't fight genetics."

"If you say so." Naal was right. He shouldn't have trusted her.

"Please, Tem. This is your life we're talking about. Try opening up about your youth. Maybe we can fix things if you talk about it."

"Why? So you can get that glimpse into Young Dome again?" He couldn't help the bitterness rising in his voice. Why was she so desperate to help him?

"No, that's not what I meant—" Neen began. Her voice was low, heavy perhaps with guilt. "I just... I want to help you."

Neen kept saying that, but all Tem could think was *why*. Why did she want to help him so badly? Desperately, even.

"What makes me so special?" he said after a moment's silence.

Neen's hand when to the pendant around her neck. She rubbed it with her fingers, unable to meet Tem's gaze.

He watched her. He said nothing. He wondered where she had gotten that half-moon pendant, trying not to betray any emotion with his face. He kept silent, but still, he wondered.

"Why me?" he repeated. "You've still never given a real answer."

Neen let the pendant fall back down across her chest. "I don't have a real answer. All I know is—" She stopped. The words seemed to catch in her throat.

Tem was trying hard to stay guarded. He shouldn't trust her. There could be no trust between males and women.

But what if—

Tem studied her face. He didn't see dishonesty. He didn't see cruelty. Neen may be misguided by her society, but she herself didn't seem evil. What would happen if Tem decided to trust her? What would happen if he let his guard down and let her in?

"I—" Now his own words were a struggle to get out. "I always finished mental tasks quicker than the others. Simple things, basic things like arithmetic. But the others, they hated me for it."

"The other Benglions?"

Tem nodded. "When I would finish reading a book faster than anyone else, that's when the taunts would begin. Little acts of violence that went unnoticed by the instructors. I thought it was just something I had to accept. Something everyone went through."

"You remind me of myself," she said. "I would read faster than my fellow Triversers. Got teased a lot, actually."

Tem sighed heavily.

"Sorry! I know I should stop comparing myself to you. It's not the same thing. Really, I'm sorry." Neen shifted in her chair. "What kind of books did you like? I always loved those books about pilot squadrons from the first war. Or the ones about the women who rang the first bell of the revolution."

Tem shook his head. "We read rulebooks. A treatise written on the inferiority of males. Reminders of our violent natures and the need for Domes."

Neen's face fell. "Right. Of course. Why would a Benglion male need to read stories or histories? I'm sorry."

Tem watched Neen's face as she seemed to make mental note of something. The creeping doubt that he shouldn't trust her kept trying to resurface, but Tem pushed it away. He had made his choice and needed to keep it.

"Once I showed myself smarter than the other boys, the bullying really started. Any opportunity they could, the others found ways of hurting me without facing consequences. Tripping me during runs. Cornering me after showers and shoving soap in my mouth. Stealing my food rations."

"Those youths were cowards," Neen replied. "They only did those things because they knew they could get away with it. You were isolated. Alone. No one willing to help."

"I should have stood up for myself." Tem's insides burned when he thought of how helpless he'd let himself become.

"No," Neen was emphatic now. "No one should have to face those things alone. It's not cowardice to need help, Tem. You were a child!"

"It is cowardice. I'm supposed to be a Benglion." As much as he hated the regime and its treatment toward males, he couldn't help but internalize the indoctrination they had given him. Benglions were strong, swift, and willing to take risks that other clans would not. Fearless. Unbreakable.

But Tem had broken. He was a defective Benglion.

"No," Neen repeated. "You were tortured as a child. I don't care if you're Benglion or not, no one could face something like that and not be affected! And you had to face it alone. I don't know where I would be if I didn't have Ems by my side when we were young. She was and is my best friend, and without her, I'm not sure I would be who I am today. We all need friendship, Tem, and the fact that you had none as a youth is not your fault. It's not your fault."

Tem tried to accept her words. Intellectually he knew they made sense. No matter what the guards and the councils of EVE might do to the males, all humans are social creatures, and they need social interaction and approval. He knew these things on a rational level, but still, he couldn't bring himself to believe them in his heart.

"You aren't alone now, Tem. You have friends. Think of Dron. Think of... me."

"We're friends?" Tem shook his head. "We barely know each other."

"Barely? Three meetings should count for something," Neen grinned.

"Well," Tem said, unable to suppress his own grin. "Maybe not barely."

"Maybe we can know each other more."

Tem didn't know what to say. Suddenly, he felt a strange tug on his heart. *Know each other more?* What did she mean? And why did he find himself wanting to say yes?

"Did I tell you," Neen said slowly, "I've been reassigned?"

Tem felt his stomach clench. No more interviews? His heart started racing. Was this the last time he'd get to talk to

Neen? Why was he suddenly so worried? What did this woman even mean to him?

"Reassigned?" he said, forcing the word out.

"Yes. Fertility Class B. My latest tests say I'm able to breed now."

"What?" Tem's mind was racing. The worries that had just overwhelmed him were replaced by a furious mix of confusion, doubt, and excitement he couldn't explain.

"Apparently my eggs are much stronger than they once were." She tried to laugh it off, but Tem could see her eyes searching his face for approval.

"Really?" The whole thing sounded suspicious, but Neen looked innocent.

"Really."

"Are you happy about this?" Why did he ask it with a clipped voice? Was he angry? Or something else?

"I wasn't at first. But then..." Her voice trailed off.

"We're being honest with each other, right?"

"I was approached by a member of the high council. There's a new program that's starting soon. They offered me a position in it, a trial run..."

Tem didn't understand what this had to do with his question. He wanted to know her feelings.

"Cross-breeding," Neen said quickly. "Clan mixing."

Tem wasn't sure he heard her right. "What?"

"The high council wants to experiment. Males and women from different clans breeding together. I've been selected for the beta testing."

Now Tem knew she was lying. Cross-breeding? Swapping genetic traits between the clans? It was preposterous.

But then why was his heart racing? Why was he wondering suddenly who Neen would pick as her mate?

"It's top secret right now," Neen continued. "But I wanted you to know."

"You wanted me to know?"

"Yes." She blushed a deep crimson. "I wanted you to know before you faced your competition."

"Clan-mixing?" he said.

Tem couldn't deny that Neen was beautiful. He had seen Benglion women most of his life, so he was used to the tall, muscular frames of that clan, but something was captivating about Neen's slender body, her long honey-brown hair that always carried with it a fresh-air scent that made his body ache.

"It could work," Neen said.

"You're hoping it does?"

Neen took a deep breath. "I am."

* * *

WHEN TEM WAS BROUGHT BACK to his cell, Dron was just being escorted out for toilet cleaning duty.

"Can I help?" Tem asked his guard.

The two female guards looked at each other and shrugged.

"Take him, he's yours," said Tem's guard, handing him over to Dron's guard.

"Are you crazy?" Dron whispered as they walked down the dank hallway. He ran a hand through his short, spiked hair. "You could've stayed put and dreamed of the breeding suite instead."

"I like helping a friend," Tem said, winking.

"Elbow-deep in shit water?" Dron replied. "I'm not sure I want a friend who's lost his mind!"

The guard poked Dron to be quiet, and the two males

walked silently the rest of the way. Tem could tell that Dron was dying to find out what happened with Neen, but talking freely would have to wait until they were back in their cell.

"Go on," the guard said, shoving both males into the latrine room. Dron realized he only had one mop.

"Better ask for another," he said to Tem.

"You go, I'll get started here."

Dron went to the guard and got permission to get another bucket and mop. She messaged for a new guard to come to stand outside while she took Dron for more supplies.

When Dron was gone, it was just Tem alone with the new guard outside the door.

He got to work right away, hoping the physical exertion could take his mind off everything swirling around his head.

Why had she told him that about the clan-mixing experiment? Was she hoping to choose him? He had dismissed the idea that Neen was interested in him like that, but then why had she said anything about breeding? About her fertility? Was she trying to encourage him? To give him something to fight for?

He heard Naal's gruff voice echoing in his head. *She's a woman. One of the enemy.*

But he had opened up to her. She seemed to really care. What if all the women weren't bad? What if some of them could be allies? Neen felt like an ally.

At last, Tem admitted it to himself. He had chosen to trust her. He wanted to see her again. He wanted to tell her the truth.

Pangs of guilt washed over him. He hadn't told her everything, had he?

The escape. His search for a plan. The desire that he and Naal, and Dron, and Lekko shared to break out of the Dome and be free.

If Neen knew what he and the others were hoping to do, she'd stop him. Just like any woman would. It was one thing for Neen to trust him when he was working within the system. She might even want to breed with him, if this new program was to be believed.

But to want a pack of males to escape? To turn a blind eye or even help?

No, that would go too far.

She would stop him without a second thought.

Tem pushed his feelings down, told himself to forget Neen and her talk of breeding. It wasn't going to happen.

He moved the mop across the floor, trying to focus on the back-and-forth motion of his arms.

But what if I passed my trial? he thought. What if I won the competition?

The fresh-air smell of Neen's hair came back to him. He imagined what it would be like to bury his face in that hair, in that smell and breathe it in...

"Thinking about breeding with the mop?" Dron said, coming back into the latrines.

Tem realized he had been resting his cheek against the mop handle. He sprung away from it, embarrassed.

"She must have done a number on you!" Dron continued. He started working alongside Tem. "Don't tell me the juicy details just yet." Dron glanced out the doorway at the two women standing guard. "But when we're alone, I want to know all about that Triverser spy!"

"She's not a spy," Tem mumbled.

Dron just laughed. He never took anything too seriously. Tem wished he could toss things off as easily as Dron. Dron was small for a Benglion, and he made up for his diminutive stature by making jokes, laughing things off, never thinking too hard about the consequences. As much as he liked Dron,

Tem could never be that way. He could never just ignore the feelings that welled up inside.

They worked together, side by side for several minutes, but their work was interrupted by a pack of males who needed to use the toilets.

As Dron and Tem moved aside to let them through, one of the males caught a look at Dron's face and his expression darkened.

"That's the fucker who took my soap ration," he growled.

Dron shrugged his shoulders and tried to look as innocent as possible, but the other male wouldn't be deterred.

"That was you," he said, shoving Dron in the shoulder.

"What can I say?" Dron said, smirking, "Your ass stinks with or without soap, so I thought you wouldn't mind!"

The gang of males surrounded him, their leader standing toe-to-toe with Dron.

"Say that again, fucker?" the male said.

Tem quickly stepped between. "Go use another toilet. We don't want any trouble."

The leader laughed. "What're you gonna do if we stay? Fight?"

The others laughed now too.

Tem's reputation was well-known.

"I don't want a fight," he answered. "But I will stand up for my friend." Tem got right into the other male's face. Whatever Dron had done, this other male was just an instigator. A bully.

"Come on, Tem," Dron said, pulling on Tem's arm. "This guy has a point. I did take the soap—"

"You need to leave," Tem said to the male. "Now."

"Yeah, okay, well," the other replied, "if you say so."

Without warning, he took a swing at Tem.

Tem ducked. He dodged another swing, and another. His adrenaline was pumping and he could feel his reflexes take over. For a split second, Tem wondered if Neen's serum really was working. He wasn't afraid.

But then the other males joined in, piling onto Tem and Dron like jackals. Someone grabbed Tem's arm, twisting it back in an unnatural angle.

Fog filled his eyes, everything swirled out of focus. He was in Young Dome again, the boys hounding him and scratching him, twisting his fingers, taunting him. He could hear Dron call out, but it was like his friend was submerged underwater, like they were separated by an endless echoing tunnel. The faces of the boys leered at him. Cruel, mocking grins of adult women encircled him. He needed to survive. That was the only thing that mattered. Survival... survival...

Tem covered his head and collapsed, trying to withstand the blows, trying to survive until the boys got bored with tormenting him.

Then, from out of the fog, another voice cut through. "Get off! Get the fuck off!"

It was Naal. Whichever bodies were piled on top of Tem were peeled off. The blows and kicks stopped.

Tem opened his eyes and he wasn't in Young Dome anymore. Lekko and Naal were driving the other males out. When Lekko grabbed their leader by the throat and started to squeeze, the male begged for mercy.

Lekko let him go and the pack quickly slinked away. The female guards outside the door chuckled to themselves as they watched the losers retreat.

Lekko and Naal helped Tem and Dron to their feet.

"What did you do this time, Dron?" Naal asked, frowning at the younger male.

"Is it a crime to want to be clean?" Dron said in his most innocent voice.

Lekko slapped him on the back. "There's not enough soap in the world for that, my friend."

The men laughed, but Tem turned away. His lip was cut and bleeding. He tried to wipe it clean, but it only stained his gray jumpsuit an ugly red color. His arm ached.

"You can all relax!" Dron called to the guards outside the door. "No broken noses to mar our delicate features!"

The guards ignored his antics, but they did call Lekko and Naal out. They had gotten their entertainment for the day, watching the males fight. The fun was over.

Tem watched his friends leave. Dron went back to mopping the floors, whistling as if nothing had happened.

But Tem couldn't make his body obey him. He was still seized with the remnants of that crippling fear.

The serum had failed.

What was he going to do when the trials came in a few days? How was he going to survive?

His heart sank. There was so much more he should have told Neen, but now he would never get the chance. Not unless he won his cohort and was selected for breeding.

An impossibility. Tem needed a miracle, and in the Dome, miracles were impossible to come by.

He reached into his pocket and fingered the small pendant inside. He let his index finger trace the straight edge of the half-moon shape, but he didn't take it out. He knew every millimeter of that pendant's surface, but he never showed it to anyone. Feeling its smoothness again made him hope. Even if miracles were impossible, maybe luck was on his side.

CHAPTER 7

EMS

THE STADIUM inside the Arena Dome was utterly silent. Ems could hear the breathing of the four pairs of Sixter males on the stadium floor. She glanced briefly at the other women in the stands, most of them Sixters like herself. They too were focused on the males down below. They all waited, listening and watching.

At last, one of the males spoke.

"I enjoy listening to the sound of water dripping slowly from a faucet."

Ems looked at Neen, who was sitting beside her. Her best friend was leaning forward, face locked in concentration, but Ems knew Neen probably couldn't make out what the male had said. He spoke in a quiet voice, too quiet for ordinary ears.

But not for the Sixter women.

The male's opponent was quiet for a long time, then replied. "Liar."

Immediately a green light flashed on all the screens around the stadium, including the handheld tablets resting on every woman's lap.

"Point to SI-1557," said a disembodied voice from the screens.

No one cheered. Everything was still perfectly quiet.

Ems dared to whisper. She leaned into Neen's ear. "I could tell before the words were even out of his mouth. Dilated pupils. Dead giveaway."

Ems was glad to have Neen by her side. It wasn't usual for women of different clans to attend the trials and competitions of another clan, but having Neen with her made Ems feel like herself again. For the past several days, she'd been cooped up with her new position within the high council. She and Neen had barely seen each other. It was nice to have her best friend by her side again.

Neen had said she'd needed a distraction. Ems could sense her friend's anxiety. Neen was nervous about something. Ems wished she would open up and talk about what was bothering her, but Neen said she didn't want to drag Ems into it.

Ems was ashamed to admit that she considered subtly influencing Neen to open up. She resisted the urge, but she couldn't deny that it was there. Herria had said this kind of subtle influencing was more like helping a person find the courage to do what they already wanted to do, but Ems wasn't so sure. If Neen wanted to tell her about these troubles, she would have. Ems didn't have the right to violate that.

It had only been a week, but already Herria was impressed with what Ems could do. Already Ems could do more than Herria could when she first started practicing her influencing powers.

Ems was ambivalent about the whole thing. Despite Herria's assurance to the contrary, the power to influence others' minds felt invasive.

If only Neen would say what was on her mind, Ems wouldn't be tempted to influence her.

Just then, Neen leaned over to say something. "Ems, listen, I know I've been guarded lately—"

Another Sixter shushed her. She scowled at Neen's Triverser jumpsuit.

Both Neen and Ems eyed each other and suppressed their giggles, staying quiet for the time being.

"The Benglion trials are later today, aren't they?" Ems asked once they were out of the Dome and mingling in the Arena Plaza outside. It was an intermission before the Sixter final competitions.

"Yes," Neen answered.

"I don't need to be a Sixter to know how nervous you are."

Neen met Ems's eyes, concern spread all over her face.

"That male of yours? Tem?"

Neen nodded. "I haven't felt like this since the day I took my Advanced Studies entrance exams. I think I'm going to be sick."

"Maybe he'll do fine."

Ems could feel the tension between them. Two weeks ago, Neen had told her what Nekka revealed about the Work Domes and the "erasure" process. Ems couldn't deny that it seemed overly harsh, barbaric even. But she worried that Neen was sticking her neck out for this male. Risking too much. They had argued about it at the time. It was the biggest argument they'd had in forever. Ems was sorry she couldn't feel as strongly about this as Neen, but she also didn't think it should come between them.

"He'll do fine," she said again.

"I wish I had your confidence."

"You did all you could, Neen."

Ems wondered if she could have done something. What

if she used her influencing powers to help Tem forget his trauma? Was that possible? Even Herria admitted she couldn't influence minds that deeply. It was more about getting others to act on thoughts they were already having. Subtle suggestions. Never overt control.

But Ems had felt more than that when she was training with Herria. She had felt as if she could go deeper, do more than just influence. Could she try to do that for Tem?

Ems was afraid to think about having that kind of power.

"I'm surprised you even decided to come to this," Neen said.

Neen knew that Herria wanted Ems to get a deferment, but Ems didn't like getting special favors. "I'm still in the breeding group," she said.

Neen's eyes widened. "What does your new boss think of that?"

"Not happy. Tried very hard to persuade me." Ems remembered Herria trying to influence her mind again, but she pushed back. She gave the councilwoman credit: Herria never told Ems not to push back, not to use her newfound power. She seemed almost pleased that Ems could resist her so well. Almost like it was another test.

"See anyone who interests you?" Neen asked.

Ems shook her head. "No one I'm pining for, I'm afraid." As soon as she said it, Ems worried Neen would take it as a jab, as if she were teasing her about Tem.

Neen did look at her strangely, trying to feel out what Ems might be implying.

Ems could feel Neen's pulse quicken with the thought of Tem.

* * *

"IS he the one who started your crisis of conscience?" Ems asked.

"Yes," Neen replied. "Naal."

They were back in their seats, awaiting the next event. Naal stood on the stadium floor, which had been transformed into a kind of obstacle course for the Benglion males to run.

"How do they possibly do it?" Ems said in awe. The challenge was for each male to run the course in under a minute. To Ems's eyes, this seemed impossible.

Neen wrinkled her nose, something she always did whenever she was calculating in her head. Ems loved when Neen focused on solving a problem.

"Two point seven seconds per element in the course," Neen murmured. "That's all the time they have."

"Impossible," Ems said again.

A loud buzzer echoed from every screen and Naal took off. The screens showed a countdown clock ticking the time away.

At first, Naal did well. He crossed several balance beams, high-stepped through a net-covered track, then dodged swinging columns that tried to knock him off balance. Then, with lightning speed and quick feet, he maintained his balance across a rotating cylindrical bridge.

Ems's eyes flitted back and forth between Naal's performance and the ticking clock. He was making good time. She didn't see anything coming up that was more difficult than the rotating bridge.

But then Naal's foot slipped. Just a simple balance beam, but it was enough. Maybe his legs had gotten tired. He didn't fall, but he teetered on the beam for a fraction of a second too long. That half-second of breathing and steadying himself was all it took. Trying to make up for the misstep, Naal ran faster, but his speed made him sloppy. More slips, more wavering, more seconds ticking away.

"He's not going to make it," Neen said under her breath.

Ems thought about what would happen to him. Before the competition, Naal and the other males were just names Neen had mentioned, just concepts that didn't register as flesh and blood for Ems. But now, seeing this male try to complete his trial — watching him try so hard only to fail — made Ems deeply uncomfortable. This Naal was certainly older than some of the other Benglions, but not that old. Graying around the temples, a slight loss of muscle mass. But his heart was beating well, even after all this exertion. Ems could tell from even this distance that Naal was not unfit. He seemed perfectly healthy.

But too slow. A fraction too slow.

Right before he crossed the finish line, the countdown hit zero and all the screens around the stadium blared harshly, flashing an angry red.

"No points awarded to ME-3441," the monotone voice announced.

The crowd of Benglion women laughed and booed. Some even shouted crude names at Naal.

Ems looked at her friend. Neen's face was pale.

"He's going to—" she began, but couldn't finish.

Ems didn't need Neen to finish. She knew.

Erased.

Her head started to ache. The trials for the Benglions were much more raucous than the ones for the Sixters. It made it hard to concentrate.

"I think I need to step out," Ems began, but Neen grabbed her arm.

"Please stay. I need you right now."

Ems looked back down at the stadium floor. Tem was standing there, awaiting his trial.

"First event: MI-1338. Strength," announced the echoing voice.

There was no question that the Benglion women found Tem attractive. But they held back their enthusiasm until they could see whether he measured up.

When the buzzer sounded, Tem grabbed the barbell and did an effortless clean and jerk. The screens showed the weight: 175 kilos. Then they flashed green.

The crowd finally allowed itself to cheer. Ems watched and listened as the women started chatting excitedly about this young male.

Ems wasn't immune either. Tem was attractive.

"You didn't tell me about that beard of his," Ems said, winking at Neen. "I didn't know you liked that on a male."

She was trying to get Neen to relax, but it didn't work. Neen's fingers were clenched together, the knuckles starting to turn white.

Next Tem ran the agility event. He made it in record time. The crowd erupted again, an even bigger cheer. The noise wasn't helping Ems's headache, but she was glad for Neen's sake. Tem seemed to be on his way toward passing the trial. He might even win his cohort, and then he'll be the pick of the litter for these women, she thought.

Event after event, Tem was nothing short of amazing. It was clear by the time he reached the penultimate event that the crowd was utterly on his side.

"Fifth event: MI-1338. Fortitude."

A massive hydraulic system lifted a huge platform from an opening in the floor. Tem stood waiting until the platform reached its final height, forty-three meters.

It was a climbing wall.

Tem put his hands and feet into the holds on the wall and started climbing. There was no countdown clock for this event, but Tem easily climbed the wall without breaking a sweat.

But once he reached the top, several jets of flame shot up from openings beneath the floor, each flame shooting up at timed intervals and in different areas around the platform. They were like blasts from the mouth of a dragon. This was the real test. Tem needed to climb back down without being hit by the flames. If he was too slow, or timed things wrong, he'd be engulfed in flames.

Neen covered her eyes. Ems put a hand on her arm to comfort her.

"He'll be alright," she said. "We've seen what he can do." Even as Ems said it, though, she worried. Other males had already been burnt horribly when they made the wrong move down the wall.

The flames shot up, always seemingly at random. Ems tried to see a pattern, but she couldn't discern one.

She listened through all the tumult in the stadium — through the cheers and chants of the women and the roar of the flames — and found Tem's heartbeat. Even from far away, Ems could find it.

He was utterly calm. No fear in the face of mortal danger.

What Neen had said about Tem didn't make sense to Ems. How could this male be worried about failing his trials?

When Tem reached the ground — unscathed — the crowd erupted. Clamorous chants and wild applause resounded around the stadium.

It was enough to make Neen open her eyes. She saw Tem standing safely on the ground.

"But he still has to fight..." she said to herself. Ems couldn't help but hear, even over the din.

The screens flashed "INTERMISSION" in bold yellow letters. Neen exhaled all the air she'd been holding in.

"Let's stretch our legs," Ems said, trying to pull her friend up, but Neen resisted.

"I'm too tense."

"All the more reason to get up and move."

Ems watched as Neen searched the stadium floor, but when she looked, she saw no trace of Tem. The guards must have removed him for the intermission

Trabador males were busy setting up the fighting ring.

Ems saw Neen's face go pale again. "Remember," she began, trying to change the subject, "how you always dreamed of being the first one to ring the bell to start the revolution?"

Neen didn't answer.

"Whatever happened to that young girl who wanted to fight the males in the streets? Win freedom for the sisterhood the world over? Now you're worried a male might lose his fight."

Neen frowned. "Yes. I am."

Ems tried smiling. "Just pointing out the irony."

Neen looked out at the raucous crowd of Benglion women.

"Look, I'm sorry," Ems said. "I just wanted to ease the tension. It's hard. I can't stop thinking about that other male... Naal. Will he really...?"

"Yes. And Tem too if he loses his bout."

"He won't, Neen. Have you seen him out there? He's fantastic."

Neen made no response.

"I have to admit, watching these Benglion trials is so

different from the Sixter ones," Ems continued. "Sixters doing target shooting or lie detection were always my favorites, but they're nothing compared to that fire tower Tem just overcame. It's quite a spectacle!"

"Watching them risk their lives?"

"I don't want them to die, if that's what you mean. But you can't deny how impressive they look when they succeed. I'm not saying I want to mate with one," Ems added quickly, "but I wonder what would happen if you combined that Benglion strength and nerve with the sensory abilities of a Sixter. I know we can't maintain the high level of enhancements if we crossbreed, but I wonder what kind of woman would result." Ems thought for a moment. "What kind of male, for that matter."

The bells rang to announce the end of the intermission.

"He just has to fight to a draw," Ems said as she and Neen took their seats again.

Tem was already in the ring when another Benglion male entered. He stalked around the ring, flexing his chest and glaring at Tem.

Neen gulped hard, and Ems squeezed her hand for support.

Ems started to wonder again if she might have the power to influence Tem. He was far away, but if she could alleviate his fears even the slightest bit, it might be enough to help him. She closed her eyes and concentrated as hard as she could on Tem's breathing, his heartbeat, his thoughts.

Sixters were only supposed to have five senses enhanced. No one should be able to perceive more than that. But Ems — and Herria — had a sixth sense. A perception of the mind. Ems focused on that now, trying with all her strength to hear the inner thoughts of Tem, to find a way to whisper into them and help him overcome his fears.

She could hear his breathing, his heartbeat, but not his thoughts. Too far away.

Ems opened her eyes and immediately her vision blurred. The headache came back like a knife to her skull. She smiled weakly at Neen who looked like a ghost.

"I should have tried something else," Neen murmured.

"You did your best," Ems said, her voice weak.

She felt so sorry for Neen. If only her friend could find a way to let go of this attachment to Tem. As horrific as it was that these males were erased and left to die in the Work Domes, what could she or Neen, or any other woman do about it? Maybe Ems could talk to Herria, get her to reverse the policy, or make it more humane. These kinds of reforms, sadly, often took time and patience.

But that didn't help Neen's suffering now. Ems thought again about what it would take to subtly influence her friend to let go of this attachment. Neen was right next to her, holding her hand.

Ems hated herself for even thinking it. She shuddered as the thoughts persisted in her head and she continued to push them out.

Having this power and resisting the urge to use it would require a lot from Ems. She worried she wouldn't be able to handle it.

The fight had already started, and when Ems looked down at the ring, she saw that Tem was doing a good job of dodging the other male's punches.

"He's barely hanging on," Neen muttered.

"But he is," Ems replied. "He is."

She squeezed her friend's hand. The countdown clock was ticking down.

"Just a few minutes more," Ems said.

The other male tackled Tem around the waist. Neen

jumped in her seat. Two blows to the head, and Tem was reeling.

Ems could hear his struggle to breathe. Neen's heart was pounding. The crowd's yelps and shouts started to crescendo.

Tem looked ready to cower, to cover his head and give up, but as Ems watched his face, her Sixter vision showing every line and crease and dilation of the eye, she noticed something strange. He looked as if he was remembering something. Not a traumatic memory, but a good one.

A look of determination. Like the one he had when he'd rushed down the burning platform. A face with something to look forward to.

"He's back up!" Neen couldn't help the excitement in her voice.

Tem managed to take a swing at his opponent, clocking him in the jaw.

"Neen!" Ems grip went tighter on Neen's hand. She could feel the cold clamminess of her friend's palm.

The buzzer sounded. Immediately, the two males stopped their fight. The crowd waited.

The screens flashed yellow and blinked the message in bold letters: "DRAW." The crowd let out a disappointed sigh. A draw meant they had passed their trial, but neither male would move on to the final competition.

"A draw... a draw..." Ems could hear Neen's thoughts reverberate in her own mind. When she looked over at her, Neen's relief was palpable.

"You didn't want him to win, did you?" Ems asked, eyebrow arched.

"What?"

"Tem. You didn't want him to lose, but you didn't want him to win either."

"How did you—" Neen started. Then she looked away. "I

lied to him. I made up a story that I was part of a new program to test crossbreeding between the clans. I told him I was going to be choosing a mate this cycle."

Now Ems raised both eyebrows. "So he..."

Neen nodded, still not looking her friend in the face.

"You thought that might inspire him?"

"Do I sound conceited if I say yes?" Neen replied.

Ems looked back down at the fighting ring. Tem was still there while guards were trying to pull him away. He seemed to be scanning the crowd for someone.

For Neen.

"He's disappointed he didn't win," Ems said.

"I don't think I can watch anymore," Neen said after a long silence. Tem had finally been taken away, back to the barracks within the Dome. "You can stay if you want. I'm sorry."

"I think I'm done too," Ems answered. "I'm going to let Herria know she can rest easy. No breeding for me this cycle."

"Really? What changed your mind?"

Ems shrugged. "Just a feeling. Or perhaps I should say a lack of feeling."

* * *

HERRIA WAS READING one of her antique books when Ems came in. Herria's love for these old-fashioned things surprised Ems initially, but when the councilwoman explained her fascination, it started to make sense.

These older technologies — books, porcelain teapots, linen lampshades — they all had a sensory pleasure that Herria found intoxicating. Ems thought they might be too overwhelming, but Herria brushed that objection aside.

"It's only overwhelming if you're afraid to trust your powers," she'd said. "If you embrace what you can do, you'll feast with your senses."

Herria beamed when Ems entered her office. "My dear!" She patted the couch cushion beside her and put her book down.

Ems sat down, still a bit awkward around her new supervisor. She instinctively checked the corners of the room, half expecting Grex to be lurking ominously. Herria's other personal assistant had an unrelenting hatred for Ems. She couldn't figure out why Herria would allow such hostility, but strangely, the councilwoman seemed oblivious to Grex's animosity towards Ems.

"There's still time," Herria said. "Say the word and I'll put in that deferment."

Ems sighed. "I think you're right. None of the males impressed me."

"Of course they didn't. So why not smile? I'll have Grex submit the forms immediately." She reached for her tablet and started to type.

Ems shifted in her seat.

Herria's finger lingered over the tablet screen. She looked Ems square in the eyes. "You feel guilty."

"We are bending the rules," Ems said. "I don't like getting special treatment."

"Ems, my dear, you are special. Haven't we established that with our little training sessions?" She patted Ems's knee like she was a child. "You've made the right decision. Breeding is impractical. Inefficient. I'd like to think that soon we can put the whole thing to rest."

"Soon?" Ems couldn't help trying to sense Herria's thoughts. How soon was soon? Didn't they just restart the program to develop laboratory breeding?

Herria's mind was hidden from her.

Ems realized she had a long way to go and more training to endure before she could hope to see into Herria's mind. She winced.

"Headache?" Herria asked, seeming concerned.

"It's nothing. Just all the noise from the Benglions in the stadium." It was a lie, and Ems hoped Herria wouldn't see through it. It was a flimsy excuse, but what else could she do?

"Get some rest, dear," Herria replied. "Don't let your mind be troubled. I'll handle everything." She started sending a message to Grex.

Ems was exhausted. All the tension of the day had finally caught up with her.

"Sleep in," Herria continued. "Indulge yourself. But don't forget our meeting tomorrow at two."

"Meeting? Right." Ems could barely keep her eyes open. She felt like she'd been hit with a sonic jet.

"Don't forget," Herria's voice sounded far away, "I've got big news, Ems. Big news."

CHAPTER 8

NEKKA

THE WORDING of the legislation needed to be precise. Nekka knew Herria would scrutinize every word, looking for loopholes, looking for some way to reject the proposal.

Nekka rubbed her temples. She was getting too old for these late nights. But what choice did she have? Committee meetings, an avalanche of reports, files to review. The work just kept piling up. And this legislation couldn't be left to her aides. Few women, even her own handpicked assistants and clerks, would understand the urgency and delicacy of what Nekka was attempting to do.

Only Neen. She could be trusted. Now that the competitions were over and breeding selection finished, perhaps it was time for Nekka to bring Neen into her inner circle. She knew it would mean undermining her own message about the importance of the interviewing program. If she was pulling Neen from the project, didn't that indicate she had lost confidence in its efficacy?

She would find a good excuse, it was just hard to think at the moment. So much to do. And Nekka felt the urgency to move quickly on all this, though she couldn't explain why.

She looked over what she'd drafted already. The first article of the proposal would completely outlaw the use of disproportionate and excessively harsh psychological manipulation on males who had committed infractions or were deemed subversive. She went over the wording several times, thinking of ways the other councilwomen could object. Her fingers ached from typing and retyping each sentence.

Making males witness videos of castration, threatening and torturing them with that information had to stop, but Nekka knew this wasn't enough. The entire policy of castration was excessive, unnecessary. So much of what they did was cruel for no reason.

Of course, the whole system was cruel. The whole edifice of EVE was a mirage that hid a blackened soul underneath.

Nekka closed her eyes. How long had she kept her innermost secrets hidden? How long had she gone along with this system that was so brutal and unjust?

If only she could get Neen into her orbit more fully, together they might affect greater change. It would be slow, Nekka knew that, but it could happen. First Neen, then others. Nekka needed to do something to counteract Herria's influence.

Perhaps tomorrow Nekka would call up Reslan and see if the Trabador councilwoman was open to more collaboration. Of all the councilwomen, Reslan seemed most open to compromise and persuasion.

Of course, Herria knew this too, which is why Nekka had to work fast. If only she was as approachable and amiable as Herria, but Nekka could never fake it.

Nekka knew her flaws. She was not a natural leader, not someone others wanted to follow. Perhaps Neen, though...

Neen was bold, attractive, perceptive. She was more than just highly intelligent. There was a fortitude in her that made her quite different from most Triversers.

Nekka went back to her draft. Still so much to do, and yet her eyes were blurring with strain.

Oh well, she thought, no one said this would be easy.

Just then, her tablet screen and the larger one on her desk both beeped loudly, signaling an alert from Sona's security office.

"What is it?" Nekka asked over the comm.

"Councilwoman," Sona's voice spoke through the tablet's speakers. "There's been an attack." Her voice was shaking.

Nekka's blood ran cold. Sona's voice never shook. Nothing rattled her.

"An attack?"

"In the breeding suites."

Nekka grabbed the edge of her desk to steady herself. In the breeding suites? This couldn't be right.

"What kind of attack?"

Sona hesitated. "Women were killed."

No. Impossible. How could this happen?

"Ten in total. We found the males covered in blood, disoriented and claiming they had no idea what happened."

"Ten," Nekka muttered. But blood? How could there be blood?

"How did they do it? There shouldn't be anything in the suites that could be used for violence."

Beds and nothing else. It was possible that a man could strangle a woman in the suite, but every suite bed was equipped with a sensor that would monitor the chips in the woman's wrist and the man's arm. And the security screens. They were designed to record and monitor all interactions within the suite. If a woman called for help or wanted a male dismissed, the screens would have picked up on it and security guards would have entered. And then there were the pills administered to all males before their breeding sessions. The drugs put them into a kind of stupor, making them compliant and at the mercy of their female partners.

"We're not finished investigating," Sona continued, "but we think the women were somehow drugged, and the males—"

"What, Sona? What about the males?"

Again, the Benglion captain hesitated. "The males... they used their teeth. They—"

Nekka didn't ask her to continue. She could imagine. Her stomach churned and she felt sick.

"I'll— I'll call an emergency meeting," Nekka said at last. "Send us the information you've gathered as soon as possible. Do we— Do we have any witnesses? What about the security screens?"

"We have one. One witness. I— I'll send you her statement." Sona's voice broke.

Nekka didn't waste any more seconds. She sent out a call for an emergency meeting of the council and gathered her things to head to the meeting room. She ended the call with Sona and rushed out.

When she got to the high council meeting room, all the other members were already there. They were alone. No clerks, no assistants. Herria was standing at the table while the others were seated, looking up at her. Nekka's entrance had interrupted the proceedings.

"What's this?" Nekka said, realizing that she was coming into something that was already underway. "I just sent out the alert."

"Nekka," Herria replied, her voice clipped. There were

no fake niceties now. "We began without you. We didn't think it prudent to wait. This is an extreme emergency."

"I concur," Nekka replied, "but how did this meeting begin so quickly? Sona just contacted me—"

"I received the news from another officer," Herria interrupted. She lowered her head, shaking it. "Shocking... Absolutely shocking. Still hard to fathom..."

"We got the summons from Herria," Forta explained, her face grim, her lips pursed. "I thought your absence was an oversight, but Herria said—"

"We all agreed that your presence might inhibit our proceedings," Herria said, giving Reslan a pointed look. "We felt you might not be willing to do what is necessary."

"What is necessary?" Nekka said, coming to the table and facing Herria. "I'm a member of this council, equal to you all. You cannot make decisions without my vote. *That* is what's necessary if we're to get to the bottom of this!"

"We've gotten to the bottom of it, Nekka," Herria said, sitting down as if to show that Nekka was intruding on the order of the meeting. "I've shared the reports with everyone. The horrors—" Herria closed her eyes as if in physical pain. "Monsters," she whispered. "They're all monsters."

"And from the sounds of it, the whole thing was coordinated," Forta added. "Despicable. Inhuman."

"That's what I don't understand," Reslan said. "How could these males have coordinated the whole thing? They weren't all from the same clan. Males from different clans don't interact. How could they have planned this?"

"What I want to know is how no one within the system even saw this coming?" said Forta. "Security forces, guards, no one had any inkling this was possible."

"Oh, I think we know who should have seen this coming,"

Herria said, a bitter sting to her voice. "Our little prodigy, Neen Salvek."

Nekka felt her legs shake. What evidence could Herria possibly have to connect Neen to any of this?"

"I don't understand," said Reslan. "What does she have to do with this? You mean to imply she knew?"

"I don't imply anything," answered Herria. "But she should have known. What were all these interviews for except to assess the males and deem them fit for breeding? The fact that several of these perpetrators were interrogated by Salvek and she failed to screen them properly has led to this. An utter failure." Herria glared at Nekka. "Your soft spot for the males has led to one of the worst acts of violence against women since the founding of EVE. So forgive me, Nekka, if I didn't call you to this meeting, but I think you've done enough damage already. This program of yours is a joke. We all knew it was pointless, but now we can see it was more than that. Not simply useless but dangerously negligent."

The others around the table glared at Nekka. Even Reslan looked pained as if she'd been betrayed.

"You have no proof of this," Nekka said, trying to stay calm. "Before we start assigning blame, we should make sure Sona and her officers have done a thorough investigation—"

"Investigation!" Herria cried. "What more needs to be done? The crimes speak for themselves! The males were covered in blood, dripping from their mouths, and the women, those poor women, savagely—" Herria stopped herself. She squeezed her eyes shut and tears welled at the corners. "The only thing left to decide," she said as she composed herself, "is what sort of punishment will follow this despicable attack."

"Punishment before trial?" Nekka said, looking around at

the other councilwomen for some semblance of reason and good judgment. "We need to find out what exactly happened. The how and the why."

"As if there could be any justification for such acts?" Herria almost spit her words at Nekka. "You tread much too closely to being a male sympathizer, Nekka, with this talk. As if the males could have any motive other than hate!"

"I am not a male sympathizer, I'm simply trying to ascertain all the facts."

"We should investigate thoroughly—" Reslan agreed.

Herria cut her off. "Of course. What do you think is happening now? No one is saying don't investigate. But Nekka thinks we should hear these males out and get their side of things, and that is simply ludicrous."

"I'm just saying—" Nekka tried to cut in, but Herria wouldn't cede any control.

"The one we should be listening to is our lone survivor," Herria continued. "She can explain everything. That will put your petty objections to rest, Nekka."

With a quick flick of her finger across her tablet, Herria signaled for a guard to bring in a trembling, bloodstained woman in a white nightgown, wrapped in a blanket. She stood before the high council, her head lowered, quiet sobs shaking her chest.

"This is Lessa," Herria said, her voice gentle and full of pity. "She's a young Sixter who managed to feign death after her attacker finished his assault. She's the one who alerted the guards once her attacker fell asleep."

The council all waited for Lessa to speak. Nekka was amazed that this woman had been able to survive, but she also wondered about the theatricality of having her testify right now in front of the council. Herria was obviously working to stir up outrage. But to what purpose? All of them were horrified by these attacks. Why move so swiftly to get Lessa in front of them?

"Go on, Lessa," Herria said, her voice like that of a mother coaxing her child. "Tell us what happened."

"I— I don't— I can't—" Lessa began, her body still shaking.

Nekka was not an overly emotional person, but seeing this trembling woman try to recount her horror made the councilwoman's heart break. Why would the males have done such a thing? Yes, the Domes and the competitions and the entire system were abusive. They were unjust.

But despite all these things, the males had never done anything like this before. Riots in the Domes, violence against one another, even the occasional attempt at violence against a female — these were things the males had done and would continue to do no matter what security measures were put into place. But occasional flare-ups of unrest were not the same as a seemingly coordinated, utterly brutal outburst of murderous violence like this.

Everything that was meant to prevent such a thing — the security screens, the sensor chips, the drugs the males were given to make them compliant — all of these things seemed to fail.

"Please, Lessa," Herria continued, "we need your testimony. You are our only witness."

Lessa swallowed hard. "Everything was going fine," she said, her voice barely above a whisper. "My male partner came in with the guard. He seemed happy. I could tell he was pleased to do whatever I asked of him. When the guard left, I told him to take off his clothes. Then I asked him to touch my neck and kiss it, then to slowly take off my nightgown—"

She started to sob, wrapping her arms around herself.

"Go on, Lessa. Please," said Herria.

"That's when I felt my vision go blurry. I don't know if it was something he did with his hands or his lips, but as soon as he started touching me, I felt sick, and I tried calling out for help, to alert the security screens, but my voice wouldn't work. I was screaming but only silence came out. And I tried fighting him off, but my hands were numb, my arms, everything was going numb, and I could feel myself falling but I couldn't stop it, and he was on top of me and then—"

Lessa cried out and slammed her eyes shut. She bent over as if in agony.

"No more, Herria, no more," said Reslan, her voice quivering.

"It's too painful to bear," said Sienax, her own face contorted by grief.

"We must know what happened," Forta countered. "But perhaps this interview need not be conducted right this minute."

"It needs to be now," said Herria. "We cannot lose this moment, not when it is fresh in her memory and so much is at stake."

What is at stake? Nekka wondered. Herria has something else going on beneath the surface, but Nekka couldn't discern what it was.

"Lessa," Herria said, "I know this is hard, but please try to recall everything you remember. You are doing the sisterhood of EVE a monumental service by telling us what you know."

Lessa took deep breaths and tried to stop crying. "I can't remember much more than that," she said. "I'm sorry. After he got on top of me, I know he tried to— I suppose he did. But I can't remember anything else. Not until I woke up and found him asleep on the floor, my blood all over him."

"What wounds did you sustain?" Forta asked.

Lessa lowered the blanket and showed her shoulder. It was bandaged, but dried blood had crusted all around it. "He hurt me here," she said. "And here." She pointed to her abdomen which was also bandaged and bloodstained.

"Hurt you," Herria repeated. "That's one way of putting it. And what did he hurt her with? There were no weapons in that room. Nothing sharp or even blunt that could be used for attack. Those aren't strangulation marks on her body, my sisters. Those are the savage marks of a beast trying to devour her flesh."

Lessa crumpled to the floor, overcome by sobs and terror. Sienax got up and put her arm around her. Forta signaled for someone to take the poor woman away.

Nekka sat there trying not to let her thoughts betray her. None of this made sense. Nothing added up. Why were the security screens not working? Why didn't the sensor chip in Lessa's wrist signal that she was in distress? Why didn't the pills keep this man compliant and non-aggressive? Everything that could possibly go wrong seemingly did, and not just once but ten other times.

Sona said the men claimed to have no memory of what happened. That they were as bewildered as anyone. Were they under some kind of outside control? For what purpose? What woman would want to see her fellow sisters brutally murdered like this?

"What more needs to be said?" Herria announced as Lessa was escorted out of the council room. "The trial must be held immediately, and the verdict swift. Execution for the males who did this."

"Execution?" Nekka tried to keep her voice under control. "You've decided the sentence before we've even convened the trial?"

"I've decided to demand justice, Nekka. Something you

have little interest in, I see. Even now, after what Lessa has just told us, you continue to cast doubt on what we know to be true. The males are dangerous. A menace. What more evidence do we need of their inhumanity?"

"Hear, hear," Forta said.

Sienax returned to her seat. "I agree. We should hold the trial immediately. Within days."

"And once these males are found guilty, we exact the harshest punishment," Herria added.

"I would like this put to a vote," Nekka said. "It must be unanimous if we're to seek the death penalty."

"I'm not aware of any such statute," Herria replied. "Majority rules, as always, Nekka."

"But in this case, shouldn't we be of one voice?" Nekka answered.

"I would welcome it. We are stronger when we're together. And we must see to it that this never happens again," Herria said. "But if one voice should waver, if one voice should want to see a weaker tomorrow, a more dangerous tomorrow, then let that voice speak. I will not stop her. We don't silence the voices of women here."

"Let us vote then," Forta said, impatience growing.

Nekka knew she had lost. She could feel it in the room, in the quiet and seething anger that poisoned the air.

"Yes, let us vote," Sienax concurred.

Herria waited — Nekka knew — to see if she would raise any more objections. Though it pained her to keep silent, Nekka couldn't risk any further antagonism. She would need to keep her head down if she wanted to find out the truth about what happened in those breeding suites.

"All in favor of seeking the death penalty for these murderers?" Herria said, looking the other three councilwomen in the eyes.

"Aye."

"Aye."

Reslan looked at Nekka. The Trabador councilwoman's face had turned a sickly green. "Aye."

"Aye," Herria said last of all. She barely glanced at Nekka.

There was a long moment of silence. Nekka sat as still as a block of stone.

"The ayes have it," Herria said, grinning darkly. "Forta, keep us abreast of what further evidence Sona and her team find, and Sienax, you and I should begin drafting a message to announce this horrendous news. Something fitting but not too sensationalist. We don't want panic in the streets. Reslan, I want the maximum security wing in the Arena Dome to be outfitted to hold these creatures in solitary confinement. I'll speak to Feldir about how to get a few Triverser engineers to allow us a special video feed into those spaces so the women of EVE can watch these males when the verdict comes down."

Herria kept speaking, kept giving commands, but Nekka had had enough. She got up slowly and walked out of the meeting room. She didn't care if the others might be shocked by her lack of protocol. She couldn't stay another moment.

When she shut the door to her office, Nekka sat down and closed her eyes. Her mind was overwhelmed with thoughts, but all of them seemed to be in an alien language, something beyond her comprehension. There was too much to think about.

She knew she should be weeping for those poor murdered women, and for Lessa too, and she wanted to weep, but the story of what happened, and the evidence they had, didn't add up.

She noticed that Sona had sent her another report. She

opened it on her tablet and read the details. The men all said they had no memory of what happened. They claimed that after they took their breeding pills, they blacked out.

They could be lying. Nekka knew she should assume they were lying. But Sona's report described the utter horror and bewilderment of these men. Could they really be so calculating, so devious, as to feign such horror? Anything was possible, but then how did men from different clans, clans that never had any interaction, manage to coordinate this attack?

Nekka tried to focus, tried to think. Her hand shook as she typed out Neen's number. She made sure it was a secure network, but even as she double-checked the security, Nekka worried. There was no guarantee that even the network of a high councilwoman was safe.

Neen needed to know. Herria's threat and suspicion of Neen was a signal of where things might lead. If Neen was called as a witness to these trials, if she was suspected in any way...

The call rang, but there was no answer. A million fearful thoughts gripped Nekka. Where was Neen?

Just then, a knock came at her door. Could it be Sona?

"Enter," Nekka said.

Much to Nekka's surprise, Herria's new assistant, Ems Davon, slipped in. She was shivering all over as if she'd been left out in the snow. She closed the door quickly.

"Ems," Nekka began, "what are you—"

"Quiet!" Ems said, looking back at the door. "Is this locked?" she whispered.

Nekka nodded.

Ems came right up to Nekka's desk. She was a tiny thing, several centimeters shorter than Nekka, and with her wide blue eyes, she looked like a pleading child.

"Can we be overheard?" Ems said in a low voice.

Nekka looked at the tablet and screen on her desk. Neither could be totally shut off, but Nekka quickly scrambled the network signals to give them a moment of privacy.

"Speak quickly," Nekka said. "This trick only works for a minute or two before someone notices."

Ems was still breathless. "Herria is lying."

This wasn't a total revelation to Nekka. She knew Herria had ulterior motives. Devious ones. What they were, Nekka wasn't quite sure, but she knew the Sixter councilwoman was not to be trusted.

"Aren't you supposed to be her personal assistant? Why are you telling me this?" Nekka asked.

"Because she's gone too far," Ems replied. "I can't— I can't keep silent."

"Silent about what?"

"The murders. Those women. It's not true."

"I have a contact in the Benglion police force, so I know it's true—"

"No, I mean, the males didn't kill them. It's all a set-up!"

Nekka was too stunned to fully process what Ems was saying. "A set-up..." she said slowly, trying to fit her mind around the implications. A set-up to frame the men, to put them on trial and execute them, to stir up fear and hatred against them...

"It was Herria," said Ems. "It was all Herria. She wants to destroy them."

"Destroy them? The suspects?"

"No, the males. All of them. She wants them all dead."

CHAPTER 9
NEEN

"ARE we sure this is a secure location?" Neen trusted Nekka, but even Nekka could be wrong. The whole world seemed arrayed against them.

"As secure as there could ever be," Nekka replied.

The four women stood together in the dimly lit bunker. Nekka had called it a bomb shelter, one of the few locations in High City where there were no networks or screens, no means of communication, nothing that could connect to the outside world.

"These were built by men before the revolution. Long before. When their warmongering had put the world at risk of annihilation. These shelters were built to withstand the most devastating bombs imaginable," Nekka explained.

"They were officially condemned as uninhabitable by the high council over a century ago," Sona added. She held a small fluorescent torch allowing them to see in the gloom. "But that didn't stop us from holding on to the keys. Just in case."

Neen knew Nekka had called Sona an ally, but she was still surprised how much the high councilwoman trusted her.

It was only the four of them — Neen, Nekka, Sona, and Ems — standing in the semi-darkness, talking about treason.

"We don't have much time," Nekka said. "These tunnels are in disuse, but that doesn't mean Herria won't wonder where we are."

"I still have trouble believing this is true," Sona said looking somewhat dismissively at Ems. "We only have this woman's word for it."

Ems's eyes flashed even in the darkness. Neen couldn't help but smile a little. Her best friend might be small in stature, but when her anger was roused, she was a force to be reckoned with.

"My word is true," Ems said, looking Sona straight in the eyes. "Herria told me her plan."

"Before it happened?" Sona replied.

Ems gritted her teeth. "After."

"Sona," Nekka said, stepping in, "you said yourself that Herria pulled you from the investigation and installed her own people. Doesn't that rouse suspicion?"

"Of course," Sona answered. "I wouldn't be here if I wasn't suspicious. But Davon's story sounds farcical. Herria murdered the women herself? Framed the males as a way to do... what, exactly? What's this all about?"

"She didn't murder them herself," Ems said. "Herria left out the details, but the plan was to blame the males and turn everyone against them."

"It's working beautifully, then," Neen murmured.

Sienax and Herria were operating overtime to blast the horrors of this crime to every corner of EVE. She had never seen this level of vitriolic messaging in her life. Every hour of every day, the screens across High City listed the names of the victims, showed footage of Lessa giving her testimony, and revealed the graphic images from the crime scene. Then, once the horrific nature of the crime was displayed, Sienax spoke the names and clans of the males, calling them murderers and savage beasts.

Neen remembered each one from her interviews, but it was hard to fathom that any of these males could have done something like this. They didn't seem the type. Maybe that hulking Benglion, Lekko, but he wasn't among the group. Every woman Neen ran into was out for blood, though, awaiting the trial and the almost-certain execution of the criminals.

"Without details, without evidence, I'm afraid there's no way to go public with this information," Sona said.

"And Herria's pet, Feldir, now leads the investigation," Nekka said, sighing. "We need proof."

"Why did you come to Nekka with this information?" Sona said to Ems. She towered over her, her ebony ponytail almost as long as Ems's torso. "How do we know you aren't a spy?"

"I trust her," Neen said, stepping shoulder to shoulder with Ems. "Ems wouldn't lie."

"I was Herria's trusted assistant," Ems said, not backing down from Sona. "That's why she confided in me. But she misjudged. What she's done, what she's justified in the name of our sisters, is beyond evil. I won't sit idly by while Herria's crimes go unpunished."

"You still *are* her assistant," Nekka said, the wheels obviously turning in her head. "Which means you still have access to her. You can gather more information. The information we need to take this to the public."

"I— I tried," Ems said. "But she's been so busy lately. Meeting with Sienax. Planning the legal proceedings."

"Legal proceedings," Sona scoffed. "There's barely been time to finish the forensic investigation."

"And the trial is set to begin tomorrow," Nekka said.

"Feldir isn't running an investigation," continued Sona. "She's running interference for Herria and the others who want a swift trial and no questions asked."

"So you believe Ems now?" Neen asked.

"I need proof," Sona said, sternly. "I'm not saying there isn't any, but we need to find it quickly."

"Ems," Nekka said, "can you gain access to Herria's office? Does she keep personal files there?"

"All such files are stored in a secure database," said Sona, not quite understanding Nekka's point. "We don't need access to Herria's office, just some way to override the security codes protecting her data."

Nekka shook her head. "For nearly all other information, yes. It's stored in the database. But I and the other high councilwomen have those security codes. We keep no secrets from each other, those of us on the council. That was how EVE has always functioned. Equal power, nothing kept secret. Officially..." Nekka swallowed hard. "But unofficially, we all have our secrets. And we keep those secrets outside the network..."

"I don't follow," said Sona. "How can anything be stored outside the network?"

Neen understood. "Paper."

"Paper?" Sona furrowed her brow. "That's ancient technology. We don't even manufacture it anymore for writing. I don't—"

"But the ancients printed books," Nekka countered. "There are some of us now who collect them..." She eyed Neen, her lips curling up in a slight smile.

"Herria's office is filled with books," said Ems. "Do you think that's how she's been communicating with her conspirators? Using the paper from the books... Or even putting messages inside and passing them?"

"Anything's possible," said Nekka.

"Then we have to get Ems into Herria's office," said Neen.

"Impossible," said Sona.

They all knew it was. Secure rooms and buildings could only be opened by those with authorization and the correct codes programmed into their wrist chips. Herria's chip was the only one that could open Herria's office. No one else had that code.

"What if she took Ems in with her?" Sona offered. "Herria trusted her enough to reveal the plan, perhaps she'll bring Ems further into the conspiracy."

Ems wrapped her arms around herself. "I don't know... I don't think I could fool her that much..."

"We need more than just something after the fact," Nekka added. "We need evidence that Herria planned these murders and the cover-up. We need evidence of her involvement from the very beginning"

"What if we reprogramed Herria's office to accept someone else's chip code?" Neen asked Sona.

"I don't see how," said Sona. "An engineer would need time to work on the interface. Are you going to risk letting anyone who walks down that hallway see you? It would be madness."

"Can my own chip be reprogramed?" Ems asked.

"Not without removing it," Neen replied. "And we don't know what Herria's security code is. Without that code, reprogramming would be meaningless."

"What if Herria did take Ems to her office, but not on any pretense related to this? Just on some other business," Sona suggested. "Is that possible, Ems?"

Ems nodded. "But how can I look through her office if she's standing right next to me?"

"That's where you'll need to be quick," Sona continued. "Something incapacitated the women in those breeding suites. A drug. Well, what's stopping us from making our own? If you drugged her that might give you time to search."

"And when Herria wakes up and wants to know what's going on, Ems will be prime suspect," Neen said, her voice rising.

"Not if she gets the information we need," Sona replied. "Herria wouldn't risk exposure. We'd have the upper hand."

Neen felt her face flush. This was a suicide mission for Ems, and she wouldn't stand for it. "How can we be sure what Herria will risk? She had ten women killed for her ambitions, why would she feel any compunction to spare Ems? Because of the risks? Herria's greater risk will be letting any of us go once we've found our evidence. Nekka, we cannot do this!"

The light flickered in Sona's hand. The dank, metallic taste of the tunnel filled Neen's mouth. Her voice reverberated off the lead walls of the bunker.

Nekka was silent for a long time. Neen wanted her to take charge, but the councilwoman seemed content to let Sona lead.

Ems broke the silence. "What if I can convince Herria she merely fell asleep? And if nothing seems disturbed, what reason would she have to suspect anything?"

"How are you going to convince her?" Neen was skeptical, and she could tell Ems wanted to prove herself to Sona. She knew her best friend. The way Ems spoke made Neen think there was something being left unsaid.

"I— I'll find a way," was all Ems could say.

"Can you make a drug to knock out Herria?" Sona asked Neen.

"Yes, that's not hard. It's the delivery method we have to think about. I can't imagine Ems will hand Herria a pill and expect her to swallow it."

"Something delivered via skin contact?" Nekka said, her eyes more alive now that there was a scientific problem to be solved.

"Possible," Neen replied. "A patch or lotion. But there's still the problem of Ems delivering it without Herria's knowledge."

"A needle?" Sona suggested.

"When's the last time you got injected with a needle and didn't know?" Neen said, unable to hide her anger. No one seemed particularly concerned that Ems was walking into a lion's den, not even Ems herself.

"Why not a patch, Neen?" Ems spoke up. "When we do our greeting, I could have it on the palm of my hand."

"There's no guarantee she'll even do the—" Neen started, but Ems shook her head.

"Herria always does the greeting," she said.

"Always?" Sona frowned.

"Always," answered Ems. "She loves the traditions of our sisterhood."

"Except the tradition that says don't murder any of us," Neen said, her stomach sick with the thought of those horrible images plastered around the city.

"Can you make such a patch?" Sona asked Neen.

Neen closed her eye and nodded.

"Quickly?"

"Yes."

"How much time do we have, Sona?" Nekka asked.

"Hard to say since I'm off the investigation. But I've

gotten reports from my Dome leaders. There's unrest in the male population. They know what's happening and they don't like it."

"And the trial starts tomorrow," Ems added.

"Then no more delay," said Nekka. "You and Neen are good friends. Nothing will seem amiss if you meet in Neen's residence and she gives you the patch. But can you contrive a way to have Herria take you to her office?"

"I think so."

"Speak of this to no one. Do not communicate via the network. No one must know."

* * *

"BACK AGAIN?" Pelon smiled at Neen through the doorway. "Officially this time too."

"Just doing some work for the head of Dome security." Sona had authorized Neen to experiment with making stronger pills to quell the males' anger about the murder trial. It was approved by both Forta and Nekka, so Herria couldn't openly object.

"Need help?" Pelon said, coming in to look over Neen's shoulder. "You know, I've been chosen for a special study this term, so I might have a trick or two up my sleeve. We're doing some really amazing stuff in advanced genetics."

Neen tried to stay relaxed. She had no reason to suspect Pelon of anything, but after the breeding suite attacks and Herria's involvement, Neen wasn't taking any chances.

"I've got it, thanks. Just testing out a new dosage for the males now that the competitions are done."

"I see." Pelon thought for a moment. "If that's all this is, why not have some low-level chemist in Pharma do it? This isn't even your department."

"It's not, but this isn't something the high council wants to be handled through normal channels. Nobody's supposed to know what's happening in the Domes."

"Oh. Right." Pelon's voice got softer. "What *is* happening in the Domes?"

"Nothing. Yet. Let's just leave it at that."

"Okay." Pelon was quiet for a moment.

Neen started to get back to her calculations, but the younger Triverser didn't leave.

"It's hard to believe," Pelon said. "Those poor women. What the males did..."

"It is hard to believe," Neen agreed. "Unfathomable."

"I've never been one for vengeance," Pelon continued, "but death is too good for those animals."

Neen didn't answer. She tried to look busy, to give Pelon the hint. She hadn't bothered with scrambling or rerouting the feeds in the lab this time. For all intents and purposes, she was doing exactly what she'd been authorized to do. But if Pelon hung around too much longer, she might notice what chemical formulas Neen was working on and then questions might arise.

"I'll let you get back to it," Pelon said, starting to tiptoe back to the doorway. "Are you working on the Benglion dose first?"

It took a moment for Neen to comprehend. "Uh— yes. Benglions first."

"You'd think we'd figure out one formula for all the clans," Pelon continued. "But I guess that wouldn't be as effective. Different brain chemistry and all. Anyway, good luck!"

Neen almost dropped her tablet.

Different brain chemistry.

It all made sense. Why hadn't she thought of it before? This would explain why the pills weren't effective on Tem.

His brain chemistry must be different from the other Benglions.

But how? How could that be?

Neen tried to focus on the task at hand. She needed a quick-acting anesthetic that would keep Herria asleep for no more than thirty minutes, enough time for Ems to search the office without arousing suspicion.

But even as she worked on calculating the formula, her mind went back to Tem. Something made him different. What was it? And how could she figure it out?

There wasn't time. Neen needed to make the patch and get it to Ems as soon as possible. She took a deep breath and got back to work.

If this formula didn't work, Ems would be at risk. There was absolutely no room for error.

"No pressure," Neen said to herself, pretending she wasn't nervous. "Just the fate of everything hanging in the balance."

CHAPTER 10

TEM

"WHY AREN'T they sending us back?" Dron asked as he and Tem laid on their cots.

Tem had wondered the same thing. Breeding should have been finished by now. It was hard to care, though. All Tem could think about was Naal.

The last moment before they took him away, Naal had managed to catch Tem's eye as he stood there waiting for his own trial to begin. Tem could tell by the grim lines on his face that Naal had failed.

And then Naal was gone.

Tem tried to distract himself, tried to pretend that he could be stoic and unbreakable, that Naal's punishment was just the way things were, that this was the system they lived under. He told himself he had to accept it.

But he couldn't. Even as he ran sprints and lifted weights, ate his meals and rested on his cot, he couldn't forget Naal. He didn't want to think about the torture they would put him through, the violence they would commit against him, but every time he told himself to forget it, the images of Naal's horror flashed across his mind.

In the end, this was every male's fate. They were each destined for the butcher's knife and eventual death. All Tem could do was survive a little while longer. He would join Naal someday, it was just a matter of time.

Still, days passed and no transfer came. No indication of when they would be taken back to their clan Domes. They trained, they ate, they did their work assignments. Day after day. Tem's mind got lost in the monotonous fog of it all, and he let himself get lost.

Lekko was off in the breeding suites. Tem wondered what it would have been like if he'd won his fighting trial. Would he now be in a breeding suite too?

Tem turned over in his cot and faced the wall.

"It's weird," Dron continued. "I thought they told us the breeding sessions only lasted three or four days. It's been, like, a week."

"What difference does it make?" Tem replied. "Here or in the Benglion Dome, it's not like our lives are any different."

"I don't know," said Dron, grinning, "this Arena mattress just doesn't have that same saggy, broken-spring feeling as the one back home." He bounced up and down a few times to demonstrate. The cot rattled on its frame. "If we stay any longer, maybe I can break it in."

Tem didn't feel like laughing. He thought of the sky and the breeze and the vast array of clouds he had seen before they transferred him from the supersonic train to the Arena Dome. Those were the only clouds he'd ever seen that weren't an image on a screen. They were like vast floating ships or strange behemoths in the sky, curling and swelling around each other in ever-shifting configurations.

He and Naal had talked about the outside world many times before. Naal was older than him, had seen the outside more times, had wanted to hike through mountains like the ones surrounding Bells, or swim across the vast ocean that separated them from the land of the Sixters. Neither Naal nor Tem had ever seen the ocean, but they had seen images on screens. They could dream.

Now Naal would never have a chance to dream again. Who knew how long it would take, but at some point, he would come up from the mines, poisoned by gasses and chemicals, fall into his cot and never wake up again. And the guards wouldn't even care. They'd just dump his body in some mass grave and get ready for the next slave to take Naal's place.

It made Tem so angry he could hardly think. He wanted to break something, to smash the glass walls of the Dome even if it did mean his death. In some ways, death was preferable to this powerless life.

"Sounds like someone's had enough," Dron said.

They both heard it. Heavy banging coming from down the hall. The walls of their cell echoed with the empty clang of thick steel.

"Pretty stupid, though," Dron continued. "He'll get a week in solitary for 'reckless disturbance.'"

The banging got louder and came nearer.

"It's not coming from inside the cells," Tem said, sitting up and listening closely.

"From outside?"

There were shouts now. Female voices. Angry ones. Calls of "animal," "beast," and "savage."

"Your time is gonna come!" wailed the guards as they slammed hard on the walls, rattling the cells. It was a wild clamor, out of control and full of wrath.

"What's going on?" Dron asked, his eyes darting from Tem to the howls and catcalls from beyond the sealed door.

"Something bad," Tem said, though he didn't move.

The banging came to their door. The pounding was furious, unhinged.

"Fuck all of you!" screamed the female voices on the other side. "You'll all pay!"

Dron was wild-eyed, standing now with his fists balled and his body ready in case of attack. He looked at Tem for some sort of answer.

Tem's lips were a thin line. He still didn't move from his cot. He met Dron's look and shook his head slightly. *Don't react,* his eyes told Dron.

Soon the banging and yells moved on, down the line to the next cell.

"What the hell was that?" Dron whispered. "Pay for what? What's going on?"

Tem had no answer, but he had a feeling it was only going to get worse.

* * *

NO ONE in the line made a sound.

Head down, eyes averted, Tem waited his turn as the guards went one by one distributing the pills.

"Open. Lift. Good."

One guard pulled down the chin, one guard placed the pill under the tongue. Close. Swallow.

"Open. Lift. Good. That's MI-1129."

Down the line they went.

"Open. Lift. Good."

MI-1130, MI-1131, MI-1132...

"Open."

Tem opened his mouth and lifted his tongue. The guard put the pill under his tongue and then closed his mouth with a shove of his chin.

"Good. Now open."

Tem opened his mouth to show he had swallowed the pill.

"That's MI-1138."

The drug wouldn't make any difference to Tem, but he wasn't about to tell the guards this. He swallowed the pill dutifully and hoped to evade any notice.

Dron wouldn't be so lucky, but Tem was used to it. His friend would still be able to crack jokes and make light of things, but there would be something pliable in his demeanor, something empty in the way he moved and talked and related to their environment.

The pills didn't inebriate them or lobotomize them, they just made the males easier to control, less aggressive, less willing to fight back. Tem had watched it happen to Dron and Naal and Lekko and everyone in their cell block. It made it hard for them to concentrate, to stay focused on finding a way out of the Dome, their long-time dream.

Being in the Arena Dome where all the males were weened off these drugs had been nice. Tem felt like he had finally gotten to know his friends in a different way, without a veil or shield between them.

That was all gone now.

"Almost ready for the show," one of the guards hissed as she flicked a finger right on a Benglion male's forehead. "Better stay awake."

Show?

Tem kept his head down, but he strained to see if he could hear any more chatter from the guard. What kind of show was she talking about?

This was the first time in forty-eight hours they had been let out of their cells. Tem dreaded being assigned to clean the chamber pots. If Dron's and his were anything to go by, it was going to make normal latrine duty look like a trip to paradise.

After the guards had banged on the walls two days ago, the men had all been left to rot in their cells. No training sessions, no assigned duties, no mess hall. Thin silicone sacks of water had been left in the drop boxes attached to their doors, but no food.

Tem's stomach growled. The two men on either side of him shifted slightly, probably hoping their own stomachs didn't rumble. No one moved. Hopefully the guards didn't hear.

Soon the last male had taken his pill, and Tem expected the guards to take them back to their cells.

But the guards were silent. They spread out along the line, holding their clubs at the ready. Tem looked at the male to his right. He expected to see a blank expression, the muscles and jawline utterly relaxed. No reaction to the guards' glowering or the raised weapons.

That's not what Tem saw.

The male beside him was breathing in quick, shallow bursts, his face contorted as if in pain. Something was wrong.

"Pigs," one of the guards said, spitting on the male in front of her.

"Monsters!" shouted another guard, whacking one of the males across the face. His head snapped sideways and sagged onto his shoulder.

"Filthy savages!" cried another guard, and soon all of them were beating the males with their clubs, some even using the electro-shock mechanism on the club to stun their targets.

Tem instinctively put his arms over his head to protect himself from the blows, though it was hard to do with the shackles on his wrists. He expected the other males to cower too, the drugs making them passive and slow to react. But when the clubs started swinging, the males erupted.

The guards were as shocked as Tem. They thought they'd have easy targets for their anger, but the males fought back.

They ran at the women, trying to tackle them. Some even tried to grab the clubs despite their shackles, forgetting that as soon as their fingers touched the surface, the security chips in their arms would send a signal to release electric currents. Males screamed in agony as they were electrocuted, others clawed awkwardly at the guards and tried to bite them.

"Stand down!" one of the guards screamed, but she was overcome by a male who bashed her in the head with his forehead. Guards were fumbling for their pistols, trying to evade the onslaught.

Tem crouched down, searching for Dron in the chaos. This shouldn't be happening. The pills should have made them easy targets. Instead, they were beasts.

"Dron!" Tem called, risking it to find his friend. They needed to get out of there or they'd be killed. Already, some of the guards had started shooting. Males were dropping to the floor, some wounded, some dead.

"Dron!" Tem saw him under the boot-heel of a guard, her pistol pointed at his head. "No, stop!" Tem cried out, running towards them.

"You're next, scum," the guard said, not taking her gun or her eyes off of Dron. "Hold your position."

Tem stopped and put his arms up. "Something's not right. The drugs should have prevented this. Please. It's not his fault."

"We've been warned the pills might not work," the guard replied. She was breathing heavily, eyes wild with desperation. "They failed those women who were murdered. You animals must have figured out a way to resist."

"No, please," Tem begged. "Look, they've stopped. We've stopped. Don't do this."

The guards had regained some control. Those males who had not been killed or knocked out were being lined up again. More guard reinforcements had come. The males were now being shackled around their feet.

The female standing over Dron lowered her gun. Quickly, two other guards lifted him and shoved him into the line. Then it was Tem's turn. Soon, all the males were shackled and subdued. Tem tried to get a look at Dron's face, but his friend hung his head and followed the line as it marched back to the cells.

* * *

DRON SAID NOTHING. He lay on his cot wearing a blank expression. This was what he should have been like before. Subdued. Compliant. Dulled.

The guards had never beaten them like that before. Not unprovoked. Was it the beating that roused the males to rage? It seemed impossible.

After a few moments, Dron fell asleep.

Tem rubbed his shoulder where a guard had clubbed him earlier. Something had roused the guards. That one female had said something about murdered women. Was there another riot elsewhere in the Dome?

Tem tried to get some rest, but his mind wouldn't let him. Everything was wrong. They were still in the Arena Dome, they'd had no word about when they'd be transferred out, the guards were out for blood, and now the strange reaction to the pills and this scrum. Something bad was happening. Tem wished he knew what it was.

He didn't expect to ever see Neen again, but all he could do at moments like these — when he was trying to block out everything else — was think of her. What was going on in the outside world? Was there trouble for the women too? Was Neen alright?

Hours passed and they didn't get released again. Dron was still sleeping, while Tem's stomach gnawed out his insides, desperate for food. Anxious thoughts seeded Tem's brain, pushing out everything else. What if they were being starved as punishment for the fight? What if they were never let out again?

Tem drifted in and out of sleep. He was exhausted from worrying, but every few hours, his stomach would cramp and wake him up. Then he'd turn back and forth in his cot, wishing Dron would say something, anything, a lame joke or even a stupid comment. But his friend was practically unconscious, sleeping so heavily that Tem couldn't rouse him. They'd had nothing in hours: no water, no contact, nothing. Tem couldn't keep track anymore of how long it had been. He was going to die here in this cell. He and Dron would be nothing but bones and ragged jumpsuits, forgotten in this domed tomb.

A clang on the door woke him. Tem sat up. Another clang. Tem went to the door. He expected something to be shoved through the drop box door.

"We got two alive in this one!" a guard called out from beyond the door. There was a scraping sound and when Tem opened the drop box, there were two pouches of water and two pouches of nutrient-enriched food puree. Tem almost tore through both food packets, but he resisted and saved one for Dron. The second water pouch, too, he saved.

He knew it was a long shot, but Tem called out to the guard. "What's going on? Why are we still here?"

There was silence on the other side.

Tem figured as much. A long shot.

"We're waiting for the trial to finish," the guard said, her voice low and close to the door.

"Trial? We finished our trials and competitions weeks ago," Tem said.

The guard barked out a laugh. "Not that trial, scum."

"I don't understand."

"You will. Soon enough. All your kind. When the verdict comes in, then you'll all understand what happens when you cross us."

"Is this about the murdered women?"

The guard sucked in a sharp breath. "Don't you dare speak of them."

"I just want to know what's going on."

"You *want*? That's all your kind does. Want. Take. Even if it means ripping out our throats to get it. Males are a disease."

Tem's head was fuzzy. The lack of food and water, the hours on end in his cell. He ached from the guards' blows. He didn't understand what this woman was saying.

"This time," the guard continued, "you'll see what happens when we take what we want from you. You'll watch your friends bleed. Then you'll know what it's like to live in fear."

That was it. The guard said no more, and Tem didn't call after her.

He had enough pieces to put together a smattering of the truth. If a group of males had indeed murdered some women, it made sense that the guards would take out their anger on Tem and the others. Maybe they were being kept in their cells until the trial was over? Then they'd return to their clan Domes?

Tem hoped. He just wanted to be gone from this place. Maybe if the women got what they wanted from this trial, they'd let things go back to normal.

It was a child's foolish hope, but Tem clung to it. It would be better for the guards to kill them all than to keep them cooped up in their cells for eternity. Tem's body ached to run and climb and jump. To forget his thoughts and just let his muscles take over.

He thought about what Neen had said about reading books. He envied her and wondered what it would be like to read books with stories in them, with ideas and beauty. He would even settle for one of those rules manuals from his days in Young Dome. Something to keep his mind from going crazy in this cell.

"Dron?"

His friend stirred, moaning from the grogginess of sleep. "What's happening... Where are we?"

"Still in our cozy Arena Dome cell," Tem answered, trying to smile. "They left us food." Tem sat next to Dron on the cot and handed him the food and water pouches. Dron sat up and rubbed his head.

"I feel like shit," he said.

"You want to know how you look?" Tem patted him on the back.

"Why are we still here?" Dron took the water from Tem and downed it in one gulp.

"I don't really know. But I think it has to do with women being murdered, and we males are to blame."

"I think I'd remember killing one of them," Dron said. "I've dreamt of it enough times."

"I don't know any details. But whoever did it is on trial

right now. That's why the guards are so hostile. We're the whipping boys. I think once the verdict is handed down, maybe they'll move us back to Benglion Dome. I hope, anyway."

"What if they don't like the verdict?" Dron said, taking the food packet from Tem and tearing into it.

"I don't think there's any doubt what the verdict will be."

"Shit, I feel weird," Dron said, wiping the puréed food off his lips. "Why don't you feel weird?"

"It was the pills," Tem answered. "They weren't right. Do you remember what it felt like after you took them?"

Dron shook his head. "I can't remember... I swallowed the little bastards and then I thought about what nice shackles we were all wearing... and then everything went blank."

"They're screwing with us," Tem said. "It's almost like they want us to fight back, cause a stir."

"So they can justify starving us?" Dron said, tipping the food packet upside-down as if there might be more hiding inside.

"But the guards seemed surprised about it," Tem said, thinking out loud. "Like they didn't expect that reaction. Like they had no idea what those pills would do. It's almost like whoever made those drugs is screwing with everybody, not just us."

"I don't remember attacking anybody." Dron rubbed his head. "But I guess I must have. I feel like a supersonic train ran me over."

"You didn't start the fight. The guards did. They were hitting us with clubs. That's when you went unhinged and fought back."

"Just me?" Dron grinned weakly. "How did you manage to stay above the fray?"

Tem didn't answer. He wasn't sure Dron needed to know

the truth just yet. "My memories are foggy too. The guards hit first. Then all hell broke loose."

"Well, let's hope hell has decided to ease up a bit. I need a break from getting my head bashed in."

Tem didn't say what he was thinking. He let Dron rest again while he went back over to the door and tried to listen. There was no sound from the other side.

Would any more punishments be coming their way? It was like someone had wanted all the males to fight back...

Not just fight back. *Win.*

And if they did, what would the women do in retaliation?

CHAPTER 11

EMS

TIME WAS RUNNING OUT, and Ems knew it.

The trial took up nearly all of Herria's time, and whenever Herria wasn't sitting in judgment in the courtroom, she was impossible to find. She had refused to resume any training sessions, and when Ems tried to contact her via the network, Herria didn't respond.

Grex would smile like a panther whenever Ems asked if Herria was available.

"She's much too busy," Grex crowed. "Perhaps after the verdict comes in."

Ems thought about barging into the courtroom and accusing Herria right then and there, but she knew it was a fool's errand. Who would believe her? The whole city was caught up in the fervor of the trial. The women wanted vengeance, and Herria was eager to give it to them. If Ems tried to stand in the way of that, she'd be torn apart.

It was like Herria knew Ems had cooled on their relationship. Had she seen into Ems's mind? Had she felt Ems's revulsion at the fact that Herria was behind the breeding suite murders?

"My headaches are getting worse." Ems hoped the message she left this time would spark Herria's sympathy. "I don't know what to do."

She sent it through the network and waited. Neen and Nekka had kept themselves scarce. No contact with Ems or Sona or anyone else. Already during the trial, Neen's name had been brought up several times by Herria. *Why hadn't she flagged these males? How could she have been so negligent?* Herria's venom seemed as targeted at Neen as at the males under trial.

Nekka wasn't even asked to sit in judgment. No one was sure what the high councilwoman was doing. No word from her, no appearances. She had become a ghost.

Ems felt so alone. Even Sona, whom she was starting to trust, ignored her whenever she passed by the high council building.

It was probably for the best. Herria couldn't suspect anything. Ems had to seem like a loyal underling.

"My dear Ems!" Herria's face blinked onto Ems's tablet screen.

Ems was sitting alone in her bedroom. She had gotten a place near Neen's in the central district.

"I'm so sorry we haven't had a chance to sit down and chat since this terrible business began. I do apologize. Truly."

"I know you're busy," Ems replied. She tried to make her face look pained, like she was having another headache.

"Nonsense!" Herria said, a feigned sympathy drawn across her thin, pale eyebrows. "I should have made time. Your training is too important. Tell me," her voice became low, confidential, "are the headaches caused by...?" She gave Ems a knowing look.

"Mmm hmm," Ems said, wincing for good measure. "But now my head throbs even when I'm not doing anything..."

"I see." Herria bit her lip. "I don't have much time, but maybe we can try something this afternoon while the trial is in recess."

"Your office?" Ems asked. She winced again, but this time because she feared her voice sounded too eager.

"Where else?" Herria said, smiling. Her teeth looked like gleaming pearls against her thin red lips. Ems was reminded of a drawing of a tiger she'd once seen in a book.

This was it. Before she left, Ems made sure the patch with the anesthetic serum was secured to her palm. Neen had given her a small scanner to store whatever information she found. They all decided it was too risky for Ems to remove any of Herria's books.

Ems worried she wouldn't have enough time. The library in Herria's office was stocked, floor to ceiling, with ancient books. She wasn't even sure what to look for.

Everything felt incredibly tenuous. This was such a desperate hope. Ems wasn't even sure why she was risking it.

She breathed deeply and closed her eyes.

Those women were murdered because of Herria. For her ambitions. A leader who was willing to kill in order to get what she wanted was worse than any male.

Herria had to be stopped.

Ems pushed through the rallies in the streets. Ever since the news was announced and the trial had begun, crowds of women filled the streets of High City, crying out for justice against the males. They chanted and shouted and marched around the high council building. They held their tablet screens up and showed photographs of the dead women from before their murders. Sixters, Benglions, Triversers, Evoxes, Trabadors: These were women who had been someone's best friend, someone's classmate, someone's lover.

The noise of the crowd was overwhelming. Ems picked

up her pace, sliding through the crush of people, using her slight frame to approach the high council building as quickly as possible. As she slipped in, she noticed special forces police were stationed outside. The women were typical Benglions: tall, broad-shouldered, stoic demeanor. They wore the same insignia as Sona, their captain.

But two of the women stood out. Their hair was nearly as white-blonde as Ems's, cropped short much like Herria's. They could have been Herria's own offspring, if Ems didn't know better.

Ems shivered. It was like these women were emulating the high councilwoman. Showing themselves to be on her side.

Choosing a side to be on.

As Ems made her way up to Herria's office, she realized she too had chosen a side.

* * *

"EMS!" Herria stood and offered her hands for the traditional greeting.

Ems forced a bright smile onto her lips and reached toward Herria. She could feel a bead of sweat on her forehead, but she kept her breathing calm, her arms relaxed. She tried to block out every thought regarding the patch hidden in her palm.

Their hands clasped.

"Together," their voices said in unison. As Herria let go of Ems's hands, she leaned in and looked Ems straight in the eyes. "Now more than ever, I'm afraid," she said, then she offered Ems a seat. Herria sat across from her, behind her desk.

Ems sat quickly.

"I don't have much time, so let's get started," Herria said. "I want you to practice the influencing, and we'll see when the headache starts. I wonder if you're still too focused on your other senses and that's causing the overload."

"Sure," Ems said, watching Herria carefully. Neen said the serum would only take a couple of minutes to work. Ems was already focusing her mind on Herria's, trying to persuade her that she was overworked and needed to rest. A long rest.

"Go on," Herria said, placidly smiling. "I won't put up my usual defenses."

Ems closed her eyes. She thought perhaps the serum would make Herria's mind more pliable, more unguarded.

It wasn't. Ems searched, concentrated, tried to see the thoughts within the other woman. But Herria's mind was a wall, a kind of fortress that she needed to push hard against to make a crack.

Why was this so difficult? Herria should be falling asleep by now.

Ems opened her eyes slightly, expecting to see the councilwoman getting groggy, but Herria sat there as calm as ever, that insidious smile on her lips.

"Go on, Ems, you can do it..."

Something was wrong. The serum should be working. Ems concentrated harder, pressing against Herria's walls.

"Keep at it," Herria said, softly. "You're doing well."

No, this wasn't right. Herria's defenses were holding up. Ems closed off all her other senses — no more sight, smell, touch, sound, taste — putting all her energy into her mind.

"Yes," Herria whispered, "that's it... Don't give up now, Ems..."

The headache struck like a thousand shards of broken glass. Ems winced and buried her head in her hands.

"Ah!" Herria said, standing up. "So close, my dear. And now the pain." She came over to Ems and put a hand on her shoulder. "Do you need to lie down?"

Ems shook her head, but she couldn't speak.

"Did you close off all your senses that time? And still a headache?"

"I want to try again," Ems said, her voice catching in her throat.

Herria looked surprised. "Wonderful! I love your dedication. This bodes well for you, truly. I know we haven't spoken much since these ghastly murders, but soon I'll be assembling an inner circle to move forward on new plans for the Domes. Your gifts will be of the utmost necessity."

Ems didn't really listen to Herria's chattering. She needed to focus. It was obvious by now that the serum had failed. She needed to find another way.

For a moment, she thought of grabbing one of Herria's ancient lamps and banging her on the head with it. But that would be suicide.

No. Ems would have to find another way. Her own way.

"Go on," Herria said, still standing with her hand on Ems's shoulder. "Try again."

Ems closed her eyes. She slowed her breathing to almost nothing. The world around her was darkness. Not only were her senses closed, but every last ounce of herself was abandoned. She felt weightless, less than air. She existed only in the realm of thought. She was a consciousness and nothing more.

This had to work. It was her last chance...

Herria's mind was before her. A wall with no beginning and no end. Ems felt her way along the wall. It was no use pushing through it. It would not break. She needed to find the doorway, the entrance that would open for her.

She glided along that wall. No struggle. No force. She could sense that Herria was starting to get anxious. No one had ever entered so calmly into her mind before.

Ems was patient. She had everything to lose and therefore nothing to hold her back.

The walls trembled. This was new. Herria had always been the master, Ems the student. But Ems didn't have to do things Herria's way anymore.

The door waited. It looked closed, but as Ems felt her way closer she saw that it was cracked open, white light spilling out from the seam. She stood in that light. She let the door open wider. She stepped through.

The walls crumbled like brittle leaves.

* * *

WHEN EMS OPENED HER EYES, Herria was on the floor, unconscious. Ems could hardly move, her head was throbbing with pain.

She didn't waste time. There was no way to know how long Herria would be out. Ems had to move fast.

First, she pulled Herria to her chair, struggling to lift the older woman. Herria was tall for a Sixter, and it took every muscle in Ems's body to drag her around the desk and put her into the seat. Even though Herria was close to sixty years old, she was as solid as a piece of steel.

Then Ems went to the bookshelf, scanning each spine to see if something was marked differently or looked amiss. There were books from hundreds of years ago, some from even older times beyond the early days of the first revolution. Ems wasn't familiar with most of them. Much of this old literature was deemed too hostile and hateful. Misogyny was the air they breathed before the revolutions. These books were considered too dangerous, too harmful to be read. But Herria had dozens of them.

One stood out for being unmarked. No name or title on the spine. Ems took it down from the shelf. The front cover was so old and faded, Ems couldn't read the title. She could barely make out the name of the author. Someone named Gilman.

Ems flipped it open, not sure what she was supposed to be looking for. A few pages at the beginning had been torn out, but otherwise, the text looked normal. Words on a page.

Finding nothing unusual, she started to put it back. That's when she noticed the edges of some pages. They were painted silver. It wasn't every page, only some. They made a strange pattern along the edges when the book was closed.

Ems opened it again and turned to a page with the silver edging. She studied the words, reading each one carefully.

That's when she saw the dots. They were as small as pinpricks, sometimes only one, sometimes half a dozen. Sometimes they were placed over the words, sometimes under. They were in black ink, blue ink, even a dark green ink. Ems couldn't see any sort of pattern, other than the dots were on pages that were edge in silver paint.

It was a cipher of some sort, but what the key was, Ems didn't know. She took out the miniature scanner Neen had engineered. At first, she planned to only scan the pages with silver edges, but she realized they might need to see the other pages too to discern any sort of pattern, so she started from the beginning.

The torn pages in the front were a mystery, but Ems didn't have the luxury to wonder where those pages might be. She scanned each page, front to back, all the while listening for any sign of Herria waking.

When she got to the last page, she slid the book back on the shelf, careful to place it where it had been before.

Ems's stomach dropped. What if this book wasn't the only one? There were dozens of books on these shelves, well over several hundred. There would be no way to check them all for the silver edges.

An alert pinged on Herria's tablet. It sounded like a gong in Ems's ears. She looked quickly at the screen and saw Grex's name pop up.

The trial. It was probably about to reconvene.

Ems typed a brief message on her tablet to Herria, thanking her for her help and wishing her a good nap. Ems hoped the thoughts she planted in Herria's mind would stick.

She knew she needed to leave in case Grex or someone else was coming to summon Herria. As calmly as possible, Ems opened the office door and looked out. The hallway was empty.

With a deep breath and her steadiest walk, Ems left Herria's office, closing the door behind her.

* * *

"CAN YOU DECIPHER IT?" Sona asked. She and Neen and Ems stood in the damp darkness of the bomb shelter.

Neen looked through the scanned images on an unassigned tablet Sona had brought with her.

"Are you sure this screen can't be traced?" Neen asked.

"It's not been hooked up to any network," Sona replied. "My Trabador contact gave it to me right off the factory floor."

"Didn't she ask questions?" Ems wondered.

Sona huffed. "She did not."

There was no questioning Sona's demands apparently.

Neen slid her finger across the screen, jumping from image to image. "I can decipher it," she said. "My best guess is that Herria's partners have a copy of the same book, and they sent numeric messages back and forth corresponding to the page numbers and words on each page. That's what the dots mean. It was Herria's way of keeping track of each word in the message until she could transcribe it. Different colors for different messages."

"How long will it take to transcribe everything?" asked Sona.

"I don't know... There's a lot here."

"We have hours, maybe less," Sona said. "The trial is in its final stage."

"What happens if we find our evidence?" asked Ems.

"Then I take it before the high council — all the members — and expose Herria's crimes," Sona said without hesitation.

"Even Nekka?" said Neen.

None of them spoke for a long minute. Nekka was supposed to be there, but no one had heard from her.

Ems could feel Neen's heart pounding. She could even smell her friend's sweat glands perspiring.

Sona, however, was utterly calm. It was true about Benglions. They didn't feel fear like the rest of the clans.

"Get to work," Sona commanded. "When you've found something, send me a message. Go ahead and use the main network, just mention that you've 'reviewed the Sixter schematics' and I'll know what you mean."

"I'm coming with you," Ems said. She didn't want to be alone in her apartment.

"Watch your backs," Sona said, looking down at them, her lips frowning. "I'd give you a security detail, but that would arouse suspicion. The streets may not be very safe. Be careful."

Ems wanted to ask Sona about the special forces she saw outside the high council building, the ones with the ice-blonde hair. But even as she was thinking of her question, Ems found herself pushing through into Sona's mind unbidden. She hadn't meant to do it. It just happened.

Sona's worries were laid out like a battle map marked for war. All the factions were represented: Nekka, Herria, the other high councilwomen, Sona, and a woman Ems didn't know. She was a few years younger than Sona, with fierce blue eyes and dark hair, cropped short against her head. Ems could feel the love Sona had for this woman. And the terror of losing her. It was there, buried within her mind. A fear that never surfaced openly, but which grew all the stronger for being nestled so deep.

Ems pulled herself out of Sona's thoughts. Her head ached, and her knees shook.

"Ems!" Neen said, catching her by the arm. "What happened?"

"I— I just need to rest," Ems said, panting.

"You've done enough, Ems Davon," said Sona. "Go home and sleep. Leave the rest to us."

"No," Ems said, steadying her legs. "I'm coming with you, Neen. I want to be there when you find out Herria's true plans."

They all looked at each other. They were pinning all their hopes on the markings of a book.

* * *

EMS SLEPT for a long time in Neen's bedroom. She dreamt strange dreams where she and Herria stood on the precipice of a towering building in the center of High City. Ems felt different. Stronger somehow. She had an uncontrollable rage building inside her as she watched Herria laugh in her face.

Then Ems was awake, Neen's hand shaking her.

"What is it?" Ems said, sitting up. "Did you find something?"

Neen nodded. Her eyes were bloodshot, her skin colorless. "I— I can't even begin to explain it. You just— you have to read it yourself."

"Does it prove Herria's connection to the murders?" Ems asked, getting out of bed and following Neen to the couch.

"Just— Just read it." Neen handed her the unassigned tablet. "And when you're done, tell me I'm not going crazy."

* * *

IT WAS ALL THERE. Herria's messages to her accomplices, her plan to pin the murders on the males by drugging them so they couldn't remember what happened. Even Lessa's involvement was detailed, her false testimony concocted as a way to prove the males had done it.

The messages made clear that Herria's operatives had gotten access to the suites through corrupt guards who were granted special favors if they allowed the operatives access to the Dome and the breeding suites. Once the males were unconscious, Herria's accomplices killed the breeding women themselves. Brutal, savage killings that Ems could hardly fathom any woman committing.

It was all there, every detail, delivered through the words of the book.

But that wasn't all the book contained. Herria and her co-conspirators mentioned strange things, things that made no sense to Ems.

Total erasure.

The final revolution.

All-Clan.

Herkeep.

"What is this?" Ems asked, pointing at one of the mentions of Herkeep. "I've never heard of such a thing."

"I think it's a place," Nee replied. "Herria mentions that the work of Herkeep is almost complete."

"What work?"

"I don't know. But it's something to do with this idea of All-Clans."

Ems rubbed her forehead. Her headache was coming back with a vengeance.

"You saw it, though, right, Ems?" Neen said. "The final revolution? Total erasure? That can only mean one thing."

"Herria's not going to stop with these ten males."

"She's not going to stop until they're all dead."

"But then how will we survive? We can't breed without the males."

"It's mass murder." Neen looked like she was going to smash the tablet screen or throw up, or both.

"She'll never be able to do it," Ems said. "She can't frame them all for murder. And the other leaders won't go along with it."

"Can you be sure?" Neen replied, bitterness in her voice. "You've seen the thirst for blood from every woman marching in the street. What's stopping Herria from harnessing that hatred? If the males in the Domes do anything even vaguely threatening, she'll have what she needs to call for their extermination."

"Did you contact Sona? We have to get this to the high council."

"I messaged her," said Neen, standing up and going to the window to look out over the city. The sun was getting lower in the sky as evening settled in. A cup of cold tea sat on the table nearby. "But there's more going on here than just this trial and these ten males." She turned to Ems. "We have to find out what's really going on."

"The high council—"

"I don't know if we can trust them, Ems. They might not be able to do anything, not if Herria is building something in secret. We have to find out more—"

"What are you saying? That we track down this Herkeep? We don't even know what it is!"

"We have to try—"

Just then, Neen's personal tablet screen buzzed. A message from Sona.

Too late.

"No..." Neen whispered. She looked back out the window.

The glass of the Arena Dome turned blinding white, and then every screen in the city switched to a feed from inside a large, brightly lit holding cell. Ten males stood around, their hands and feet shackled, their faces gaunt and sallow, glassy-eyed and bewildered.

"These are the savages," Sienax's voice announced over the video feed. There was a relish to her words as she spoke. "The beasts who killed your sisters. They have been tried and found guilty by a unanimous vote of the high council. By decree, thus, their lives are forfeit. Let the execution commence immediately. Justice has been served."

The bright room's lights flickered, and the males looked around wildly as if some condition in the cell had changed. Then they each fell simultaneously to their knees, clutching their arms where the sensor chips were embedded. They started foaming at the mouth, convulsing and shaking, their limbs spasming in unnatural angles.

They jerked and shook, and blood poured out of their ears and noses.

It went on for over a minute, the shaking and convulsing, then their bodies were still. They lay in a heap on the floor, unmoving, drowning in shallow pools of their own bodily fluids.

The image faded to black and was replaced by pictures of the murdered women, all of them young and happy. Their names were listed under their pictures, each woman a martyr to a cause that had just begun to take hold.

"We're too late," Ems said, turning away from the screens. She felt sick, like her stomach was a pit of crawling worms. The injustice of it all, the way these executions were being celebrated: all of it made Ems physically ill.

"No," Neen answered. Her face was twisted with agony, but Ems could see her friend trying to keep her emotions in check. "We're not. This is only the beginning."

Herkeep. Ems could hear Neen's thoughts.

"But we don't even know where to look?" Ems said.

"We have to try."

"Neen..." Ems had been holding back from her friend for too long. She was tired of keeping secrets. "I should have told you earlier..."

"What is it, Ems?" Neen sat down next to her.

"I— That serum you made— It didn't work."

"What?"

"Nothing happened to Herria. She didn't fall asleep."

"But then how—"

"I shouldn't have kept this from you. I was too caught up in Herria's promises. I'm sorry."

"Sorry for what?"

"For not telling you." Ems took a deep breath. She held Neen's hand in her own but didn't look at her. "There's something I can do... something Herria can do too, but I think I might be stronger than her..."

When Ems was finished explaining, Neen stood up and started pacing around the room.

"Are you— are you mad at me?" Ems asked. "For not telling you sooner?"

"What? No. Definitely not. I just... I need to think..."

Ems waited while Neen paced around a while longer.

"Herria doesn't suspect?" Neen said, finally.

"I— I don't think so. I planted the thought in her mind that she was tired and fell asleep."

"So you could meet with her again?"

"Yes, but why?"

"To make another suggestion. To use your influence."

Neen didn't have to say it out loud. Ems understood.

To find the location of Herkeep.

CHAPTER 12
NEEN

"IT'S NOT A PLACE, Neen. It's a people. They are everywhere. Every industry. Every position."

Those were the last words Ems had said. Neen deleted the message as soon as she heard it, hoping it didn't get intercepted or filed. A desperate hope. Everything was filed, everything recorded.

Neen had been to Ems's apartment three times already, but still, there was no answer. After she got Ems's message on her tablet, Neen immediately tried to contact her, to no avail. Ems didn't respond to video or text communication. So Neen went to see her face-to-face. Only to find no one home.

"It's not a place, Neen. It's a people."

Neen wished she could get in touch with Nekka or Sona, but they too didn't respond to networked communications, and Neen didn't want to risk too much contact with them. Since the execution of the "ten beasts," as every woman on the street was calling the males who had been framed for the murders, police were everywhere: stalking through the streets, hanging around shops, waiting outside living residences.

Or maybe they were always there, Neen thought, and it's only now that I've noticed them.

She hardly left her apartment except for food and essentials. She couldn't stand to see the rallies and mass gatherings of women who took to the streets to celebrate the executions in the name of "justice." She also couldn't help feeling the target on her back. During the trial, Herria had all but accused her of dereliction of duty, and Neen knew there were women who believed she was complicit in the murders.

The irony was not lost on her.

"It's not a place, Neen."

How could Herkeep not be a place? What did Ems mean? Even if it was a network of people, they still had to gather somewhere, had to interact somehow. Had Ems found that place? Is that where she was now? Why didn't she wait for Neen?

Unless she had no choice.

When Neen knocked on Ems's door a fourth time that day, there was still no answer. Neen couldn't get in. Her wrist chip wouldn't open Ems's door, and breaking the lock was impossible

Guilt was gnawing at her insides. It was her plan that made Ems go back to Herria, her plan that had led to this.

And now Neen didn't know where to turn. If Ems was caught, if she had been found out...

They had tried and failed to find evidence of Herria's plan in time to save the executed males. Now they were going to fail in this too. And Ems would pay the price.

Not just Ems, all of them who stood in Herria's way...

How could they possibly fight against something that was everywhere and could be anyone? Even if she showed the high council the evidence they had against Herria, would they even believe her? Herria had poisoned Neen's reputation.

What Neen needed most were allies, and yet all her allies had disappeared. As she stood in the hallway of Ems's residence building, she turned to look out the window at the vast Arena Dome in the distance. She was too far away to see much, but she could see one thing: There were no males visible to the outside world. There was no one training or working or doing anything that could be seen from the Dome windows.

Neen could only imagine what they were being subjected to. If the rallies in the streets proved anything, it was that the women of High City were ready to scapegoat all the males for those murders.

Was Tem there now, at the mercy of guards who hated him?

Neen tried not to think of Tem too much since the competition had ended. She'd done her part to help him. He'd made it through.

But the murders and the trial and everything else made him intrude on her thoughts more than ever. She found herself inexplicably grateful that he hadn't been one of the breeding males. If he had, he might have been one of the executed...

Herria was playing for keeps. That much was certain. It wasn't just the males who were in danger now.

Neen went to the window pane and stared down at the street. From behind that glass, the world looked serene. Beautiful. Women making their way through the city, children playing in the nearby green space, ivory and glass buildings gleaming like icicles on a sun-kissed winter's day. It was a perfect world.

But only from behind that glass. Only when seen from the surface.

Ems had said Herkeep was everywhere. In the people themselves, hiding in plain sight. Any of those women on the street could be part of it.

Neen had no leads, no clues other than Ems's final message. If she hoped to find her friend, she'd have to start looking somewhere.

"If Herkeep is everywhere," Neen said to herself as she watched the street below, "then that's where I'll start."

* * *

"I'M PUTTING in an application to come back as a junior instructor," Neen said as she and Pelon sat down outside the provost's office.

"Really?" Pelon replied. "I always thought you couldn't wait to get out of here."

Ems had said Herkeep was in every industry. Why not in education? Neen thought.

Pelon was right that she had no interest in teaching Bio-Chemistry or Genetics or anything else, but the provost at the Advanced Studies Institute didn't have to know that.

"I have to do something now that my other assignment fizzled," Neen said.

Pelon winced. "Oh. Right." She was sufficiently embarrassed — or scared — to make any further mention of Neen's work in the Dome.

"Thanks for keeping me company while I wait," Neen said. "I hope I'm not keeping you from a lab session or something."

"Not at all. I'm doing a special study this term. Didn't I tell you?"

Yes, you did, Neen thought. It was a long shot, but Herria and her accomplices had used strange new drugs to commit the murders and frame the males. Maybe Pelon's special studies were connected. Though Neen found it hard to believe Pelon would knowingly go along with the extremities of Herria's plans, she might have been recruited to this cause without knowing the full extent of it.

Even if this was a long shot, Neen was running out of options. It had been seventy-two hours since Ems sent that final message. When Neen finally risked getting in touch with Sona, she received an automated message that Sona was busy with official business. Nekka's office didn't even have an automated message, just total silence. Neen was on her own.

"After I'm done here, would you mind taking me on a tour of your special study labs?" Neen said as innocently as she could.

"Definitely!" Pelon replied. "I was hoping you'd ask."

"You were?"

"Are you kidding? Who wouldn't want your input? You're, like, a genius Neen. Any tips you can give me on this project would be amazing!"

Tips.

Pelon seemed so innocent. But then, none of the women who cheered for the execution of the males thought they were doing anything wrong either. The whole system was excused and celebrated because the males were deemed to be nothing more than beasts.

"Great," Neen said, forcing a smile.

"I'll wait for you on level three."

Neen nodded. Then the provost called her in.

* * *

"WHAT KIND of work are you doing?" Neen asked.

Pelon scanned her wrist across the door sensor. "Quick!" she said. "And stay close. I'm not sure if your chip will set off an alarm or not."

"If I'm not supposed to be here, then—"

"No, it's fine. They're just super strict about things. You know how it is."

Security in the institute was never lax, that much was true. They didn't want non-students wandering around and popping into classrooms or labs. But it wasn't what Neen would call overly strict. Was this related to the increased police presence around the city, or was this something more?

Neen's stomach clenched. *It's a people. It's everywhere.*

Pelon looked so excited. She led Neen down a white-walled hallway.

"Can I know a little bit about this project before we get there?" Neen asked.

"You know they've restarted the lab breeding program, right?"

"Yes." Herria had pushed that through the high council several weeks ago. Neen remembered Nekka's concerns that successful lab breeding might spell danger for the males. If they were obsolete...

"This is an offshoot of that," Pelon continued. "Really amazing stuff. You'll see."

Neen's skin started to prickle. Pelon was so cheerful, so innocent. They walked further down the hallway, passing unmarked doors on either side.

"I don't remember this area," Neen said.

"It was off-limits to students, for high-level special projects only. I'm surprised you forgot."

Neen hadn't forgotten. The special projects wing was on level nine. She knew that. And it wasn't strictly off-limits to students because she worked on a study there with Instructor Redma during her final term.

But this wasn't level nine, and Neen had never seen this hallway or all these unmarked doors before. This was level three. Neuroscience and Endocrinology. Neen had taken classes here. She would have remembered this hallway.

But she didn't recognize it now.

"Here we are," said Pelon, stopping at a door without any markings or windows. She passed her wrist across the sensor in the door and it unlocked. "Keep your voice low. We don't want any sudden interruptions."

Neen followed her in.

The room was set up like a hospital ward, with rows of beds along the opposite wall, monitors everywhere, and workstations to the right. On the left side of the room were several freezers, incubators, and shelves of chemicals.

The beds were empty, except for one.

Her tiny body was almost as small as a child, her face elfin in features. She wore a surgical cap on her head, but Neen didn't need to see the white-blonde curls underneath to know who it was.

Her blood froze. She stood just inside the doorway, paralyzed.

"It's okay, she's asleep," whispered Pelon, pulling Neen by the arm. "Just volunteered the other day. Case study number one-hundred-thirty-six. I wasn't involved in those other studies. One-thirty-six is my first."

Neen couldn't speak. She watched as Pelon went over to the monitor and checked the vitals.

"I know what you're thinking," Pelon continued in a low voice, going to one of the lab desks and entering data into a tablet. "This doesn't look like embryonic research. But that's just it. We don't have to breed traits anymore.

No more genetic enhancements in the fertilization stage." She looked up at Neen. "We've taken gene therapy to a new level."

"Are you—" Neen couldn't take her eyes off Ems lying unconscious in that bed, "—implanting a zygote—"

Pelon grinned. "No, that's just it. We don't need to do it that early. The enhancements can be done at any stage. Any stage, Neen. Isn't that incredible?"

"I don't—" Neen willed her legs to carry herself to Ems's bedside. "What are you saying?"

"This is only her third day of treatment," Pelon said. "But by tomorrow evening, she'll have received all four injections. One for each enhancement. Did you know the other one-hundred-thirty-five cases have been out and about in High City for months now? Years even. I guess the program started elsewhere, maybe even in one of the clan lands, they're pretty sketchy about giving us all the details. This is the final stage before we roll it out publicly. But so far, side effects have been minimal. Headaches, some elevated testosterone levels, but nothing even remotely dangerous. This is it, Neen, the thing we've been waiting for. No more breeding with the males."

"But this woman already has her enhanced traits," Neen said, scanning the room for security screens. To her astonishment, there didn't seem to be any security whatsoever except the lock on the door. "And you just said you're not implanting a zygote. I don't see how this eliminates breeding."

"Laboratory fertilization has been around since the ancient days," Pelon explained. "We all know that. But the enhancements couldn't be guaranteed in the lab. That's why we needed the males. Breeding directly was the only way. But now—" she went to one of the freezers and took out a tray of sealed vials— "we can do the enhancements at any stage. Even in fully matured adult females."

Neen read the labels on the tray.

Benglion. Triverser. Evox. Trabador. Sixter.

"It's a new day, Neen," Pelon said, eyes shining. "Hard to believe, but it's true. No more separate clans. No more breeding sessions. No more limits. All clans as one."

All clans. *The final revolution.*

Neen could feel her stomach churn. What had they done to Ems? How was she going to get her out?

"So—" Neen tried to keep her voice steady, "—what did you want from me? It seems like you've got things well in hand."

Pelon put the tray of vials back in the freezer. "Well, I was thinking about that serum you made before... You know, the one for the male."

Neen had never told Pelon what that serum was for.

"I'm not an idiot, Neen. I saw what chemicals you were using. Serotonin. Oxytocin. Mood enhancers. Fear inhibitors. I don't know why you were trying to help a male overcome his fears, but I figured out eventually what you were doing."

Pelon's face wasn't cheerful anymore. There was an unusual seriousness to her expression. She walked over to Ems's bedside and checked her vitals again.

"What I want to know is," Pelon continued, not looking at Neen directly, "did it work? Were you able to get rid of his fear?"

"I—" Neen felt the room get smaller. Ems was just lying there, calmly asleep. Pelon wasn't doing anything threatening. Just talking. Monitoring her patient. Entirely professional.

But then why was Neen's heart racing?

"If I could find a way to further decrease the fear-response in our subjects, of somehow boosting the Benglion traits for risk-taking, I might get the project leaders to keep me on for the next phase. Maybe put me in charge of the roll-out."

"The roll-out?"

"We're getting ready to go wide, Neen. This isn't just for experiments anymore. This is the future."

Pelon walked over to the other side of the bed, close to Neen. She showed Neen the formula she was calculating on her tablet.

"Am I on the right track? It's been a bit of guesswork since one-hundred-thirty-six here isn't male or Benglion..."

"Let me see," Neen said, taking the tablet. As she did, she grabbed Pelon's arm and twisted it sideways.

Pelon yelped.

Neen dropped the tablet and grabbed her now with both hands. Using all her strength, she threw the younger woman down. Pelon's head hit the side of the monitor with a dull thud, then her body slumped on the floor.

Neen was gasping for breath. She had never done anything like that before. She stood over Pelon's body for several long seconds, waiting for the other woman to move or cry out or do something. But Pelon didn't move.

Neen didn't have much time. "Ems, wake up." She removed the heart monitor and the IV. "Come on."

Ems didn't move.

Neen put her arms under Ems's back and lifted her from the bed. "Come on!" Pelon was still unconscious on the floor, but Neen had no idea if there were security screens hidden somewhere in the room, or even if Pelon's wrist chip was being monitored.

Luckily Ems was small enough that Neen could drag her

out if she needed to. But anyone who saw them would immediately know something was wrong.

"Ems, please!"

Her head lolled back and forth, and she groaned. "Neen?"

"We have to get out of here. Do you have clothes?"

Ems shook her head and hung weakly in Neen's arms.

"Okay, lean on me for support. I'll figure something out." Lifting Ems out of the bed, she shuffled the two of them toward the door. Maybe the hallway would be as empty going out as it had been going in. It was a faint hope, but it was the only thing Neen had.

Neen used her opposite shoulder to shove open the door.

I wouldn't budge.

It needed a chip code. Pelon's chip code.

"Wait here," she said, setting Ems down and leaning her against the wall. "I'm about to do something I hope I don't regret."

Ems's head sagged forward, and she moaned softly. "Herria... she's not..."

But Neen wasn't listening. She was searching through drawers and cabinets looking for what she needed. Thankfully this lab was equipped for medical purposes...

"Neen... listen..."

"We need to get out of here, Ems, or we'll be caught. Just give me a second." Neen found what she was looking for, then she turned to the still-unconscious Pelon. She wanted to say she was sorry, but she knew it wouldn't matter. She put on the surgical gloves.

"...you don't understand," Ems said, her head lifting slightly. "I saw inside her... went too deep... She's not what she says she is..."

Neen had to concentrate. With deft swiftness, she

jabbed a syringe into Pelon's forearm. Then, steadying her shaking hand as best she could, she cleaned the area and lowered the scalpel, hoping the local anesthesia had done its job.

"I'm sorry, Pelon," she said, "but we need it for the other door too..."

As soon as she cut into the skin, a thick trail of blood spurted out. Neen was ready for it. Bloody sponge after bloody sponge soaked up the gore, while Neen searched under the skin to find the chip. Both women's brown and white jumpsuits were stained with splotches of bright red blood.

Finding the chip wouldn't be too hard. Neen knew where to look. But all the blood everywhere made her fingers slippery, the tweezers unwieldy in her slick hand. Who knew how long they had until someone came in, until security forces found them...

"Got it!" Neen lifted the chip out with her tweezers. Dumping it in a small tray, she moved quickly to bandage Pelon's wrists. The metallic smell of blood mixed with the isopropyl alcohol and latex. Neen's heart pounded.

Pelon groaned and started to shift as the last bandage was secured.

Neen scooped up the tray with the chip in it, then scrambled over to lift Ems. She knew she was leaving Pelon trapped in the room, but all she could do was hope someone came by eventually and found her.

With the bloody chip in hand, Neen unlocked the door.

The hallway outside was empty. The white walls made her feel exposed like she was a dark stain streaking across the clean surface.

"Neen," Ems groaned, her eyes squeezed shut. "Herkeep—"

"I know, Ems. That's why I'm her."

"But there's more... So much more..."

"Not now, sister. Keep quiet."

The hallway's length stretched on and on. It was an eternity. Each unmarked door they passed could be the one that would open, exposing their escape. Neen tried to go as fast as she could, but dragging Ems along was proving more difficult than she expected.

"Herria..." Ems gasped and then flopped her head forward. She had passed out.

The main door to this wing was in sight. Neen was sweating, her shoulder aching from holding Ems up.

What would they do once they were in the common areas of the Institute? How could Neen possibly escape? Her clothes were still stained with blood.

They reached the exit door.

Neen waved the small chip in front of the sensor. It pinged and the lock clicked open.

"Here we go."

Outside the door, there were a few women walking to their classes or to a meeting. Neen held her breath and waited. Anyone seeing them would immediately wonder what was going on. It was like the universe was laughing at them, keeping her and Ems from being trapped in that lab room, only to have them get caught now.

"Oh my!" One of the women saw Neen struggling to hold Ems up. She rushed over. A broad-faced Triverser with flaxen hair. "Let me call someone. Med staff are just a few levels above us." She didn't appear to suspect anything, just trying to help two women who seemed in distress.

Neen almost said no, but stopped herself. "Call special forces," she said quickly. "Ask for Sona Lohen. Captain. Tell her to come right away."

The woman's eyes grew big, but she didn't question. With a couple of flicks of her fingers, she sent out a call through her wrist screen.

"What happened?" she asked. "I didn't think we had any patient studies in this department right now..."

"Special project," Neen said, parroting Pelon. "Lab breeding."

"Oh," the woman looked perplexed. "But I thought—"

"It's not something we can discuss. This patient is having an adverse reaction to the treatment and I need to get her to Captain Lohen."

"Captain Lohen? But that—"

Neen didn't wait for any more questions. She shifted Ems in her arms and pushed past the woman.

It was a ridiculous lie, but Neen hoped confusion and shock would be on her side. She tried to stay as confident as possible even as other women stopped and stared.

"I'm working with special forces," she said as she passed by their stares. "Go about your business and don't ask questions."

As soon as the women heard the words "special forces," they looked away and pretended not to notice. Apparently, Neen wasn't the only one who had found the police force to be an overbearing presence these days.

All she had to do now was get to the exit and hope Sona had gotten her message...

* * *

"I'M glad you got in touch, Neen Salvek." Sona stood outside her official vehicle. "I have orders to take you to the high council building." Sona betrayed no hint of shock at seeing Ems in a hospital gown and clinging to consciousness, Neen struggling to support her. Without another word, Sona whisked the two women into her vehicle and got into the driver's seat.

While her eyes watched the street as she drove away from the Institute, Sona put a finger to her mouth, a shush barely escaping her lips. Neen swiftly concluded that the vehicle wasn't secure.

Neen didn't feel like speaking. She sank into the smooth synthetic fabric of her cushioned seat and closed her eyes. Ems sat next to her, moaning softly. The low hum of the traffic and the outside world lulled Neen into a semi-sleep, but even as she closed her eyes and relaxed, she still kept her fingers gripped tightly to the chip she'd stolen from Pelon.

* * *

WHEN SHE WOKE UP, Neen was on the cold, hard floor of the bomb shelter.

"I'm sorry I've been hard to reach," Sona said, squatting beside her, her voice low. "Things are, as you might imagine, precarious right now..."

Neen understood. She flexed her arm and felt its stiffness. Her shoulder ached. "How's Ems?" she managed to whisper.

Sona stood up, and Neen could see Ems sitting against the opposite wall. The only light was Sona's battery-powered torch, but even in the dimness, Neen could see the hollow, glassy look in Ems's eyes.

"She's doing better now, but whatever they gave her in that lab had made her vomit." Sona nodded toward a rusty bucket a few yards away.

"We have to find Nekka," Neen said, her exhaustion fading as she remembered everything that had happened with Pelon at the Institute. "Herria has figured out some kind of process for altering women's genetic traits after birth. It's not just breeding in the lab. It's something much bigger."

"I haven't been able to get in contact with Nekka for over a week," Sona replied. "I worry that somehow Herria has—"

"Herria." Ems spoke sharply, a bitterness to her voice that Neen had never heard before.

"Yes, I think Herria—" Sona continued again.

"She's not who you think she is," said Ems. She was still staring straight ahead, not looking at either of the women.

"I got your message about Herkeep," Neen said. "I think I understand now. Pelon is involved, most likely others as well. I don't know how wittingly they're involved, but Herria has them working on experiments—"

"No!" Ems said, her voice rising. "Listen to me! Herria is not who you think she is. We've been wrong about her this whole time. I saw..." Ems shivered. "I saw inside her mind. When I was trying to find out more about Herkeep. She took me to her office again, I started suggesting things to her, steering her thoughts toward what she was planning, what this all meant. I steered... too hard."

Ems swallowed and looked like she was going to throw up again. She closed her eyes and took several deep breaths.

"I went in too deep," she continued. "That's when I saw it. All of it. Memories. From Herria's childhood. Her mother... Her... father."

Sona's hawk-like eyes narrowed. "Father?"

"You mean the male her mother bred with?" Neen asked. "How could Herria know who that was? Or have any memory of him?"

Ems shook her head. "No... I don't mean that. I mean her father."

"Ems, are you okay?" Sona asked. "Whatever they did to

you in that lab, we can't be sure they didn't manipulate your mind—"

"I know what I saw." Ems's eyes had a far-off look. "He was a cruel man. He beat her mother. Herria was terrified of him. She used to hide under her bed when he went into his rages."

Neen drew her knees up to her chest. This sounded like something out of their history textbooks. Males used to beat and assault women all the time, and the police of that era did nothing to stop it. Sometimes, in fact, the police males were the worst offenders. The implication of what Ems was saying was simply impossible. If Herria was a child with a father and a mother... a father who beat them...

"Three hundred years," Ems said, her voice barely above a whisper. "That's how long—"

"Ems, listen to what you're saying," Neen replied. "This is impossible. Are you claiming Herria was born before the revolutions? That's ludicrous."

Ems's eyes flashed. They seemed to see Neen for the first time. Ems leaped up and practically snarled at her. "I know what I saw! It seems impossible, but it's true. Herria has memories from before the bells rang. She was there when it all began, the beginning of everything. She's older than the founding of EVE, older than what's humanly possible, but it's true! They did something to her, those first women, a splinter group or something. They experimented with enhancing traits, before we developed the clans and advanced breeding. They did something to her..."

Ems's shoulders slumped and her anger dissipated. She retreated into herself again.

"They wanted her to have multiple traits, not just one," Ems said, sinking again to the floor and leaning on the wall. "She's not a Sixter. Not really. She's more... she's..."

"All clans as one," Neen said, her voice sounding hollow in that empty tunnel. "That's what Pelon called it." She looked at Ems — sweet, joyful, wonderful Ems — and saw the pain in her best friend's face, the trauma of what she'd just gone through. "That's what they've done to you, Ems. Given you all the traits of the clans."

Ems lowered her head. She shivered and wrapped her arms around herself.

"If this is true," Neen began, "we have to tell the high council. We have to expose what's happening. It's hard to believe, but Pelon said the experiments were working. Herria's after more than just a few male lives. She's going to alter the very nature of society. Of every woman. Every male..."

The Domes, the breeding process, all of it would be obsolete. Including Tem.

Neen tried not to show it, but her entire insides were roiling.

Sona was pacing the area, hands on her hips. "We have nothing to corroborate this but your testimony, Ems. And frankly, the fact that you claim to have seen all this inside of Herria's mind... I don't know what I'm supposed to do with that. I can't go to the high council with it."

"Why not?" Neen demanded. This was life or death now, more than she ever realized. "I have proof that Herria's been experimenting with these genetic alterations. I was there in the lab!"

"You can't walk into the high council's meeting room and accuse the Sixter councilwoman of being three hundred years old!" Sona cried. "We'll be locked up as delusional! It's suicide! "

"We have to try," Neen said, coming to her feet. She was a head shorter than Sona but that didn't stop her from facing down the Benglion captain. "Who else can stop Herria? Who else knows the extent of her lies and what she's planning to do? We have to try."

Sona turned away, shaking her head. "It's suicide."

"If we don't risk it now," Neen replied, "then there won't be anything worth saving when Herria's through. Whatever they've done to Ems and the others, they won't stop there. It's coming for all of us one way or another. Unless we stop them. We have to try."

Sona sighed. Then she smiled to herself. "Who says our clans determine our natures? Here I am, a proud Benglion, showing less courage than a Triverser." She held out her hands.

Neen understood. She clasped them. Neither woman said anything, but they didn't have to.

At last, Sona nodded. "Alright, prodigy," she said. "Let's try."

CHAPTER 13

NEKKA

THE ROOM WAS NOT UNCOMFORTABLE. She had to give Herria credit for that.

Nekka sat on a suede upholstered wingback chair, while the room dazzled with color from the mint-condition glass lampshades in two corners. Patterned to look like violet and lavender lilies, the glass on the shades filtered the light, casting a warm glow over everything. How Herria managed to acquire all these antiques was confounding to Nekka. The time and effort needed to find them were indulgences Nekka could hardly understand.

She sniffed the stale air and tried not to look at her jailer, who stood in the corner like a disapproving vulture.

Grex had just come to replace the previous guard, one of Herria's many foot soldiers. That was Nekka's name for them, seeing as they acted like some kind of pseudo-military unit, taking orders only from the high councilwoman.

Nekka remembered the night they stormed into her office and took her away. She was shocked at the time, but thinking back, she should have expected no less. Herria knew the threat Nekka posed. It was only a matter of time before she took action to neutralize that threat.

Nekka had been keeping track of the days she'd been held in this little suite. A sitting room, a small bedroom, and a latrine were all she had for living space, but the rooms were not bad. Herria's taste in decor was eccentric but pleasant in its way. It made the weeks bearable, perhaps.

Of course, Nekka had no idea where she was, whether still in the high council building or elsewhere. The foot soldiers hadn't given her the privilege of staying awake during her capture. After they knocked her out, the next thing she knew, she was waking up to the dazzling light of these lampshades.

Grex seemed unhappy about her post, standing in the corner with a scowl on her face and hunched shoulders.

But then when did Grex ever seem happy?

Herria's pet. Cowed and controlled. But miserable too.

"Anything to report?" Nekka said in mock seriousness.

Grex pursed her lips and turned her head as if Nekka had breathed out bad air.

"I may be getting old and senile," Nekka continued, "but my memory doesn't recall you ever keeping watch before. Where did all the hulking Benglions go? The ones Herria's recruited for bodyguards?"

Grex scoffed, but a sly smile crept along her lips at the same time. "Those weren't Benglions," she said, smugness dripping from her tongue like poison.

Nekka decided not to play Grex's game. She could tell Grex wanted nothing more than for Nekka to beg her for an explanation. She wouldn't give Herria's little creature the satisfaction.

Instead, Nekka went back to her daydreams, to her

memories of long ago. They were the only things keeping her sane during these long, tiresome days of captivity.

She thought of those wild wheat fields in late summer, her escape from the rigors of writing clan reports and meeting with capital city officials. She insisted on working all the way through her final trimester, even though her ankles were as swollen as melons. Those wheat fields were like blankets of golden brown, ripe and ready for harvest. Just like Nekka felt, her belly swollen with life.

It had taken a lot of doing to make sure no one asked too many questions when the child was born. Having a position in Triverser leadership helped. Files could always be amended if one knew the right channels to pursue. And Nekka always knew the right answers to any problem.

She thought of his hair, so dark it was almost black, and his eyes like the rich brown of a roe deer's fur, so deep and round that she could get lost in them if she stared too long.

It had taken a lot of doing to make sure no one asked too many questions then too. When she had pursued him and taken him for her own.

Bargo.

She could still taste the faint saltiness of his skin, could feel the firmness of his arms as she ran her hands along them.

Before Nekka knew it, she had started to doze. She woke up with a start, jumping a little in the chair and drawing the withering gaze of Grex.

"Do you ever feel happy, Grex?" Nekka said. "Or did Herria suck all the joy out of you too along with the rest of your emotions?"

"I know I'll enjoy watching you suffer," Grex replied. "Just wait, Nekka. The storm is coming soon."

Nekka paid no mind to Grex's posturing. It wasn't that she didn't fear Herria's plans. It was obvious by now that

Neen and the others hadn't been able to expose Herria's conspiracy, and what Herria had planned next, Nekka could only guess. But panicking or lashing out wouldn't help. She needed to be patient and wait for an opportunity. If Herria had wanted her dead, she would be already. So there must be a reason she was still alive.

"If my inklings are correct," Nekka said, "we're due for another meeting of the high council any day now. I assume Herria plans to claim I'm ill or indisposed?"

"Not at all," said Grex. "Herria wouldn't dream of keeping you away from that meeting."

"Is that so?"

"She wouldn't want you to miss it. Your final defeat."

"I see." Of course. A vote of no-confidence. Then Nekka's removal and a special election. Herria would have no one standing in her way on the council, and then she could proceed with whatever plans she had without any legal ramifications.

Nekka kept her face as calm as possible. Worrying wouldn't help. She still had sway, if only she could speak her piece to the council. Reslan was amenable. Perhaps even Forta. What she needed was evidence. Some way for Ems to testify before the council. Even without definitive proof, if she could make the accusations against Herria, then perhaps something would happen...

Grex was staring at Nekka. She seemed on the cusp of saying something, like she was holding something in that wanted to be let out.

"Go on, Grex. I won't stop you. Say your piece."

"Herria..." Grex began, her voice quivering. It was the first time Nekka had ever detected a hint of genuine emotion from the woman. "She saved me. She rescued me from despair."

"Yes, I know about your breakdown." Nekka didn't mean to speak so bluntly. She really did feel some pity for Grex's previous trauma, but it was simply beyond her abilities to speak delicately about such things. "Unfortunately not uncommon for Evoxes. But Herria's methods... whatever they were... did you no favors, Grex. You should have gotten real help from a trained specialist—"

"Specialist!" Grex hissed. "They would have put me in hospital. Forced me into menial work. Painting pictures for elderly homes or something equally useless. Kept me from rising in the ranks."

"Perhaps that would've been for the best," Nekka said softly.

Grex squeezed her eyes shut. Her face contorted as if in pain.

"I shouldn't have upset you," said Nekka.

Grex shook her head, still wincing.

"Why don't you get back to gloating over how great Herria is? I'll be a good prisoner and listen."

"No..." Grex said, voice strained. "You'll see... I won't be weak anymore. The final revolution is coming..."

Nekka didn't respond. But Grex's words chilled her spine. Herria wanted revolution. She could only imagine what that might mean...

A knock on the door. "The councilwoman is wanted," came the muffled voice on the other side of the door.

Grex's lips twisted into a grin. She opened the door and two armed guards came in. They lifted Nekka from her chair and shoved her out of the room.

She could see now that she was still in the high council building, the familiar hallways leading her to a familiar room.

The high council meeting room.

"Together."

"Together."

"Together."

Around they went, giving the greeting. It came to Nekka's turn, Herria's outstretched hands waiting for her.

"Together." The words felt like dust in Nekka's mouth. She could see what this was. Herria's grip was vice-like, like talons clutching their prey. Nekka had to suffer it in silence. She wouldn't give Herria any satisfaction if she could help it.

"First item on the agenda," Forta began, "is—"

"Riots." Herria's voice was clear as a bell ringing.

Nekka watched the faces of the other councilwomen. Only Reslan reacted in apprehension. Everyone else seemed to know what was going on.

"Conflagrations breaking out everywhere," Herria continued. "The males are out of control. Something must be done."

Despite her weakened position, Nekka couldn't let such unreason stand. "How is it possible the males are out of control if we've administered the necessary pills—"

Herria stifled a laugh. "Oh wise and cunning Nekka, how could we possibly function without you? What a genius you are! Just pop some pills in the males' mouths and all will be well!"

Forta and Sienax laughed openly.

Nekka tried to speak again, but Herria cut her off. "Do you think we didn't?" she said, deadly serious. "Did you think us fools?"

"The guards know how to administer the correct pharmaceuticals," Forta added, frowning. "But the males' rage cannot be contained any longer."

"Then increase the dosage," Nekka cut in. "We shouldn't be having riots in the Domes if this council was doing its job properly."

The die had been cast. Nekka could feel the cold stares of the other women at the table, even Reslan.

"Unless riots are to someone's advantage," Nekka continued, looking straight at Herria. "Chaos breeds opportunity, doesn't it, Herria? Perhaps someone is purposefully altering the drugs—"

"Chaos breeds chaos," Herria answered, cutting Nekka off. "Which is why we need a stronger hand. The males will never learn if we treat them with kid gloves. You've spent years on this council advocating for those beasts, pretending they were reformable. We all know that was foolishness. Now we see the rotten fruit of your policies, Nekka. Something must be done."

"Like what? Shock them into submission?" Nekka replied, her voice rising in anger. "Beat them? Keep them in solitary confinement? Starve them? What? What do you plan to do?"

Herria looked around the table, a serene smile on her lips. "I wasn't talking about the males, Nekka. I was talking about you."

All eyes were on Herria. No one even glanced Nekka's way.

"I'm calling for a vote of no-confidence for Nekka Trovek, high council representative for Clan Triverser," said Herria. "All in favor?"

This was it. Herria had wasted no time.

They all voted. No hesitation, not even Reslan. All it took was Nekka's absence for two weeks and Herria had seized complete control.

"That's settled," Herria said, resisting a triumphant note. "We'll call for a new election next month. Before that time, Nekka, you may stay on as a non-voting member of the council."

Nekka didn't bother saying anything. It was just as she predicted.

"As regards the riots breaking out in the Domes," Herria continued, "I think it best we increase the number of special forces and push more males into the Work Domes if possible. As a deterrent, of course."

* * *

"NO," Sienax said, trembling. "No, no. It's not possible..."

"Care to share with the rest of us?" Herria asked. She seemed utterly calm. Forta and Reslan looked at Sienax and then at their aides and assistants. Their confusion was evident.

"It can't be..." Sienax said again, handing the tablet back to her aide. "I've just— I've just had a report from Evox Dome..."

Herria leaned in, waiting for the other woman to elaborate.

"What kind of report?" Forta demanded.

"They're all..." Sienax couldn't help her emotions. They flowed out of her like a rising tide, filling her eyes with tears. "Nearly every guard is dead."

"Dead?" Forta stood up.

"What are you saying, Sienax?" Herria asked.

"The males," Sienax continued, "they revolted. All of them. Attacked the women, killed them. Just like in the breeding suites."

"No." Forta's face was pale.

Reslan looked around helplessly.

"Grex," Herria said, taking command. "Get in touch with Feldir. Now."

"There's a chance the males could get out," Sienax said, trying to stem her grief.

"Impossible!" cried Forta. "Any attempt to breach the Dome's walls will mean instant death. Their security chips—"

"My sources say the males have removed them," Sienax continued. "Carved them out."

"Sisters, this is what we've most feared," said Herria standing up and moving toward the door of the meeting room. "We knew our ambivalent stance towards the males could lead to this. There's no more time to waste. We must take care of the males once and for all."

"Take care of the males?" asked Reslan.

Herria motioned to Grex, who went to the door and opened it.

Feldir entered leading a squad of two dozen women behind her. Nekka recognized several of them immediately. Her jailers. They were tall like Benglions, with impassive, emotionless faces. But Grex had said they weren't Benglion. Nekka felt dread in the pit of her stomach.

"We need a new special force to deal with these insurrections," Herria began, motioning to Feldir and the squad. "This is only a handful of the dozens I've been training for such an emergency as this."

"I don't recognize these women—" Forta began, but Herria's cunning smile stopped her short.

"They are not Benglion. Nor are they Triverser. Nor Trabador. Nor Sixter. Nor Evox." Herria waited for her words to sink in. "For many months, I've been working with scientists to develop new therapeutic treatments: Genetic modifications that can be injected into fully-matured adult human females without side effects. Modifications that can enhance their traits. All their traits." Herria let the words sink in. "These women have increased strength, increased speed, increased sensory abilities, increased intelligence, increased focus and endurance, increased emotional awareness. In essence, they are all the clans in one."

Nekka could see that Forta and Reslan were dumbfounded at Herria's claims. Sienax, though still overcome by grief, didn't seem as surprised.

"This is our future," Herria continued. "A future without breeding. Without clans." She turned her gaze on Nekka, her eyes shining in triumph. "Without males."

"Herria, what—" Forta began.

"Is this what you want, sisters?" Nekka said. There was no point in holding back. Herria had defeated her, but Nekka still had a voice. "You've heard her words. She's speaking of genocide. Now that she's made these 'treatments,' there's no use for the men. They're to be worked in the mines until death. We'll have made ourselves no better than they, casting an entire group into slavery for our benefit. Violence and death for our enemies. Is that it? Is that what we want? But who is the enemy here? Is it the men? Or is it us?"

"Men?" Herria pretended to choke on the word. "You have always been a fool, Nekka. Always taking the side of those beasts against your own kind. Would you have another Evox Dome? Would you let your fellow women die at the hands of these animals again? Because that is what will happen unless we act now, stamp out their kind, and end this foolish breeding business. We are at the forefront of a new revolution. The final revolution."

Herria waited to see what the others would say. Nekka waited too. The choice was clear.

"How long have you been experimenting with these therapeutic treatments?" Reslan said, her voice shaking.

Nekka smiled at her. Reslan had always been a follower,

the youngest of the council, and fear had always ruled her decisions, but perhaps Herria had misjudged her fear. Perhaps it wasn't strong enough to justify the extinction of the men.

"Quite some time," Herria replied. "We're in the final stages. Next step is rolling it out to the general public."

"But—" Reslan quivered, "—this wasn't approved. How could you have started all this without taking it to a vote?"

Herria's pale face flushed red. She balled her fists until the knuckles turned white. "What difference does it make?" she hissed. "It worked. The treatments are perfect."

"But are you sure there are no side effects?" Reslan asked.

Herria didn't answer. She cocked her head, listening. Feldir and the other special forces also seemed to hear something that Nekka and the others could not.

"Down the hall," Herria said to Feldir. "Intercept them."

Feldir and four others ran out of the room. Within seconds they returned, shoving three women onto the floor at Herria's feet.

"They were armed," Feldir said, holding three pistols in her hands.

"What is the meaning of this?" Forta said. "Sona? Explain yourself."

Sona, Neen, and Ems stood up and looked around at the council.

"I'm sorry councilwoman Forta," Sona began, "but we have highly sensitive information related to one of the high councilwomen. Information we believe you are entitled to know."

Herria took her seat at the table again and folded her hands, looking expectantly at Sona. "Go on, Captain Lohen. Tell them what you've discovered."

Sona hesitated, and Nekka could see that she was puzzled by Herria's calmness.

"It's too late," Nekka said. "She's already told them. They know everything."

"Everything?" said Neen. "What do you mean—"

"Look around you, Neen Salvek," Herria said, eyes gleaming like a hunter that's spotted her prey. "These women are the future." She motioned to Feldir and the others.

"But that's not all we know!" Ems cried. "Herria is hiding more secrets! I know she's not who she claims to be!"

"Not who she claims to be?" Forta asked.

Herria chuckled softly to herself. "And how, exactly, dear Ems, did you find out all these 'secrets' about me?"

"I—" Ems began. "I saw—"

"You saw? What did you see? How?" Herria's smile mocked the young woman.

Nekka couldn't understand why Ems didn't answer, but she could see that something warred within her.

"So this council is ready to massacre every male in the Domes?" Neen shouted. "Is that what we've become?"

"They massacred us first," Sienax replied. "Nearly every woman in Evox Dome is dead. It's past time we dealt with them."

Forta sighed but nodded her head. "I can't argue with that. It's a security risk. We can't go back to the way things were. How can we ever allow women to be in a breeding suite again? If there's a way to keep our enhancements and end contact with the males, why shouldn't we take it?"

Nekka looked to Reslan. The war within was happening on her face too.

"We don't have to destroy them," she said. "Just send them to the Work Domes. We still need the mines."

"Indeed we do," Herria chimed in. "Salvek here and her

rabble-rousers make it sound like we're planning to murder the males, but that's ludicrous. We need them as workers. We don't need the other Domes, of course, but more Work Domes can be built. Reslan, that will be a wonderful project for the Trabadors. And once the males are put into the Work Domes, we can begin work on increasing automation. Eventually, the minerals we need to power our networks can be mined with robots. Males will have served their purpose, and after that—"

"Extinction," Neen said. "That's your final goal."

Herria shrugged. "The males will have outlived their usefulness."

No one spoke. Nekka watched as Feldir and her squad moved slowly to surround Neen, Sona, and Ems. She studied the faces of the other high councilwomen. Had Herria's words unnerved them, or were they ready to embrace this grim future?

"This is still a meeting of the high council," Nekka piped up. "Perhaps before Herria starts building statues in her own honor we might vote on this plan? Are we really going to move ahead with injecting all the women of EVE with this new treatment? Are we going to move all the men to Work Domes? Are we really going to let an entire population of humans work themselves into extinction simply because we have no further use for them? If that is what you want, then vote on it and let your consciences suffer the consequences."

"But not you, Nekka," Herria said. "Your vote no longer counts."

Nekka nodded, eyes downcast. She stood up from the table and came to stand next to Neen. If she was going to be defeated, at least she would stand with the few allies she had left.

Every bone in her body ached. She had been struggling so hard to stay strong, her limit had finally been reached.

Neen and the others looked to the high council, hope still clinging to their young faces. But Nekka knew better. There was no hope to be found anymore.

She closed her eyes. Bargo's firm hands caressed her cheeks. His lips were so soft against her skin. She breathed in his smell, her face buried in the folds of his dark locks.

If only she could go back to those days. When she still hoped the world might be made better.

"What does the council say?" Herria spoke. Her voice was hollow in Nekka's ears. A distant voice. It intruded on her memories.

The other councilwomen spoke. As each one voiced her ascent, it was like pillars of stone — one by one — came crashing down around Nekka, turning everything into rubble and ruin, burying her and Bargo and her little son until they were ghosts who wandered a barren field, searching for but never finding each other ever again.

"The motion is passed," Herria said. "And now," she continued, and Nekka opened her eyes to see Herria staring straight at her, "it's time to arrest these traitors."

Hands grabbed them, stronger than any Nekka had ever felt before.

This was it. There was no escape.

CHAPTER 14

NEEN

"NO!" Ems cried, sliding out of the other woman's grip and twisting her arm until it snapped.

Neen struggled against her own captor, a tall blonde woman with a wide forehead and beady eyes, but it was no use. It was like being trapped by a block of ice.

How had Ems managed to do it? She had twisted that woman's arm like a twig.

Sona grappled with her captor, trying to clear a way to Feldir and the pistols.

"Enough!" Ems screamed, squeezing her eyes shut. Her high-pitched voice cut through the other noises in the room.

A sharp pain jabbed into Neen's head like long fingers were prying open her skull. She crumpled to the ground and realized that the other woman's hand had fallen away. Everyone in the room had collapsed, all of them writhing around in pain. Even Herria, who still had her eyes open and was groping towards Ems with halting, tortured movements.

Then the prying fingers were gone, and Neen's head was free. All the stabbing pain had ceased, and she could breathe freely again.

Sona rose from the floor and went over to Nekka, helping her up. Herria was still struggling towards them, teeth gritted in obvious pain.

Ems's eyes were shut, her face contorted.

"We have to go," Sona said, giving Neen a hand.

"Ems," Neen said, shaking her on the shoulder. But Ems didn't react. She was lost in the depths of her mind. Everyone in the room lay on the floor, looking like peaceful sleepers, except Herria, who had stopped her crawl and was fighting back tears.

"Get out!" she gasped under her breath. "Get out of my head!"

"Let her go, Ems," Neen pleaded. "We have to leave!"

Sona handed pistols to Neen and Nekka, keeping one for herself too. "Follow me."

Neen pulled at Ems's shoulder, trying to break her out of the trance.

"Hurry!" Sona said, leading Nekka out of the room.

Neen didn't know what to do. Herria had fought through whatever control Ems was trying to exert and was crawling toward them again.

"Ems!" Neen grabbed her friend's hand and squeezed.

Ems's eyelashes fluttered, and then her entire body went limp. Neen picked her up, and Ems gave her a faint smile, eyes heavy-lidded.

Herria had regained her feet, though she still moved slowly.

"Come on," Neen said, helping Ems move. They ran after Sona and Nekka, with Herria in pursuit.

"I—" Ems mumbled, "I don't know how long they'll be out..."

"Don't talk, just move."

Sona and Nekka were at the end of the hallway, a huge

window in front of them, filtering streaks of sunlight across the floor. Sona aimed her pistol and shot the glass three times, shattering it.

Neen bit her lip, hoping her plan worked. It had to work. Herria had regained her strength and was charging toward them.

Sona lifted Nekka like she was a child and tossed her out the window. Then she leaped through the shattered opening. They disappeared into the cloudless day.

"Come on, Ems," Neen said, pulling her friend along. Ems had not recovered nearly as quickly as Herria. She was still weakened and shuffling awkwardly. Neen gasped for breath, her chest burning as she sprinted toward the broken window.

"Please let this work, please," she mumbled under her breath.

Herria was gaining. Neen twisted around and pointed her pistol at her. A shot ricocheted off the wall. Herria didn't even react. She just kept charging at them.

Neen redoubled her efforts. The muscles in her legs felt like they were going to explode. "Here we go," she said, practically tossing Ems up the window opening. Ems wobbled on her feet, but then she fell, out the window and into the sky.

Neen leaped after her, holding her breath.

When her feet hit the surface of the hovercraft, she felt it buckle. Four women was a heavy load for the drone to carry, but after it dipped several feet due to Neen's added weight, it steadied itself and didn't sink further.

A voice spoke through Sona's wrist screen. "All set?"

"Take us out, Li," Sona replied.

"You owe me, love," Li's voice said through the small screen.

"Always," Sona answered.

The drone sped off, sailing over the streets of the city, zig-zagging around the buildings until it came to the outskirts.

Neen looked behind her as they flew. The high council building could still be seen, a majestic white tower ascending to the sky. But Herria was nowhere in sight. Neen only wondered what was happening now as Herria most likely called forth whatever force of multi-powered women she had created. A squadron of enhanced warriors who would be tearing the city apart to find them.

* * *

"WE CAN'T STAY HERE," Sona said as they locked the doors inside the bomb shelter. "We're in a terrible tactical position, and it's only a matter of time before Herria takes control of the airspace around the city. We need to move now."

Nekka sat down to catch her breath. Her eyes looked sunken and her body smaller and more frail since the last time Neen had seen her.

"I must say," Nekka began, "I wasn't expecting that hovercraft. I thought Sona was throwing me to my doom. It proved quite effective though."

"It was Neen's idea," Sona said, nodding at Neen.

There was admiration there, and Neen couldn't help but feel some measure of pride. She was a scientist, an engineer, a woman more comfortable working out equations than firing a pistol, but it felt nice having the good opinion of a trained warrior like Sona.

"But a hovercraft drone can't carry us all the way to Bells," Sona finished.

"Bells?" Neen asked. They hadn't discussed anything about fleeing to the Benglion capital. "Why not Triverser lands? Nekka is still our representative on the council. She can rally the women there."

Sona shook her head. "Rally them to do what? Herria's forces aren't ordinary women. They've been altered to fight. We need an army if we want to stop them."

An army?

"Can we get an army?" Nekka said. She looked at Sona.

"We can try," Sona answered. "With your permission, Nekka, I'll order an aircraft to bring us to Bells. I don't know if we have any kind of jump on Herria, but we have to try."

"Can you manage that?" asked Neen. "Will the Dome police respond to your orders?"

"I still have women loyal to me." Sona tapped a few times on her wrist screen. "The transport crafts aren't being used right now since the males have been returned to their clan Domes. I'll try to commission one."

"And if that doesn't work?" Neen asked.

Sona met her gaze. "You have your pistol."

Neen swallowed hard. The walls of the shelter had never felt colder. It was like waiting inside a tomb.

"Make the call, Sona," Nekka said. "We must get to Bells."

Ems had slumped against a far wall, her chin resting against her chest. Her eyes were closed but she wasn't sleeping.

"Sister," Neen said softly, kneeling by her side. "You saved us back there. You were amazing."

Ems groaned a little and tried lifting her head. Her eyes were rimmed red like she hadn't slept in a week. "Herria didn't think so."

"No," Neen replied. "She didn't know she'd created a monster." She smiled at her friend, but Ems turned away.

"I am a monster," she whispered.

"You are incredible. You can do something nobody

thought possible. These mind powers are beyond any capabilities we've ever seen. Even Herria was shocked—"

"No, Neen. It's more than that. I can feel something..." Ems squeezed her eyes shut and grimaced. "Something is happening inside me."

Ems didn't have to say anymore. Neen knew what she meant.

The treatments. Genetic enhancements. All the powers of the clans.

"Rest," Neen said. "I'll wake you when Sona's aircraft gets here."

Ems shook her head. She opened her eyes, and when she looked at Neen, there was panic in them. "I can't rest," she said. "I can't think straight. I want to tear open that steel door and rip it to shreds. I have never felt more alive, Neen. Every sound, every smell. I can taste it all like it's on my tongue. I can feel your fear and your adrenaline like they're my own. I can feel your longing too, and Nekka's, and Sona's. Your desire to be with the ones you love. I can feel it like it's my own heartbeat. I finally know what it's like for you, for your brain to be whirling all the time, always studying, observing, always thinking. I can't shut any of it off. It's all of these things at once. I'm crawling out of my skin just sitting here."

Ems leaped up and started pacing around the tunnel. She rubbed at her arms and huffed heavy breaths. Her eyes were wild with pent-up energy and restlessness.

Neen didn't know what to do. This was what Herria's experiments had done to Ems. She glanced at Nekka who was watching them from a distance.

"Come, Neen," she said. "Sit with me while we wait."

Neen didn't want to leave Ems, but there was nothing she could do for her. Ems stalked up and down the length of the main tunnel like an anxious leopard.

"This is what Herria calls progress," Nekka said when Neen sat beside her. "Women who have more power than they can control."

"Feldir and the others looked in control," Neen responded.

"I wonder," was all Nekka said. She studied Neen's face, and her eyes fell on the small half-moon pendant Neen still wore around her neck. "Did that bring you luck?"

"I thought so. Tem passed his trial. He was spared from the Work Dome... But now it doesn't matter, does it? He and all the other males are doomed."

Nekka didn't say anything. She reached out her hand and put it on top of Neen's. It was a strangely maternal gesture, something Neen would never have expected from the councilwoman. She saw tears gathering in the corners of Nekka's eyes.

"I—" Nekka began. "Remember how I told you we councilwomen kept secret communications? Herria has her books... I have my own papers..." She reached into a pocket in her jumpsuit and pulled out an old-fashioned piece of stationary in a cream-colored envelope. "This is something I've carried with me for a long time," she said, pressing the envelope into Neen's hand. "Don't open it now. I never meant to write it, but when we saw each other last, I had a terrible feeling these might be my final days."

Neen tried to protest, but Nekka waved her off.

"No, Neen. No need for cheap words. If our world is to have any kind of future, it will be you who delivers it, not me. My time is past. But this letter, this letter is my confession. All my faults, all my hopes. Don't read it now. I'm not sure I can bear to have my truth exposed while I'm alive... but when I'm gone..."

Neen took the envelope and put it in her pocket. She

held Nekka's hand and tried to smile. "You're not going anywhere," she said. "Once we get to Bells and rally the city behind us, we'll put up a resistance. Sona is Benglion. They'll trust her before they trust anything they hear from Herria."

Even as Neen said the words she doubted them. Hadn't Forta and all the rest of the high council gone along with Herria's proposal? Hadn't they all voted for this new world order? She could only imagine what messages were going out this very moment to the clan lands.

"I knew what I was doing when I picked you," Nekka said. "You have spirit. You can see the truth even when others would rather look away."

"Others will see the truth too. Once we tell them who Herria really is, the lie she's been living all this time—"

"I don't know if I'd call it a lie," Nekka said. "Herria never hid her disdain for the men. It was I who refused to see her for what she was."

Neen realized Nekka didn't know what Ems had seen in Herria's mind. "No," she replied, "you couldn't possibly have seen the truth." She told Nekka what Ems had learned. Even as she spoke the words they sounded impossible, but Nekka never once blanched, never once dismissed her. When she finished, Neen waited for Nekka to tear the story apart with flawless logic and rationality.

But the older woman sat very still and said nothing.

"I know it sounds impossible," Neen began, "but I think the earliest revolutionaries were experimenting with genetic enhancements long before the official histories were recorded. It's possible whatever methods Herria used to create the enhancements given to Ems and the others were developed centuries ago by these early scientists."

Nekka nodded. "And Herria was one of the first. These kinds of enhancements, theoretically, could slow down the cellular aging process. She looks like a fifty-year-old woman because on a molecular level, her cells aren't aging as fast."

Neen looked at Ems. She was still pacing back and forth, her body a taut string ready to snap. Is this what would happen to her too? Her body's aging slowed to a crawl, her life extended for hundreds of years?

"It's almost time," Sona said, checking her wrist screen and coming over to Nekka and Neen.

"It is time," said Ems, who had appeared suddenly at the door. It was like she had moved in the blink of an eye. "They're five miles away."

Carefully, Sona unlocked the shelter's main door. She insisted on going first, her pistol ready. Ems followed, then Neen and Nekka. Ems sniffed the air like a bloodhound. She hadn't made eye contact with Neen since their last conversation. Already Neen could feel a distance growing between them.

"Come on!" Sona motioned them to an area north of the shelter's entrance. They were in a field of wild grasses and late summer flowers. It was almost twilight, and the clouds were shades of orchid and pink as the sun sank toward the horizon. In the sky, approaching from the south, came a transport aircraft.

It landed in a whirl of noise and exhaust, the faint outline of High City off in the distance behind it. The hatch opened and a Benglion officer stood waiting.

"A bit overkill for just four people," she said smiling at Sona, "but it's all we could spare."

"We'll take it," Sona replied, stepping onto the craft. "Thanks, Senta."

"No problem, Captain. But where are we taking it to?"

"The mountains," said Sona. "Home."

CHAPTER 15

NEEN

NEEN TRIED CONTACTING SONA AGAIN, but for the third time, she was rebuffed. She stared at her hand-held tablet and watched as images of the shimmering towers of High City floated across the screen. When she sent another message to Sona's device, all she got was a glaring red response:

Busy.

Since arriving in Bells, Sona had been in constant closed-door meetings with the top officials of the city and Clan Benglion. Neither Neen nor Nekka was allowed in, and Ems was now confined to a room in one of the city's medical wards.

Neen tried not to think about Ems too much. It was too upsetting. Her headaches had grown worse, and her mood could swing unpredictably. The doctors kept her semi-sedated until they could figure out a way to ease the headaches and bring her back to normal. Neen had the sinking feeling that "normal" for Ems was a vanishing possibility.

Neen felt almost as trapped here as she did in High City. Herria and her squad might not be chasing them through the streets at the moment, but that was small comfort. Instead, Herria's presence felt like an ever-encroaching shadow, a storm that was reaching its dark fingers across the entire continent and beyond. If they didn't act soon, they would be engulfed. But Sona wouldn't speak to her, and Neen couldn't get even a foot in the door to one of those meetings.

The suspicion between the clans was bearing rotten fruit just at the moment when they all needed to work together.

Nekka lay on a mattress in the corner of the room. "It won't be enough," she said, her voice flat. She had retreated into herself since leaving High City.

Neen and Nekka had been put into a sparsely furnished, barracks-like room by the Bells high command. They weren't supposed to leave without permission from the security guard outside the door. The comforts of Neen's apartment, and all of High City, were seemingly anathema to the women of Clan Benglion. Neen found herself constantly shivering. It didn't help that the city was nestled high up amid a range of snowcapped mountains. Bells was as much a fortified encampment as a city.

Neen felt Nekka's letter in her pocket. It seemed too important to risk keeping it anywhere but on her person. She resisted the urge to open it, but it was a struggle. What did Nekka want her to know, and why couldn't she tell her now?

"There's a strategic stockpile of weapons and defense systems," Neen replied. "That should count for something."

"Not enough," Nekka repeated. She gazed at the ceiling.

Neen tried to pretend this was just Nekka's age speaking. She was weary and at the end of her mental strength. Everything she had been striving for seemed wiped out in an instant, in the very moment when the council had voted to approve Herria's plans. Neen couldn't blame her for being defeatist.

But then why did Neen feel so hopeless too?

Even if Sona could convince the leaders of Clan Benglion to form a resistance against Herria's new All-Clans army, would it be enough? What if the other cities fell? Could Bells stand alone?

Neen knew the answer. Whatever her qualms might be with the leadership of EVE, they had gotten one thing right over the years. They were always stronger together.

Together.

Neen felt the letter in her pocket again. "Nekka," she said, "what if we've been thinking about this all wrong? What if the answer isn't in resistance but in liberation?"

"What do you mean 'liberation'? You saw the high council's acquiescence. They want what Herria wants. No one in EVE is interested in being liberated."

"I can think of a whole population who wants to be liberated."

Nekka looked at Neen, the spark of understanding flickering on her face. But just as quickly as the spark ignited, it fizzled out. Nekka laid back down. "I know what you're thinking. It'll never work. Too many years, centuries, in fact, have rubbed that idea right out of existence. No woman will agree to it."

"I would," Neen replied. "You would too. Don't we count?"

Nekka scoffed. "Try it then. Ask Sona the next time you see her. If you ever see her. For all we know, the leaders of Bells have jammed her in a cell somewhere for aiding and abetting a couple of known Triverser subversives."

Neen's tablet buzzed. The serene images of High City were replaced with notification that Sona was calling.

"Neen," only Sona's voice came through, no video. "They want Ems to be interviewed. Herria's already sent communications to every clan capital, and frankly, her proposals are persuasive to the majority. They don't quite understand this idea of the All-Clans, but they like the idea of ending the breeding program. We need something to sway them. If Ems can give her testimony—"

"She's not ready," Neen replied. "You don't understand the pain she's in—"

"What choice do we have? Herria's position is too strong."

"Let me talk to them."

"Don't take offense, Neen, but why would the leaders listen to you if they won't listen to me?"

"Because I have an idea that might sway them."

Sona hesitated. "I don't know—"

"Do the leaders of Clan Benglion think they'll have any sort of power once Herria's army has taken over the city? It's clear that Herria sees her multi-powered All-Clan women as the future of EVE, but where does that leave the rest of us? If your clan leaders capitulate to Herria's plan, they'll be cementing their status as second-class citizens. We all will, unless we consent to have our physiology altered through Herria's 'treatments.' I don't want that."

"Nor do I."

"And you've seen what's happened to Ems."

"Yes, that's why I think she should testify. The clan leaders might understand what's at stake if they can see what Ems is facing—"

"But even if they do, it won't be enough."

Sona was silent.

"Even if you convince them, even if Ems testifies, can this city hold out against Herria's forces?"

"We have weapons, we have—"

"It's not enough. Herria will bring the full might of High City, the full weight of the government and her special forces to bear on this city. You have weapons, but so does she. We need more than that. We need... more."

Sona didn't respond for a long time. Neen wondered if maybe she had disconnected the call. But the screen still showed Sona's name.

"What are you suggesting?" Sona said at last.

"I'm suggesting we find allies in the fight."

"Allies?"

"Let me talk to the clan leaders."

"Neen Salvek, what exactly are you proposing?"

* * *

IF A PIN HAD DROPPED in the furthest corner of the vast leadership chamber, Neen would have no doubt been able to hear it. Her words had reduced the Benglion leadership to utter, impenetrable, disbelieving silence. Neen worried she had grown two heads based on the shocked look Sona was giving her. Still, she stood by her proposal.

"You want to free them?" The eldest of the three city leaders stared down at Neen from the high bench where she and the others sat. As the clan which specialized in risk-taking, physical prowess, and law enforcement, Benglions preferred a stripped-down, militaristic aesthetic to their buildings and civic areas. The leadership chamber resembled a courtroom more than it did a meeting room, with straight-backed benches for sitting and a metallic coldness that reminded Neen of the old bomb shelter. The three leaders sat on a raised dais at the far end of the long chamber, their stern faces peering down over Neen and Sona with mounting disgust.

"I think it's our only chance of stopping Herria," Neen replied.

The eldest Benglion leader pursed her lips as if she'd just swallowed a piece of rancid fish.

"And what if we decide we don't want to stop Herria?" said another leader, this one much younger. Her narrow face reminded Neen of a greyhound.

"If you want to make peace with Herria, then I can't stop you," said Neen, barely concealing her disgust. "But if you want to live as free women, if you want to stay in control of your own clan and not become a twisted science experiment for Herria's pleasure, then you need to fight back. This city is well-positioned for a siege, but how long can it hold out? What I'm proposing is that we take the fight to Herria, not just wait like sitting ducks."

"By releasing the males?" The eldest leader's voice screeched like a gull. "Utter madness!"

"It's not madness!" Neen countered. "It's what we should've done a long time ago! Sona's already told you that Herria framed those males in the breeding suites. They have just as much reason to fight against her as we do. More in fact. They will help us if only we ask them."

"Captain Lohen informs us that your friend, Ems Davon, has been injected with the genetic alterations Herria wishes to impose on everyone," the third leader interjected. She was a hulking, bull-like woman with biceps that could rival that male Lekko. Of the three, Neen noticed she was the least hostile to the idea of enlisting the males' help. No scowls or pursed lips. "Is it true that she's become erratic and prone to outbursts since receiving these injections?"

Neen nodded. "Herria claims these treatments have no side effects, but it's a lie. Ems is proof of that."

"Then we should see for ourselves," the third leader continued. "Sona, why haven't you fulfilled my request for an interview with Ems Davon?"

Sona stood up. "I'm in the process of doing so. But Davon is in severe pain from headaches and has been sedated for the past twenty-four hours. It will take time before she's ready to testify."

The third leader frowned. "I was hoping for a different answer."

"You don't need Ems to tell you what needs to be done," said Neen. She felt particularly tiny in that vast, high-ceilinged room, but she wasn't ready to back down yet. "Speak to an envoy from the Dome, a representative of the Benglion males. See what he tells you and whether he'll help us fight."

The youngest leader laughed. "An envoy? As if we're just arranging a meeting with a diplomat? These are males, Neen Salvek. Dangerous beasts."

"We've demonized them for too long. I've spoken with dozens of males, spent time with them, gotten to know their fears and desires. They're not beasts even if we insist on treating them that way."

The eldest narrowed her watery eyes. "Careful, Triverser. The high council warned us that you were subversive, but we didn't want to judge without proof. The fact that Captain Lohen vouches for you doesn't prevent us from charging you with sedition."

"It's not sedition to want a better world!" Neen knew she shouldn't shout, but it was hard holding back. "We can compromise with the males. Working with them doesn't mean letting them have free reign. They'll still have their arm chips, we can still restrict their movements."

"But we'll have to deprogram the chips to allow them to use firearms," the third leader said. "You do see how that poses a problem? What would prevent them from turning those weapons on us?"

"They won't. Not if we talk to them reasonably. Form a truce." Neen looked at Sona and nodded.

Sona stepped forward. "We have a representative from the Domes waiting," she said, holding her chin high despite the trepidation Neen knew was building inside her.

"You have him waiting?" The eldest leader's face was red with fury. "How dare you—"

"Let him come," said the youngest leader. "If the males are really interested in helping, then they should hear our terms first. They may not be so keen on a truce if they know what it will cost."

Sona excused herself and left the chamber, leaving Neen alone in the oppressive silence. She knew this was a huge gamble, but what choice did they have? She had been thinking about it more and more as the days wore on, since Herria's take over and the execution of the males, since the revelation of what Herria's plans really were. The status quo couldn't be maintained. Either they went along with the destruction of every single male, or they found a way to live with the males that didn't involve their imprisonment and exploitation. The time to choose was now.

When Sona returned, she had Tem with her. He was shackled around the wrists and ankles, and Neen could see that he had been beaten. His lip was swollen and cracked with blood, and bruises colored his face an ugly dark purple. She almost cried out when she saw him, the first time since the breeding competition. He looked so defeated.

A guard accompanied him, a somewhat smallish woman with short, spiky brown hair. Neen was surprised that a Benglion guard could be so short, but the way this woman moved left no doubt about her clan. She was like a live wire, pulsing with energy and ready to spring at any moment. And her face — utterly confident, even defiant — was not what Neen expected. This woman handled Tem not as one who hated him but as one who respected him. It was clear that this guard was not the one who had beaten him.

"This is MI-1338," Sona announced. "Also known as Tem. He is one of our Benglion males. He has been chosen as a representative to speak with you."

Neen realized she was holding her breath. She felt a desperate need to speak to Tem, to be close to him. She feared what might happen now that he was standing in front of the city's leadership. Her plan now felt not only desperate but utterly reckless.

"Tem," the third leader said, her face a mask. "You know what this meeting is about?"

"Yes." Tem's voice was clear and unafraid.

"You understand that any alliance between Clan Benglion and the males will be temporary?"

Tem didn't answer.

The younger leader leaned forward, her thin nose peering down at him. "Any alliance between us will be temporary. It will be in service to stopping Herria Skalon's take-over of our clan lands, nothing more. Do you accept that?"

Despite the bruising and swelling on his face, Tem met the leader's eyes. "We do not accept such terms."

There was an angry murmur from the clan leaders. Even Sona looked at the guard near Tem and frowned.

Neen couldn't help but notice that the guard seemed almost proud of Tem's reply. A small smile had crept into the corner of her lips.

"We will fight on your behalf," Tem continued, "but when we achieve victory and Herria is defeated, we want a change to our status."

The eldest leader laughed. "Change to your status, eh? What *changes* do you propose?"

"More freedom of movement. If you insist that we stay in the Dome under supervision, then at least allow us some time outside, in the fresh air. At least let us spend our time how we want. Give us access to education. Reading material. Give us some measure of dignity—"

"Dignity?" The old Benglion spat the word. "You wouldn't know what to do with dignity. What could a Benglion male want with education? What would be the purpose of letting you out into the open air? It would just give you more opportunity for manipulation. For violence. You want us to give you access to the outside world so you can assault and violate any woman you choose? Ludicrous demands!"

"That's not what I'm saying at all—" Tem protested, but the third leader, the more reasonable one held up a hand.

"If the conditions in the Dome are too harsh, we can discuss some amenities. But I think allowing males access to open spaces is a mistake. Too many ways for security to be breached."

"Then you're not interested in an alliance," Tem replied. "You're interested in keeping us slaves. We fight for you and then you throw us back in our prisons—"

"Enough," the youngest leader said. Her nostrils flared

with anger. "This meeting is finished. We've heard all we need to hear. Take the male back to the Dome."

The guard nodded, though Neen could see the frustration on her face. Sona, too, hung her head.

"Captain Lohen," said the third leader, "return Salvek to her room and wait for us to finish our deliberation. We'll contact you when a decision has been made."

* * *

AS THEY WALKED BACK through the city, both women were silent. Neen didn't want to face Nekka and tell her the bad news. She didn't blame Tem for making his demands, but they were never going to be accepted by the leaders. Those women still saw the males as subhuman. The idea that males might need to see the sun shining or feel the breeze on their faces more than a handful of times in their lives was an incomprehensible thought for most women. The Benglion leaders were no different.

When they neared the compound where Neen and Nekka were staying, Neen noticed a plaza around the corner filled with monuments and statues.

"Wait," she said to Sona. "Just a quick detour."

Before Sona could say anything, Neen bounded off to the plaza. The sky opened up before her, the monuments gleaming in the bright daylight. There were statues of the first women revolutionaries, plaques dedicated to all the women who fell in that first battle for freedom, and in the center of the plaza, a monument to the bells, the very bells which rang out the song of women's freedom and started the uprising against their oppressors.

Oppressors.

Neen had wanted to see these bells since she was a child.

Her dream had always been to be one of the revolutionaries, one of the first women to fight for her rights against the male regime that suppressed them.

The glories of EVE. The triumph of the Sisterhood.

But what glories were they really? In their fight for freedom, they had enslaved another group. In their stance against oppression, they had become the oppressors.

In the brightness of that plaza, the monuments shimmering in the sunlight, Neen felt the hollowness of it all.

EVE was built on a false premise. The idea that women could only have peace and justice if they kept the males in Domes was a lie. It had always been a lie, but now Neen could see it. An alliance to fight Herria wasn't enough. Even Tem's terms weren't enough.

Sona stood beside her looking up at the bells. "I don't see how we can get out of this, Neen," she said. "Despite knowing the truth about Herria, I'm struggling to commit to an alliance with the males. It's too hard. And if I'm struggling, there's no way the clan leadership will go along with it. Maybe we try to work for good *within* the regime. Accept our fate."

"Did these women accept their fate?" Neen nodded to the statues. "Did they go along with the regime? When they saw evil, they did something about it. They fought back. If EVE stands for anything, it should stand for that."

Sona didn't reply. Neen turned and strode in the opposite direction of the housing compound.

"Where are you going?" Sona called.

"To start my own revolution!"

* * *

IT WAS TOO EARLY for the evening broadcast, but that didn't stop every screen in Bells from shifting into a mandatory video address. The white face and red lips of Herria filled each screen, including the Benglion Dome, which made Herria appear like some kind of goddess amidst the ant-like people in the street.

She smiled warmly and called every woman of the city to attention. "My dear sisters," she began, eyes bright with anticipation, "I'm sure word has reached you about the successful laboratory breeding program. No longer do we need to rely upon breeding with the males to achieve our genetic enhancements. And what's more, every woman may now have the enhancements of every clan. No more segmentation or separation. No more division. It's what we've always dreamed about. A real and lasting sisterhood. A togetherness we could have only dreamed of until now.

"No more males, no more breeding, no more fear. Within the next hour, my special delegation will arrive. Then we can begin the work of transferring all the males within your Dome to the Work Domes near the mines. We'll begin signing women up for their first genetic treatments. We'll begin the exciting work of transforming our society into something truly special."

She licked her lips and smiled. "We are on the cusp of a new era, my sisters. Soon my ambassadors will be at your city gates. Welcome them with open arms. Usher them in and you will be ushering in a new EVE. A new beginning. A final revolution."

Herria's face faded from the screens and was replaced by an image of a vast group of women, all of them wearing a new uniform, stark white, no clan symbols or colors. They were women of every clan, but they looked different, their eyes devoid of any sort of compassion or gentleness. They looked hungry. Ravenous. Their faces were seething, barely controlling an insatiable rage. At the front of the group was Feldir, a twisted smile on her lips. She almost seemed to resemble Herria, her face pale and her lips red. And along the edges of her hairline, her normally brown hair was starting to turn white.

Feldir's hungry face was the last thing the screens showed before they faded to black.

CHAPTER 16

TEM

TEM TRIED NOT to think about Herria's message. He closed his eyes and remembered the sun instead. His guard led him down the long underground tunnel that was the only way for males to enter or leave the Dome.

It surprised Tem when the guard spoke to him.

"I thought you did well," she whispered. "I'm sorry they didn't give you a chance."

Tem stopped. He knew it was a risk to turn and face her. Such a move could be interpreted as hostile. He did it anyway.

"Are you... do you know Neen?" he asked.

The guard smiled. "Not really. But I know someone else who does. And I trust that someone with my life. So if she vouches for Neen, it's good enough for me. And if Neen vouches for you... well, I can't say I've never thought about what it's like for you here in this Dome. I've seen what we do to the males." The guard looked down. "I've felt this way for a long time, I guess. Just didn't realize others did too. Like Neen."

"But you're a guard."

"Which is why I know firsthand. It never sat right with me. The way we drug you, the way we keep you locked up in these Domes your whole lives. Being a guard opened my eyes to all this."

"You're the only one, then," Tem said grimly. "Most guards relish a chance to impose their authority." His face throbbed with pain, and even though his lip had started to scab, it still stung a little whenever he talked.

"I'm sorry things couldn't be different," the guard said. She motioned for Tem to start walking again.

If Herria's words came true, the next time Tem came back down this passageway it would be en route to the Work Dome.

He wasn't going to let that happen.

* * *

"DRON," Tem whispered. "We're on our own. The females won't help."

Dron was curled up on his cot, not asleep but in a hazy stupor. The drugs were doing their job. As soon as the guard had locked their cell and left them alone, Tem wasted no time.

"In a few hours, they're going to start shipping us out to the Work Dome. Herria broadcast it to the whole city. She's sending her forces here right now. When we're in that transport tunnel, that's when we bolt. It's the only place where the sensors in our arms won't work if we make a run for it."

Dron grunted but his eyes were half-closed. It seemed like the drugs were even worse than usual. Tem worried that Dron had been dosed a second time.

"Hey, Dron." Tem tried shaking him, but Dron just rolled over and faced the wall.

This was bad. Even if it was long odds for the two of them to escape, one man all alone, no partner to help, was as good as dead.

What difference did it make, though? Dead in that tunnel or dead in the mines, it was all the same really.

Tem closed his eyes and tried to imagine the sun again. Instead, Neen's face filled his mind's eye. She had looked so fierce, so proud. There was pity there too, for his injuries, but it was mixed with a defiance that gave him strength. She had called for him. She had believed he could sway the leaders.

Too bad he'd failed. Maybe he'd asked for too much in asking for more freedoms, but he didn't regret it. The only thing he did regret was not being able to speak to Neen one more time.

He went over the plan again and again in his head, all the while, rubbing his fingers over the pendant in his pocket. It calmed him to feel the smooth edge of the pendant against his skin.

When the guards took them out of the tunnel, they'd all be shackled. He wouldn't be able to run fast. He'd have to make sure to get out of the chaos as quickly as possible and then hope the guards were distracted enough not to notice.

He'd feel a lot better with a pistol in his hand, but unless he found a way to remove the chip in his arm, that was a non-starter. No male in the Dome was ever allowed a sharp object.

Waiting was the hardest part. Herria's message had said within the hour. But how long after that would it take for the males to be transferred to the Work Dome?

"Dron," Tem said under his breath, watching his friend drool onto his cot in a stupor. Even if Tem could start something, what good would it do if all the males were as drugged out as Dron?

He had to try. Even if his plan was doomed to failure, he had to try.

Tem closed his eyes and waited.

* * *

"MOVE! LET'S GO!"

The guards shoved them into two lines and marched them down to the tunnel. Guns at the ready, it looked like nearly every Dome guard was there, lining the walls, poised to strike in case the males got unruly.

There was no chance of that, though. Just like Dron, every male shuffled along in a drugged-out haze, head hanging low, mouths drooling. Tem played along just so no one got suspicious. He could see Dron a few feet ahead. It would be hard to get to him unless things played out just right, but Tem decided he would try.

Now it was just a matter of timing things perfectly...

"Head down!" A guard shoved Tem in the shoulder. "Keep moving!"

He resisted the urge to look back at the woman. He needed to stay calm until the very last moment.

The end of the tunnel was up ahead. He worried the other males were too sedated to react, but it was too late to change plans now.

Tem thought of Naal. What Naal would've given to be part of this. Dron and Lekko wanted freedom too, but not like Naal. Naal had believed. He had truly hoped it was possible. Not just something to talk about at meal times or in weight training, not just a faint daydream, but something real. Something possible.

Tem tried to find Lekko amongst the throng, but he was nowhere to be seen. The light at the end of the tunnel was growing stronger. This was it. The last faint hope for freedom.

Tem clutched the pendant in his pocket and made a silent vow.

Then he shoved the male in front of him.

The drugs were a boon, it turned out, because the male he shoved was so caught off guard that he toppled forward, taking a group of males out with him. As they piled into a heap, the guards yelled out. Tem hurled his body at the males beside him, pushing them into the crowd, and soon there was falling and shoving and jostling, all the males around him wailing and disoriented, trying to regain their balance or lashing out in their confusion.

The guards cried for order and raised their pistols, but the confusion only swelled. The mass of males surged forward like a wave. Tem didn't move to the outside yet, there were too many guards around the perimeter. They would either start shooting into the chaos or charge in themselves to restore order. Tem was hoping they'd charge in, giving him his chance. If they decided to start shooting...

Tem kept his head up as best he could and tried to avoid being knocked down. He needed to find Dron, to drag him along if need be.

"Order!" cried the guards, panic setting in.

"Back in line!"

"Get up!"

"Order!"

A shot was fired. The crowd of males lunged forward, stupor replaced by blind fear. They all charged for the exit of the tunnel.

"Hold!" The guards started collapsing on the mob, moving in to pull the males back, to stop them from fleeing.

This was Tem's moment. Crouching low, he ran for the edge of the tunnel, past the guards who were trying to regain control of the panicked males. Maybe he could see Dron better from the edge of things. If he couldn't...

Sunlight streamed into the tunnel from outside...

Maybe he'd have to go alone...

"Shut the hatch! Shut it!" Guards were racing for the entrance to try and bar the way.

Tem would have to sprint to make it.

Something hard hit the back of his head.

"Nobody gave you permission to leave," a guard said, hitting Tem in the back with the butt of her rifle. "Get down, scum."

Tem fell to his knees. More shots were fired from up ahead. The mob reared back. The guard grabbed Tem's wrist shackles and lifted him up. She pointed the gun right at his chest.

"Back in line," she hissed.

Tem's vision was blurred. His head throbbed. The crowd was still surging forward and then back and then forward again, a roiling, confused mess.

"Back in line!" the guard screamed and struck Tem again with her rifle.

He fell into the crowd, jostled one way, then another, then he was pinned between two males, both bigger than him. They were like a dead weight against his body. If he fell now, he'd be trampled. Already some males had fallen and their bodies were crushed under the weight of the rest.

Tem tried to squeeze out, to find air and the edge of the tunnel again, but the guards had closed in. There was no escape.

This was it. The end. Tem had tried... at least he had tried...

A shadow cut through the sunlight at the end of the tunnel. Then another shadow. And another.

Three figures cast long shadows on the wall. One of them stepped forward and blocked out the rest.

"Stop!" cried a shrill, commanding voice.

All at once, every guard collapsed. The surging mob of males froze. Tem was able to break free from where he had been pinned. He looked at the end of the tunnel. A tiny woman with curly blonde hair stood before the throng, her face twisted in rage. She looked to be concentrating on something off in the distance, as if she was holding back a wave with her mind.

Behind her was an elderly woman and another young woman, both in Triverser garb.

Neen.

"Men of Benglion Dome!" Neen called out to the gaping mob. "Do not panic, do not resist! We don't have much time! There are forces in the city who would see you dead, who are coming here right now to destroy you. If you want to live, you need to follow us. We've bought you some time, but you need to hurry!"

The smaller woman beside Neen faltered. She started to collapse and Neen caught her just in time.

"Now is the time to rise up and be free!" cried the older woman behind Neen.

At first, the males didn't move. They were still in a state of terror and confusion. Tem grabbed the nearest male and shook him.

"Come on, this is our chance," he said. "Come on!" he said to anyone who was near. "Dron!" Tem saw his friend staring dumbfounded at Neen and the others. "This is it! Come on!"

Tem yanked on Dron's arm and pulled him up through the crowd. He couldn't see Neen very well from this angle, but he shoved his way toward her as best he could, Dron dragging behind.

Then there was a scream. A high-pitched scream, almost like a child's. The crowd lurched back. Tem and Dron were pushed back with it. Then the crowd rushed forward, like a stampede of frenzied animals. Tem and Dron were swept up in the surge. They had to run or they'd be trampled.

Tem looked everywhere for Neen.

Guns fired.

The guards were still all unconscious on the floor, but up ahead was a cacophony of women's voices. Tem headed for the tunnel's opening, swept up in the stampede. He clung to Dron's arm with all his strength.

There was Neen. She was carrying the body of the smaller woman, struggling to get out of the way of the males.

"Nekka!" Neen screamed. Her face was drained of color as she searched the crowd.

"Neen!" Tem called to her. He pulled Dron with him and pushed his way toward Neen's position.

She saw him. But then she and the woman she was carrying were swept out of sight by the mob. Tem tried to follow.

That's when the surging mob crashed against a wall of women, all of them dressed in white uniforms, guns at the ready. They fired into the crowd. They relished the sight of dead males dropping at their feet. The males, like a scourge of starlings, changed course and fled back down the tunnel. Tem and Dron were going to be crushed by the fleeing mob before the guns even reached them.

"Tem!" Neen was there, limping and staggering along,

holding her friend in her arms. They were going to be crushed too.

"We have to get to the perimeter!" Tem called.

"Nekka! I have to find Nekka!"

Tem looked around wildly. There was no sign of the older woman. The mob was bearing down on them.

"No time!"

"We can't leave her!"

Tem looked again. There was a gap further up the tunnel, a small opening in the crowd of males. A gray-haired head bobbed up from within that gap.

Tem wasted no time. He pulled Dron along, hoping Neen would follow. He had to shove males out of the way to fight against the tide. He was almost to the older woman, Nekka. He could see her trying to fend off the crush of males around her.

Then she fell.

Neen cried out, but Tem couldn't hear her clearly. He pushed through to where Nekka had fallen. She was there, on the tunnel floor, eyes wide open but lifeless. Blood and bruises marked her face and arms. Boot prints indented into her skin.

Tem turned to Dron. "Follow me. Stay as close as you can." He wasn't sure if Dron understood him, but he had to hope. Then, bending down, Tem lifted Nekka's body.

When Neen saw Nekka's body, she screamed.

They had no time to mourn. The crowd was still coming, and that new squadron of women was still blocking the exit, firing into the mob.

"There's no way out!" Tem cried.

The Dome guards were starting to wake up. Soon they would be surrounded.

"I'm not giving up," Neen said, pushing her way back

toward the tunnel exit, struggling to carry her unconscious friend. Tears filled Neen's eyes, but she was still defiant.

Tem felt his stomach dip. It wasn't for fear or despair. It was for something he'd never felt before. Neen's determined face stirred something inside that he wanted to hold onto forever. He knew they couldn't escape, but he followed her anyway.

"You're going the wrong way!" said a female voice from behind Tem. He knew that voice.

The guard from before, the one who had taken him to the Benglion leaders, was standing there, that brash smile once more on her face.

"We've never formally met, Neen," the guard said, eyeing the woman in Neen's arms, "but let's save formalities for later. Follow me!"

She guided them back down the tunnel, toward the Dome, following the flow of the panicked crowd. They pushed their way to the front of the retreating males and soon came to the locked entrance to the Dome. Frenzied males were pounding on the doors, scratching their fingers bloody trying to open them.

The guard shoved several males aside and used her wrist chip to open the lock. The males flooded in, but not before the guard squeezed Tem and the others through the door with her. Tem, carrying Nekka, followed the guard as she ran down one of the side hallways. He glanced back and was glad to see Dron was still with them. His friend's face was starting to look more alert.

"Glad you decided to stick around," Tem teased.

Dron gave a weak smile but no witty comeback.

"You're speechless?" Tem said. "I didn't think that was possible."

The guard unlocked the shackles on Tem and Dron's

wrists and ankles, then led them all through a secure door and into a locker room. "This'll give us time to think," the guard said.

"How do you know us?" Neen asked, laying her friend down on a bench. The blonde-haired woman was still unconscious.

"It's my side gig to help you out of scrapes," the woman replied. She flashed her puckish smile. "Drone escapes, Dome breakouts. I blame Sona, frankly."

"Sona?" Understanding dawned on Neen's face. "You're Li."

"The one and only." Li held out her hands. "It's good to finally meet you, Neen."

Neen returned the formal greeting.

Tem laid Nekka's body down. They all stood looking at her in silence.

"I can't believe it," Li said at last. "She was the first one who made me believe our world could change..."

"You knew her?" Neen said.

"Only what Sona told me. We quarreled about it, sometimes. I took Nekka's side when it came to the males. I saw what it was like for them on the inside. Sona was sympathetic, don't get me wrong. She believed in reform too. But not a radical like me." Li brushed her hand across Nekka's face.

Neen knelt down beside Nekka. Tem could see she was crying. She bowed her head and rested it on Nekka's arm. Through her tears, Neen took the necklace from around her own neck and lifted it over Nekka's head. The bright blue of the half-moon pendant made a stark contrast with Nekka's white and brown jumpsuit.

As Neen started to turn away, Tem approached her. He

reached into his pocket and drew out his own pendant. He placed it in Neen's hand.

"I've had this with me since before I could remember," Tem said. "I don't know where it came from or how I got it. When I saw you wearing the other half, that day in the interrogation room... I wondered what it meant. I thought maybe we were connected somehow."

"It was Nekka's," Neen said. "She gave it to me for good luck."

"I'm sorry I couldn't save her," Tem said.

Neen took his pendant and placed it next to the other one. The two half-moons formed a whole.

"She insisted on coming," Neen said almost to herself. "I told her to stay back, to wait. But she said she wanted to see the men claim their freedom."

Neen started to cry again. Tem almost put his hand on her shoulder. He wanted to take her hand in his own, to pull her close to him. Instead, he stepped back.

"This is a hard loss," Li said, "but I'm afraid we can't stay here. Herria's goons will be coming into the Dome soon enough."

"How are we supposed to get out?" Neen asked.

"I guess I didn't think that far ahead," Li said, shrugging. "Give me something to fight and I'm your ace, but strategic planning? Not my strong suit."

"The Dome glass is practically unbreakable," Neen said.

"We might be able to rig an explosive," Li said, a gleam in her eye. "I know where all the artillery is hiding."

"But Dron and I can't go through the glass," Tem said. "If we cross that perimeter, the chips in our arms will release the toxin."

Li's face fell. "Oh, right."

Neen grimaced, but she faced Tem square.

He couldn't help but draw a little closer to her, to catch the faint smell of her hair. That wind-swept scent.

"You're not going to like my suggestion," she said. "But please know that I've had a little practice already..."

* * *

NEEN USED LI'S KNIFE. There was nothing but soap to sterilize the skin, and nothing to numb it, but Li had a leather belt that Tem could bite down on.

"This will hurt," Neen said.

"And leave a nasty scar," Li added.

Tem nodded. He wasn't afraid of pain.

It didn't matter, though. He still screamed when it happened.

The chip clinked onto the floor when Neen was done. They tied a shirt around his arm to stanch the bleeding and used another shirt as a bandage.

Dron was shaking his head. "No way, no fucking way..."

Tem tried to say something, but he could barely get words through his gritted teeth.

"It's our only option," Neen said.

"No way," Dron repeated. "Can't you give me a pill or something first?"

Li shrugged. "Sorry, that's not my department. I could knock you out, though."

"Maybe?" Dron said, looking expectantly at Li.

"Just get it over with," Tem said. "We're running out of time."

Dron screamed his head off, but in the end, Neen removed his chip too.

"If Herria's squad wasn't already looking for us, you bet they'll be coming now," Li said.

Dron looked like he was ready to pass out, and Tem felt about the same. He wasn't sure he could outrun any soldiers if it came to that.

"So how do we break the Dome glass?" asked Neen.

"Leave that to me." The small blonde woman was awake now, sitting up on the bench. She looked ashen and ragged, but the swelling rage from earlier was gone. If Tem didn't know better he would've thought she was a sickly child.

"Ems!" Neen ran over to her friend and embraced her. "You've done enough, sister. Please. You need to rest."

"We don't have time," Ems said. "Li, take us to the glass walls."

They crept as silently as possible through the Dome corridors. It was eerie having no one around. No guards, no males. The Dome felt abandoned.

Despite the pain in his arm and the loss of blood, Tem insisted on carrying Nekka. It felt wrong to leave her body to Herria's forces.

"Here," said Li as they entered a wide passageway. Tem recognized it as one of the main hubs that connected to the training rooms.

"Ems, how are you—" Neen started, but she stopped when Ems reached out her hand and placed it on the mirrored glass.

"They can see us, can't they?" Ems asked.

"The women in the streets?" Li responded. "Yeah, I guess so. Let's hope they're not paying too much attention."

"I almost wish they were," said Ems. "To show that Herria hasn't defeated us."

Then she closed her eyes and concentrated. That same seething fury from before filled her face.

"Stand back," Ems growled.

"Ems, what are you—" But Neen didn't finish. With a

wild yowl, Ems balled her fingers into a fist, drew back, and smashed the glass with one strike.

Shards sprayed everywhere.

Li whooped in excitement, Neen shielded her face, and Tem and Dron stared in amazement at the burnt orange hues of the clouds in the sky. The sun was setting. A breeze wafted through the broken glass, hitting their faces like a cool, clean breath.

"Good luck," Li said, patting Tem and Dron on the back. "Maybe we'll see each other again someday."

"You're not coming with us?" Tem asked.

Li shook her head, grinning. "Not this time. Somebody's gotta stay behind and form a resistance."

"We'd better go," said Ems. "I can hear people coming."

"You can hear people coming?" Dron said. The street just outside was empty. "You can smash your hand through Dome glass, and now you can hear like a Sixter. What clan are you, woman?"

"Does it matter?" Ems asked. Then she stepped through the opening. "Do you want to be free or not?"

Dron grinned. "I'll take freedom, please."

"Hurry," Neen said, pointing for Tem to go next.

Tem stopped and faced her. "Why did you come to the Dome? Did you really hope to free all of us?"

Neen looked down. "A foolish hope. We were too late."

"It was more than I ever expected from any woman... I didn't think it was possible..."

"I thought if we fought back, if we didn't back down, maybe we could stop Herria. I was naive."

"I'm glad you came back."

"But the other men..."

"I know. I wish we could've..."

"We have to go, Tem. If we hurry, maybe we can get out of the city before they find us."

"We?"

Neen looked at him. "That's what I said. We're in this together now."

With Nekka's body in his arms, Tem stepped through the broken glass. His feet hit the pavement, and for the first time in his life, he was free.

CHAPTER 17

SONA

IT WAS MERELY by suggestion that Herria convinced the leaders of Bells to hold the transfer of power in the monument plaza.

Sona was not directly involved, but since she was still in the city, and since she had extensive experience with coordinating security forces, she was tasked with making sure the high councilwoman would be safe in the open square.

It was luck, and quite a bit of groveling, that allowed Sona to stay on as part of the Benglion special forces. A personal apology to Herria, including the excuse that she had only followed Nekka out of misplaced loyalty to a former high councilwoman, meant Sona got to keep her position as head of security.

It had been hard to keep a straight face when she humbled herself in front of Herria and offered her deepest, most sincere mea culpa, but it was the only way she'd be allowed to protect her today. Sona hoped it would be worth it.

The overcast day seemed fitting for this particular venture. Not only did the gray clouds cast a somber mood over everything, but they washed out Herria as well, her all-white jumpsuit, white hair, and pale face blending into the vague whiteness of the muted daylight.

Sona betrayed not a hint of these thoughts as she watched the city leaders approach Herria's entourage from the west side of the plaza. She stood as still as one of the statues of the foremothers who started the revolution. The irony of what was happening was not lost on her.

The leaders met Herria right beside the monument to the bells. All of them exchanged the customary greeting, but the mantra was different this time.

"All-Clans. Together," they intoned in unison.

Then Herria smiled and addressed the carefully managed audience in the plaza, along with every woman in the city, all of them forced to watch via the video feed transmitting the meeting.

"My sisters," Herria began, utterly comfortable in her role as an elder stateswoman and supreme leader, "thank you for welcoming us to your capital city. We were fortunate to arrive when we did so as to could quell the riot that was breaking out within your Dome. I'm happy to report, not a single woman's life was lost that day."

She didn't mention the two dozen males who escaped, though. Of course not. Herria needed to project total command of the situation, no missteps, no mistakes. To admit that in all the chaos Herria's special squadron of multi-powered women had let a pack of males slip through their fingers was to admit weakness. Herria could never admit that.

"For such a resounding success in quelling the riot and protecting our sisters, we have Feldir and her squadron of peacekeepers to thank," Herria continued.

Here she motioned to the woman standing slightly behind her.

Sona remembered Feldir well. The hatred that was coursing through her veins burned hot as she watched Feldir accept a medal of honor from Herria, but Sona kept her face impassive, her eyes unflinching. She wouldn't let Feldir have the satisfaction of seeing her lose her cool.

"For the sisterhood," Herria said, clasping Feldir's hands and nodding.

Behind the two women was another sycophant, but this one looked much less pleased by the saccharine display than the others. She wasn't wearing the all-white jumpsuits of Feldir's squadron. Instead, she wore the insignia of the Evoxes.

Sona remembered her, vaguely. Herria's pet, Grex.

Grex's obvious displeasure was directed at the praise being heaped upon Feldir. Sona watched as the Evox wrinkled her nose like there was a bad smell in the air.

That might be something to work with, Sona thought. In due time.

Herria was yammering on again, thanking the city leaders, fawning over them and flattering them. Sona was surprised that even Tensa Lihen, the only leader who had shown any interest in Neen's plan, looked pleased by Herria's compliments. All these politicians were alike, apparently, even the Benglions. Hungry for adulation and desperate to be close to the engine of power.

"A new world is upon us," Herria proclaimed. "A world without the need for breeding. A world in which any woman, any clan may have the full spectrum of genetic enhancements. No more copulation with the males. No more need for their bodies except as machines to help us build a better, more peaceful world.

"We've already begun the process of stockpiling sperm and soon the males of your Dome will be airlifted to the Work Domes where they will be sterilized and put to good use in the mines — much better use than they ever had as breeding stock."

Herria's heavily curated audience in the plaza cheered. The councilwoman basked in the adulation.

Sona watched the three city leaders carefully to see what their reactions were. The eldest had a thin, self-satisfied smile on her lips. The youngest was eyeing Feldir, and if Sona wasn't mistaken, her eyes shined with a kind of hunger.

Of course. What Herria promised was hard to believe, and if Sona hadn't seen it with her own eyes, she wouldn't believe it. But she'd seen what Feldir and the others could do. She'd seen Ems. And it was clear that the youngest leader of Bells — like many other women in the city — wanted what Herria promised. To have not only one genetic enhancement but five. It was a tempting promise. Irresistible, even.

But Sona had seen the side effects. She had seen Ems Davon's roiling anger, irrational behavior, painful headaches, and mental instability. Was this something unique to Ems, or was this a condition that any woman who took Herria's "treatments" might face? She had tried to warn the city leaders, but those warnings now evaporated into the clouds. Herria's smooth words proved too alluring.

Sona shivered to think of what would happen to their society if it was filled with women who couldn't control their anger or their desire for violence. And what would happen if some women wanted to forgo the treatments? Was that even an option?

The crowd cheered again, and Sona cursed herself for not paying attention. She scanned the perimeter, making sure all of her guards were in position. And that one of her guards was not.

Sona tried not to let her hands get too sweaty. It was rare that she felt any sort of nerves about anything, but today, it was hard not to. Too many chances for error. Too risky.

But what do Benglions love more than risk?

"There will be no need to register," the youngest leader of the city said, Herria standing beside her with a hand on her shoulder. "We'll begin the process in a few weeks. You'll receive an alert on your wrist screen and a date and time to appear for your first treatment. The Dome, as soon as it's unoccupied, will serve as our central hub for administering and monitoring women as they proceed through the enhancement process. In only a few short months, every woman in Bells will be able to say she is part of the All-Clans!"

There were wild cheers, but Herria held up a hand. "Not just Bells," she said. "Every woman, from Sunset City to High City, from every corner of EVE, from every clan. Each of you will know the power and satisfaction of being without limits, of being unstoppable. No male can ever again hurt us. No male can ever again put us down. We will be the dominant sex, from now until eternity. The final revolution has begun!"

Now the crowd erupted. Euphoria swept over everyone like a gust of wind. As if on cue, the sun started to peak through the clouds, casting a hallowed glow over Herria's white hair. She hugged the city leaders, clasped Feldir's hand and held it up in the air with her own, and waved to the adoring crowd.

Sona held her breath. The leaders took a step back, giving Herria her moment of victory, Herria released Feldir's hand and waved with both arms to the crowd. She was flanked by her assistants and the city officials, but she stood in front of them, the councilwoman who had made herself supreme leader. Sona eyed the other security guards. They were doing their job, staying alert and watching the crowd. There were even a few positioned on top of the surrounding buildings, watching the overcast sky for any sign of danger.

The shouts of the crowd were growing louder and louder. Feldir and the other squadron members didn't seem too bothered by the noise level. Perhaps they were dampening their sensory abilities to avoid overstimulation.

Sona hoped so.

The monument to the bells stood as background to Herria's triumph. The massive brass bells hung from rafters behind Herria's head. Sona locked her eyes on the bells, looking for any sign of a disturbance.

There was none.

Herria continued to wave, the crowd continued to cheer.

Sona's hands were sweating now, no doubt about it. Her guards were at attention. Their first instinct would be to look up. A drone perhaps. Someone on the rooftops. Then they'd look to the sidestreets that branched off from the plaza. They'd be looking everywhere but where they needed to look. Sona would call out commands, rush to Herria's side, signal for backup. It would be too late. There would be nothing anyone could do.

The scenarios played out in Sona's mind as she waited. The seconds stretched out into eternity. The crowd's roar would soon fade. The time had to be now. Now that Herria was basking in her moment of glory.

"Herria!" Feldir's cry went up just as the shot rang out. With a speed no Benglion could ever match, Feldir lunged for Herria and tackled her to the ground. The security forces and Herria's personal guard leaped into action, searching for where the bullet had come from, from where the assailant might be.

They did just as Sona had expected. The rooftops. A drone. The sidestreets where an assassin might flee.

Sona played her part too. She rushed to Herria's side, waving her arms and screaming for the city leaders and other functionaries to clear the area. She barked at Herria's squadron to surround the city leaders and protect them. She had her pistol out and stood over Herria and Feldir to make sure another shot didn't get through.

"Is she?" Grex was standing beside them, her face drained of all color. She vibrated like a tuning fork that had been struck against a rock, every muscle of her body quivering and agitated. Something was simmering beneath her, a chamber of magma that was fighting to get out, and a hard rock surface struggling to keep it all in.

Sona squeezed her pistol, standing guard over Herria and Feldir, hoping for the answer she wanted to hear...

"She's fine," Feldir said, standing up and holding out a hand for Herria.

"No harm done!" Herria said, dusting sidewalk debris off her white jumpsuit.

Sona couldn't let anyone know she felt sick. She had to keep playing the part.

Feldir immediately went into command mode. She barked into her wrist screen. "No excuses! Find the one who did this!"

"Just a subversive," Herria said, nonplussed. "We'll have more of them, I'm afraid. Tell your lieutenants to be on the lookout for anyone matching Salvek's description."

"Or Davon's," Feldir added.

Sona's heart was racing. Security forces spread out around the plaza, went into the streets, searched the rooftops. She realized she needed to communicate with her own guards.

"No sign of anyone," Feldir said, bitter venom dripping from her tongue.

The city leaders and other officials had regained their composure, and Herria calmed them all with her unperturbed demeanor.

"Let's get the crowd out of here," Sona heard herself saying into her wrist screen. "Then lock down the perimeter."

"No need," Herria said, overhearing Sona's command. "Whoever attempted this recklessness is gone now. I'm sure of it. I certainly don't sense anything amiss."

Sona nodded and tried to keep her heartbeat calm. She didn't want to give anything away to Herria or the others. The best thing to do was to get everyone out of there as soon as possible.

"I don't have enhanced senses," Sona replied, "but I do know we should move all leadership personnel to a secure location."

"Agreed," said leader Lihen. "Then we can discuss next steps."

"Yes," Herria said, looking at Sona and not the city leader. "Next steps."

* * *

"I DIDN'T ASK for an oath of loyalty," Herria began. She sat on the high dais in the leadership chamber, the city leaders on either side of her. "Nor did I accuse you of helping the subversive Neen Salvek escape the city. You claimed no knowledge of her plans, and I believed you. I have a way of discerning the truth from people."

"Good, then you'll know I'm telling the truth now. As far as I'm aware, neither Neen nor Ems nor Nekka had anything to do with the assassination attempt today." Sona didn't need to calm her breathing or her heart rate. There was no deception in her words. At least, not in the way Herria thought.

"As you've said," Herria continued. "But that still doesn't mean you've earned my complete trust, Sona. You did help Neen and her accomplices in High City. I haven't forgotten."

"That was because of Davon's lies," Sona replied. "She had me convinced you were trying to destroy EVE. It's obvious now that she has a deranged mind. I was a fool for believing her."

"It doesn't feel good to play the fool, does it? And yet I acquiesced to your leaders and granted you amnesty in the spirit of our new project. Was I a fool for doing so? Are you playing me now?"

"No."

"That amnesty is conditional, Sona. You were in charge of security today and that security failed us. If it hadn't been for Feldir's quick reflexes, I would be dead right now."

Feldir stood next to Sona like a jailor, smirking and jutting her chin.

"We took every precaution," Sona said. "And the investigation is underway. Whoever took that shot will be found and prosecuted—"

"Oh, yes. Yes, of course. I'm sure justice will be served." Herria nodded to Feldir. "In the meantime, I thought you might like to know that we're moving ahead with our first enhancement treatments."

Sona didn't say anything. It twisted her stomach to know

that she had failed this time, but she tried to keep her thoughts as empty as possible. She remembered what Neen had said about Herria's powers of influence. She didn't want to give Herria any opportunity to see into her head.

"I'll say no more for fear of ruining the surprise," Herria said, grinning. "Go home and get some rest, my dear. We won't need your services anymore today."

Feldir stepped closer to Sona, a sick grin on her face. She was invading Sona's space, trying to intimidate her. It was clear that Sona needed to go.

When she got to Li's residence, she wasn't expecting anyone to be home. The plan was for Li to wait until nightfall before coming back. The sound of movement in the bedroom made Sona tense up. She put a hand on her pistol and crept toward the half-open bedroom door.

Li was packing a duffle bag with clothes. She was still wearing the all-black jumpsuit, her black mask pushed up on her forehead. Spikes of brown hair poked through the eye holes of the mask.

"You came in broad daylight?" Sona asked incredulously. "That wasn't the plan!"

"Sorry, love," Li said, hastily shoving clothing into the bag. "Plans change. I've got your stuff packed already. Grab some soap out of the bathroom, will you?"

"What is going on? Did someone see you?" Sona's heart froze. Li wasn't supposed to leave her hiding spot in the bell until things were all clear. Had Herria's squad spotted her?

"No one saw me," Li replied.

"What did you do with the gun?"

"Why are you treating me like I'm a child?" Li's voice did that inflection that made her sound like a petulant schoolgirl getting scolded.

Sona felt her skin get warm and her stomach flutter. It

annoyed Li that Sona found her so attractive whenever she was in one of these fiery moods, but Sona couldn't help it. She wanted to press her lips against Li's and feel the warmth of her mouth.

"I'm just worried, that's all," Sona said, stepping closer to Li. "You came home early and now you're packing our bags? What happened to the plan?"

"I tossed the gun, okay. And I'm packing our bags because we have to leave."

"Leave? I know we didn't get the result we wanted today, but there'll be other chances."

"You don't understand," Li said, facing Sona. "I got an alert on my wrist screen. I'm up. First to get the treatments. They want me to report to the Dome in forty-eight hours."

"The treatments?" Sona's head swam. She put a hand down on the bed to steady herself. "They want you to get the treatments?"

"It's either a coincidence or they *know* and this is their way of neutralizing me. I'm sure once I get the first injection there'll be some unforeseen side effects. 'So sorry, we did all we could.' I can see Herria's face all twisted up with mock tears as she delivers the bad news to you. And who knows if I ever come out of the Dome again after that."

"Wait, Li, let's talk about this. There might be another way. If we run now, they'll know it was us. We'll be fugitives like Neen. There has to be a way to stay and undermine Herria from within."

"I don't see how. Just the two of us? How many more assassination attempts can we plan?"

"We can undermine in other ways."

"Not if we're sedated and undergoing the treatments."

Sona sat down on the bed and Li stood beside her still holding a handful of clothes. Li wasn't one to give up, but even Sona could see that she was right. She studied her lover's face, her wide eyes and high cheekbones, the way her hair could never quite behave. Sona reached out her hand and took Li's fingers in her own.

"You're right. They're coming for you."

"Which is why we need to leave. Now."

Sona sighed. "No."

"What?" Li almost pulled her hand away, but Sona squeezed her fingers.

"We aren't leaving." She swallowed hard. "You are."

"Sona—"

"I'm staying. Someone needs to be on the inside. Someone needs to fight Herria from within."

"Baby, you can't—"

"I will. And if I get caught, I'll face the consequences. But for right now, I can do more good here. I don't want to leave you—" Sona couldn't say anymore. She felt her throat burn with the words she wanted to say.

Li held Sona's head against her chest, running her fingers through Sona's long, dark hair.

"The ruins in the north valley past the mountains," Sona said. Her voice was flat, weary. "From before the first revolution."

"I know the place."

Sona smiled. "I know you do." When they had first started seeing each other, Sona had taken Li hiking in the northern mountains. They hadn't meant to find the old abandoned settlement, but once they did, it became a kind of romantic retreat.

"We haven't been there since you accepted the position in High City."

"I know." Sona didn't want to dredge up old fights and

disagreements. Now wasn't the time. "But it's a good place to hide. Wait things out."

"It'll be hard. I don't like waiting for you."

"You never did." Sona lifted her head. Li leaned towards her face. Those lips were as warm as Sona had hoped. She closed her eyes and drank in that warm breath.

When Sona opened her eyes, Li was gone.

CHAPTER 18

NEEN

THE CAVE where they laid her was just a narrow tear in the rock face. But Nekka was not very large, and her small, delicate frame fit snuggly into the makeshift grave.

The ceremonies of Triverser burial were not feasible in the low mountains. They had no means of cremating the body — a problem that Neen knew would only prove worse as night approached and they needed heat — and no way for Nekka's accomplishments to be officially documented and honored in the database of the dead.

All Neen could do was speak what she felt. But when she tried, the words caught in her throat.

"I wish—" she began, but if she said another word, the tears would flow uncontrollably. Tem stood behind her, Dron too, and Ems was almost too weak to move, mental and physical exhaustion having overtaken her shortly after they entered the hills. Dron had to carry her most of the way into the mountains.

Neen felt Tem's hand on her shoulder. It was heavy but firm. It gave her strength.

"Nekka saw something that most women didn't. She

believed in... the humanity of all people." Neen thought she felt Tem's hand squeeze her shoulder slightly. "And she wanted a better world. A world that didn't reduce men to animals. A world that didn't reduce women to oppressors. I'm sorry... I'm sorry I failed her. I'm sorry we couldn't make her vision of the world a reality..."

Neen couldn't say anymore. She turned away, arms wrapped around herself, and walked to the edge of a copse of pines that sloped down the side of the mountain.

No one followed. After a while, without any words exchanged between them, they left.

* * *

THE SIGN WAS A RUSTED, faded hull atop a metal pole. What words were once on it were lost to oblivion. It was the marker for the building that lay behind it: a squat, rectangular shed-like building with a sagging metal roof and no windows. Long ago, weeds and tree saplings had invaded that building and made it a wild garden, home to rodents and snakes and cockroaches. There was a canopy next to the building: rusted steel, all the paint chipped away centuries ago, supported by beams that also had some kind of defunct computer devices installed in booths at their bases.

Neen studied the computer devices. They were inoperable, their screens now just a haven for dust. There seemed to be some kind of card reader next to the computer screen, and a hydraulics-style pump next to that, with a handle attached to a rubber tube that snaked its way up into the booth and disappeared.

"Fuel," Neen said. "These were filling stations for vehicles before the revolutions. People pumped oil out of the ground and used that for energy."

"Does that mean we're near a human settlement?" Tem asked. He wiped dust from the computer screen and rubbed his fingers together, causing the powdery dust to drift into the air.

Dron was lingering on the edge of the fuel station, standing protectively over Ems who had sat down to rest. Since their escape, Dron had tried to help Ems as much as possible, giving her support when she was weary, guarding her when she needed to lay down. Since breaking the Dome glass, Ems was more exhausted than Neen had ever seen. She barely spoke, barely acknowledged the presence of the others. Neen was tired too, and hungry. They needed to find shelter soon and begin foraging for food.

"It might," Neen replied, looking past the fuel pumps toward the sagging building behind them. "It also means we might have a way to make a fire."

She jogged over to the decrepit building and went inside its darkened doors. There wasn't much light from the empty windows, but there was enough to see shapes and the outlines of objects. Tilted, broken shelves lined the store in rows. Most of the items on the shelves had either been reduced to dust or were rusted and mildewed, but some things still remained usable. Neen found what she was looking for and returned to the others outside.

"This should work," she said, holding up a handful of little plastic tubes.

"What are they?" Dron asked, coming over. Ems had stood up and was wandering around under the canopy, looking with lifeless eyes at the ancient structure.

"Lighters," said Neen. "There's a rudimentary flint and steel mechanism at the top." She pointed to the little metal wheel atop a steel cap. "The plastic part is the gas reservoir. If we can shave off some of this plastic, we can use it for tinder too. Or find dry wood for kindling."

Tem asked to hold one of the lighters. He studied it, turning the lighter over in his hand, rubbing his finger on the spark wheel. He understood immediately how it worked. With a quick flick of his thumb, he spun the wheel. A tiny spark jumped out from the hood.

"Whoa!" said Dron, impressed.

Neen was ashamed to see how little education the Benglion males were given. Dron's reaction to something as simple as this lighter was a testament to how restrictive and demeaning the lives of these men had been. Another reminder of the cruelties of a society Neen had once championed.

"We'd better keep moving," she said, looking up at the sky. It was still daylight, but the sun was traveling quickly to the western horizon.

"Wait." Ems had moved close to them now. Neen hadn't even realized her friend was standing beside her when she spoke. It was like Ems could move as silently and swiftly as an owl. "I hear something."

They all stood completely still, listening.

"Should we hide?" Tem whispered.

Neen nodded, and they retreated into the dark building. They waited, Neen and Tem taking turns peeking out the windows to see what was coming.

Tem immediately recognized the first one who came into view. Neen did too. Those massive, bulging muscles were unmistakable. He towered over his companions, looking like a piece of the mountain had broken free and walked amongst them.

Tem started to get up, to go out to the men who approached the canopy, but Neen pulled him back down.

"We don't know—" she started, but Tem pulled his arm free.

"I do. That's my friend." He stepped into the doorway, slowly, his hands held up to show he wasn't a threat.

"Lekko." Tem smiled.

Lekko and a gang of about twenty men stopped short when they saw Tem. At first, Lekko's eyes widened, then as the reality of the situation seemed to settle in, he grinned from cheek to cheek.

"Tem!" He strode over to Tem and the two men embraced. Lekko's companions hung back, unsure of the situation, but not hostile. "I hoped you had escaped. I said to myself, 'If anyone will know what to do in all this madness, it's Tem. He's too clever to let a good opportunity slip by.'" Lekko laughed and slapped Tem on the back. "Come on, meet the others."

"Wait," Tem said, "I'm not alone."

"Eh?" Lekko tilted his head to try to see behind Tem into the building.

Neen held her breath and crouched down even lower. She stole a glance at Ems who was scowling, and Dron who looked eager to stand up. Neen shook her head at him. Tem and Dron might trust Neen and Ems, but these other men wouldn't be so amenable. Neen remembered Lekko's hostility from his interview.

"But promise me," Tem continued, "you won't do anything until I've had a chance to explain."

"Explain?" Lekko said. "What's there to explain?"

Neen had a sinking feeling. Why was Tem doing this? Was he really so trusting as to believe Lekko and the others wouldn't want to take revenge on a couple of women? Ems was starting to pant, an irrational look in her eyes. What if she was about to lose control?

Neen looked around the building for another door, an exit out the back, something. But there were no other exits.

"We didn't escape on our own," Tem said, his voice calm and natural. "We had help. I want you to leave your feelings aside, Lekko, and trust me. They might look like the enemy, but they're not."

"The enemy?" One of the men in Lekko's group spoke up. He was almost as tall as Lekko but not as brawny. Still, he was young and fit, and when he heard the word "enemy," his body tensed. He had a narrow face and pointed chin that reminded Neen of an upside-down arrowhead. She remembered his face, but as much as she tried, she couldn't remember his name.

"They're not the enemy," Tem repeated. "Trust me."

"I trust you, brother," Lekko said. "We've got to look out for each other if we want to survive out here."

"Exactly," said Tem. He took a step back into the building and turned to Neen and the others crouching beneath the window. "It's okay," he said to her. "Come out."

Dron stood up right away, arms swinging breezily, and went out to meet Lekko and the others.

"Dron!" Lekko said, slapping him on the back. "I missed that shit-eating grin!"

"Is this who we're supposed to think is an enemy?" the narrow-faced man said. His scowl had deepened as he watched Dron shake hands with the other men in the group.

"No, it's us," said Neen. She stepped into the open doorway. She held Ems's hand and squeezed it tightly. "Stay calm, sister," she said under her breath. "We have to trust that Tem knows what he's doing."

The men all stopped talking and stared. Suspicion and hatred darkened their faces. Neen felt exposed, as if she stood before a pack of ravenous wolves waiting to devour her.

But Tem was nearby, his solidness, his warmth comforting her. She had to trust him.

"They saved us, brother," Tem said to Lekko. "Remember when the riot was happening, three women came and the guards collapsed and those three women told us to fight for our freedom? These are those same women."

"There's only two here," said Lekko, all the jovial camaraderie in his voice gone. Neen could tell that he recognized her by the way his face had gone as still as stone.

"One died," said Tem, casting his eyes down. "She was old, but she was the one who started Neen on this journey. To help us. To see us as humans."

Neen could barely hear what they were saying, all her thoughts were with Ems, hoping her friend wouldn't lose control. She pulled Ems a little closer to her own body, hoping it would settle Ems's nerves. If Ems could read her thoughts at all, she hoped she could hear Neen's inner voice saying, "Be calm, be calm, be calm..."

Lekko's grim frown didn't change, but he did nod at last to Neen and Ems. "Okay, Tem," he said. "If these women are willing to be allies, then let's call a truce."

Ems's body relaxed, and Neen put her arm around her shoulders to steady her. She almost looked like she was going to collapse. Dron, always on the spot whenever Ems needed something, was by her side in half a second, taking her under his arm and supporting her.

"This one here," he said, smiling, "is practically unstoppable. She broke the Dome glass with one hand! I'm telling you, lads, she's not to be messed with. Small size but big strength!"

Though Dron was trying to lighten things up, Neen could see that the narrow-faced man was not convinced. He stood apart from the others, glaring at Neen and Ems with cold eyes.

"We're looking for a settlement," Tem said to Lekko. "There should be one near here. It was good fortune we found each other."

Lekko smirked. "You didn't hide your trail very well. We took a gamble and hoped other males might have escaped too. When we found your footprints, we followed."

Neen bit her lip. Why hadn't she considered that? If their trail could be found so easily, that meant Herria could track them too. They needed to be more careful going forward.

"Come on," she said. "We don't have much daylight left to find shelter."

An uneasy but peaceful alliance now formed, the fugitives set off down into the valley.

* * *

AS THE SUN disappeared behind the peaks, they came to the ruins of an ancient settlement. Following along a dirt path through the mountains, the trail opened into a box canyon where the remains of houses and buildings from centuries ago sat like silent tombs. A concrete road snaked down to their east, forming the main thoroughfare into the empty town, but as they drew closer, it was clear that nature had begun to reclaim this spot, with the concrete streets cracked and uneven, wedged apart by the determined will of the wild grasses and weeds which pushed their way up into the open air. Many of the buildings had also been reclaimed by nature, with trees growing inside buildings, their limbs finding passage through sunken and caved-in roofs. Nestled to the west of the main road was a cluster of dwellings that looked like they must have once formed a community, a residential area of some sort. Many of the houses were two or three stories high, but their peeked roofs were sagging and sometimes destroyed, worn away by time. Some houses had turrets and bay windows along their front sides, and some were simpler but with huge windows that stretched almost from top to bottom. Some windows were intact, but most were broken or non-existent, destroyed by weather or war. Neen wasn't sure it mattered.

"Not exactly a resort," she said. "But what choice do we have?"

Ems swooned. "Neen," she said weakly. She clutched her stomach and bent over.

"I know the feeling," said Dron, by her side. "I'm not saying I want to go back to the Dome, but at least they fed us. Occasionally."

They needed food. But they also needed to find safe shelter as nightfall approached. Neen described the kinds of plants and berries that would be edible and Lekko volunteered himself and the other men to start foraging.

"We should have been looking already," the sour-faced man with the narrow chin grumbled. "It's almost dark."

"Yes, and that's my fault," said Neen. "I'm not at my best right now."

She had always loved being outside, going on hikes and enjoying nature. But it was hard to think clearly when things felt so hopeless. She hadn't spoken about it to anyone, but the chances of their survival were minimal at best. They had no food, no means of protection except for a few guns, nothing but the clothes on their backs. It was almost like they had won the men's freedom as a final gasp of life, one last shining moment before death found them all.

"We'll find something," Lekko said, nodding to Tem.

"Don't worry." He never looked at Neen when he spoke, but addressed everything to Tem. Neen didn't really mind, but it gave her an uneasy feeling.

The dark, cold eyes of the other man, the sour one who didn't trust Neen, glared at her before he turned to follow Lekko and the others to find food.

Neen was glad for the respite. Lekko and the other men never said anything, but there was an uneasiness between them and the women. A sense that they always had to be on their guard. Neen, too, felt more guarded with them around.

Tem and Dron decided to stay behind with Neen and Ems to help find shelter for the night. Many of the houses were too exposed to the elements to be useful for sleeping in, but a few of them had rooms where the ceilings hadn't collapsed and they could take shelter. Dron found a place where Ems could lie down, a room that was mostly clear of debris. Then he went out to look for kindling so they could start a fire.

Neen wandered through a nearby house that still had some walls intact. So much of it was littered with metal and plastic remains: cooking appliances, refrigerators, stoves, washing machines. These things weren't altogether different from what they used now, just different designs, different technologies. The grime and rust and dullness of them were depressing to look at. These things were all once new, but now they were nothing more than dead relics. Neen tried to imagine the people who had lived there, what kind of lives they led, what kind of relationships. There were plastic picture frames that had fallen to the floor, covered in centuries of dust and mildew. The glass over the pictures had kept some of the moisture out, and Neen thought she could make out the faded outlines of human figures in the images. Were these people a family? It was a word that didn't get used much in Neen's society. Like the dead refrigerators, families were relics from the ancient past.

She knelt down to get a closer look at the pictures and felt the letter in her pocket crinkle.

Nekka's letter.

She'd forgotten it in all this chaos. Reaching into her pocket, she took it out. She was trembling as she started to unfold it. The sound of footsteps stopped her.

It was Tem. "I didn't know you in here," he said, then seeing the letter and Neen's face, he backed away. "I'll give you some space."

"No, wait." Neen still held the letter in her hand, but she remembered something else. "Can I ask you something?"

"Are we doing another interview?" Tem said, raising his eyebrows and smirking.

Neen shook her head and laughed. He had a way of teasing her that was playful without being cruel.

"Not this time," said Neen. "You don't have to answer if you don't want to."

"I'm game. What is it?"

"That half-moon pendant? Where did you get it?"

Tem's mirthful smile faded and he looked away. "I've always had it," he said softly. "Even in Young Dome. I don't remember a time when I didn't have it, but we weren't supposed to have personal possessions, so I kept it hidden. Someone must have given it to me as a child. Someone who wanted me to have something of my own..."

"Nekka gave me this letter and said not to open it until she was dead." Neen showed him the folded letter. "I thought she was being dramatic, that she was overreacting to Herria's takeover. But maybe she sensed something I couldn't see."

"I'm sorry. I'll let you read it in peace. I didn't mean to intrude—"

"But you didn't," Neen said quickly. "You came at just the right time. I think... I think you should hear this letter too."

Tem nodded.

"Dear Neen," she read. "If you are reading this letter, that means I've passed on from this world. Don't weep for me, please. I was just one woman, no more, no less. What I had accomplished was smaller than what I had hoped for, which is the way it is for most people. Our grand plans often come to little more than paltry half-measures.

"But if my victories in politics have been minuscule, if my legacy is tarnished and ultimately disgraced, I still have one thing for which I can hold my head up high. One thing I might be proud of. I have loved and been loved in return.

"His name was Bargo. I saw him for the first time in the Arena Dome as he fought with the other Benglion males and won his cohort easily. I'm ashamed to admit that it was really only lust that made me pursue him. He was the strongest, tallest man I had ever seen, and I wanted him. I was already rising the ranks of leadership. You'd be surprised how easy it was to bribe the other breeding women. Extra food points, extra rest days, a new assignment with less stress. I could make those things happen, and because I could, I was able to bribe the guards and bring Bargo to my breeding suite.

"Those three glorious days were indescribable. I wanted him and I took him. But what I wasn't expecting was his tenderness. He was so patient with me, a woman who hadn't been alone with a man before. He wanted to talk to me, to know about me, and I, in turn, wanted to know about him. I looked forward to each session with giddy anticipation. I know he did too.

"After the breeding sessions concluded, I still hungered for him. I felt bereft without his company. I realized that I had grown attached to him, something we were often warned to guard against. 'Males are cunning and dangerous. They will manipulate your feelings if you let them.' That was what we trumpeted all the time, on every screen, in every broadcast through the clan lands. But Bargo didn't seem dangerous to me. He didn't seem cunning. He was soft-spoken, and gentle, and a little bit shy. He wasn't the picture I'd been inundated with of the savage, subhuman male who only wanted one thing from a woman. He was kind. He was a person.

"That's when I knew my mission in life was to change the system, to help women see that men were not monsters, that each man was an individual, just as each woman was. I wanted to build a better world. For me, for Bargo... for my son."

Neen stopped reading. She didn't look up at Tem but could feel his eyes on her.

"Tem," she said, "Nekka gave me that necklace with the half-moon pendant. She said it would bring me good luck." She still didn't take her eyes off the letter, the black marks on the page all swirling together into an inky soup. She felt Tem move closer.

"And did it?" he asked.

"I think it helped bring us together."

"Neen," Tem said, his voice soft, "keep reading."

Her eyes focused and the words swam into sense again.

"It took more bribery and calling in favors," she read, "but I had the boy placed in the Benglion group in Young Dome. It was a faint hope, but I thought perhaps he might meet Bargo one day when he reached maturity. But it was worse than that. Bargo's copulation with me was exposed. I don't know who revealed it to the high council, but he was immediately castrated and sent to the Work Dome. I was spared punishment, though. Whoever targeted Bargo didn't mention my name to the authorities. All they said was that a woman from a different clan had been assaulted by this Benglion male. That was enough. Accusation only, no evidence, no trial.

"I never saw Bargo again. And when my son was born, he too was whisked away, taken from my arms not long after the birth to be raised by the nurses in Young Dome. That is what we do to male children born in this glorious paradise of ours.

"He was marked and tagged and given a name by strangers who never loved him or even wanted to care for him, but I made sure that he would have something to remember me by, something to cling to when he felt alone or bereft. I used my influence one more time and took an assignment inspecting the male children of Young Dome. Reports needed to be written, policies made. I found out which boy was my son, angled my way into speaking with him, and before I left, gave him a half-moon pendant, one piece of the pendant I always wore around my neck. I almost couldn't speak when I knelt down to see him. The words all dried up in my mouth when I realized that this child was my child. This boy was Bargo's son. He had the same dark brown hair, the same intelligent, searching eyes. He was only two or three years old, but I gave him the pendant and found some way to tell him to keep it secret, to never show anyone, and to keep it always near. It was a small gesture, not nearly enough for what a child deserves from his mother. But it was all I had to give.

"That was the last time I saw my son. My beautiful boy. My greatest accomplishment."

Neen trembled as she held the paper. She blinked and a pool of tears overflowed. When she looked up, Tem had tears in his eyes too.

"I can't believe it," he said, his voice hoarse.

"I can. It explains a lot. You were always different, Tem. You said so yourself."

"My mother... I never thought..." He was lost in a thousand what-ifs and faded memories.

Neen handed him the letter. "I think this belongs to you much more than it does to me."

Tem was about to reply when Dron popped his head into the room. "Dinner is served!" he grinned. "We have a dandelion salad with wild fennel, mallow leaves, and some little red berries that I can't remember the name of. A feast!"

Tem and Neen both let out small laughs, happy to have something to break the tension and sadness. It was good that the men had found some food. At least they wouldn't go to bed totally famished.

"We also found a spring nearby," Dron continued as they made their way to where Lekko and the others gathered: a yard behind one of the ruined houses. "I found some glass containers in one of the buildings and filled them up," Dron explained, proud of his handiwork.

"Let me start the fire, then," Neen said. "We'll need to boil the water to kill off bacteria."

While Neen started the fire with her plastic lighters, Tem and Lekko made sure the food was divided fairly. There was some disagreement about Ems's ration.

"She's nearly unconscious," Tem argued. "She needs a bigger portion."

"Everyone gets the same," Lekko replied. "No special favors, especially for the females." He seemed to relish saying that word.

Neen tried to ignore the insult. "Fine, no special favors," she said. "Give me her ration. I'll take it to her."

As Neen went inside the house, she could feel the eyes of the other man, the narrow-faced one, watching her. It made her skin crawl, but she tried to ignore it. They needed to work together with these men. It wouldn't do to start accusing them of scowling looks.

Ems ate a little and drank a bit more, but then she fell back into sleep and restless dreams. Neen rejoined the others and they all ate their foraged greens in gloomy silence.

The sun had set by now, the night closing in fast.

Most of the men decided to sleep by the fire, but Neen wanted to be alone. There was a long, low table still intact in one of the rooms, and she thought it might serve as a place to lie down. Luckily it wasn't a cold night, the summer heat still lingering on after dark even in these altitudes.

Neen laid down to a restless, half-sleep. Her mind was whirling with thoughts and questions and regrets. The contents of Nekka's letter had both confirmed for her what she had suspected about Tem, and shocked her with the story of Nekka and Bargo. To think that Nekka — aloof, clinical, too-blunt Nekka — could be so in love with a man, so willing to risk her position within society to be with him.

What would it feel like to have that kind of love? Neen lay awake thinking about it, her mind drifting from these abstract questions to the very real situation she now found herself in. What would it feel like if she gave herself over to loving someone else? Was she capable of it? Would he love her in return?

A door creaked on its hinges. Neen didn't sit up, but she shifted her body over so she could see who was coming into the house. A man stood in the doorway to the room where she lay. He wasn't large like Lekko, but he was tall and sinewy.

For a split second, Neen thought it was Tem. Her stomach fluttered.

But then it sank and clenched tight when she saw it was the narrow-faced man.

"Hard to sleep on the ground," he said. "Thought I might try my luck in here."

Neen sat up. "There aren't many good places here either, I'm afraid. Most of the furniture has rotted away."

"Mind if we talk, then?" He took two quick strides and was right next to her, looming over her like a swaying cobra.

"I need to sleep," Neen replied.

"Aw, come on. We've chatted before, you know." He leered at her, teeth gleaming in the traces of moonlight that streamed through the door and windows.

"I don't think—"

"Back in the Dome. Don't you remember? You came to interrogate all us males, make sure we were fit to touch your precious womanly bodies."

Neen had a vague recollection of his face, but she couldn't remember his name. "I'm sorry, but I don't remember—"

"That's funny. 'Cause I remember. I remember the way you sat there swiping your tablet screen, typing stuff in, judging and ranking me, measuring me against all the rest. You passed me through, so I guess I should be grateful. Only when it came time for my competition, for getting the chance to breed, your kind rejected me. I never got my time in the breeding suite..."

He bent over her now, bringing his face close to hers. Neen wanted to scream, to call for help, but then the delicate peace they were clinging to would fall apart.

"I'm sorry you didn't get what you wanted," Neen said, trying to stay calm. "But you could have been one of the men framed for murder. Be grateful you were spared."

"I don't wanna be spared now," he replied, grabbing her

neck and pulling her up towards his face, his thumb stroking her lips back and forth. "Maybe this time you can remember my name..."

Neen tried to pull away, but he thrust her back onto the table, slamming her head hard against the wood. Then he put his hand over her mouth.

"Did anyone ever tell you you look good for a Triverser?" he said, licking his lips.

Neen tried again to get out of his grip, but he was unbelievably strong. All she could do was try to keep squirming and hope to slip out of his grasp.

Another shadow was there, a tall shape behind him that reached out and grabbed his arm. Neen wriggled free and backed against the wall, keeping the table between her and the man. The shadow twisted the man's arm. He cried out. Then the shadow threw him to the ground.

"Get away from her," the shadow growled, eyes aglow with fury.

It was Tem.

The man tried to lunge for Tem's legs, but Tem was too quick. Then the man was on his feet again, and Tem was at an awkward angle. The man delivered a punch right to Tem's jaw.

Neen tensed. Tem crumbled after the blow, sinking to one knee, his body bent over. The man came in for another strike. Tem was still hunched down. The man hit Tem again, another blow to the head.

Neen looked for a way to get out. She needed to warn Dron and Lekko. Tem was going to be killed.

"I... said... get... away from her..." Tem spit blood and before the man could take another swing, he tackled him, the two of them wrestling on the floor, writhing around like snakes.

Neen started to run for the door, to get out and find the others, but when she looked again, Tem was on top of the man, his fists pounding their way into the bone and flesh of that narrow face, blood spurting onto Tem's knuckles and clothes.

"Tem!" Neen said. If he didn't stop now, he'd kill the man.

Tem's fist was raised over the mashed-up face, but he let it hang in the air, his chest heaving in and out, his mouth panting.

"Enough, Tem. Enough."

Tem closed his eyes, then opened them again and got off the man's chest. He turned away from the sight of it. "Get out of here," he said to the man. His voice was low, but his anger simmered just below the surface. "Leave this settlement. Never come back."

The man struggled to get up. When he finally tottered to his feet, Neen could see that his eyes were starting to swell shut and his face was all mashed and formless. He staggered out of the room and into the night.

Tem was still breathing heavily. Neen didn't know what to say.

"Some of us are animals," Tem said, in that same low, hateful voice. "That part Herria got right."

"Tem, I—"

"I'm sorry you had to see that. But I'm glad I did it."

"Tem." Neen was shaking, and she wanted to thank him, but she also didn't want to face him. He would have killed that man if Neen hadn't stopped him. She wasn't sure how she felt about that.

"I'll leave you alone now," he said.

"No, don't... I mean, I want to thank you."

Tem turned to look at her. "Neen..."

"How did you know to come?"

Tem took a step towards her. "I just... I felt it. Something. I knew you needed me."

"I'm glad you came."

"Should I stay? In case he comes back?"

Neen nodded.

"Don't worry, I'll sleep on the floor." He tried to smile. He lay down on the floor next to the table. Neen went back to the low table and lay down too.

Neither of them said anything as they lay in the darkness, but it was clear both were still awake. Neen's hands were folded on top of each other on her stomach, but slowly, she let her left hand slip down the side and hang over the edge of the table. She wasn't sure what she was expecting.

Then she felt it. The faint touch of Tem's fingers as they reached up to hold her hand.

* * *

THE NEXT DAY, they didn't know what to expect, but they never expected to find a library. It had been while they were exploring other parts of the ancient city, further onto the main road that led into the center of town. Most of the buildings looked like they had been shops or businesses of various kinds, but one of the buildings was large and square, made of red brick, two double doors of solid oak still guarding the entrance. Above the door was a chiseled plaque that read, "Information, Knowledge, Wisdom."

"A library," Neen said, squeezing Tem's hand. They hadn't mentioned what happened the night before, but throughout the morning, Neen found her hand often drifting to Tem's, and his to hers.

"A library?"

Neen could see Tem's eyes widen. She took her hand and swept the hair from across his forehead. "What are you waiting for?"

The thrill was tempered once they got inside. Most of the books were brittle and pages turned to dust when they touched them. But as they got deeper into the stacks, away from the windows and the lights, some of the books were still intact and able to be read.

Tem pulled a heavy tome down from one of the shelves. It was a thick book with a leather-bound cover. Delicately, he leafed through the pages, eyes staring in wonder at the faded illustrations and artwork. His eyes scanned the words and he began to read.

"They're... they're stories," he said at last, breathless.

"No more rulebooks or propaganda," Neen replied.

She drew close to him and was surprised to find him weeping. Huge tears fell down his cheeks, making his brown eyes glisten.

"I can read them all," he said, a wide smile spreading across his face, mingling with his tears.

"And no one can stop you," Neen added.

Tem gulped out a laugh and then wiped the tears away. "Thank you, Neen."

"For what? Taking you to the library?"

"For helping me be free."

Neen wasn't sure when he had set the book down, but somehow his hands weren't holding it any longer. They were holding her arms, gently. And his face was pulling closer and closer to her own...

Neen could smell the pleasant musk of his skin, the sandalwood smell of his hair. She could almost taste the slight tinge of saltiness in his mouth. She could feel the gentle pressure of his lips against her own. Then the warmth of his breath, and the saltiness mixed with sweetness, his mouth opening to hers...

The kiss lasted only a moment, but for Neen, it was a moment frozen in time. Even after they stepped apart, she could feel the imprint of his lips on hers. She could still taste him.

"I'm sorry..." Tem said. He blushed and fumbled around trying to pick up the book again.

Neen brushed her fingers through his hair again. "I'm not."

The light outside hurt their eyes when they emerged from the darkened library. Lekko and a few others were walking down the middle of the street toward them. They didn't look happy.

"She says you know her," Lekko said, scowling at Neen.

"Who?" Neen and Tem both looked at each other.

* * *

LI STOOD BY THEIR CAMPFIRE, hands on her hips. Several men hovered around her like buzzards waiting to pick her bones.

"You're lucky I showed up when I did," she said, scanning the campsite and the houses nearby. "You have no supplies. Nothing. If we're going to survive out here, we'll need more than a few jugs of water and a plate of weeds."

Neen embraced Li, and Tem and Dron awkwardly shook her hand. There were grumbles from Lekko and the others, and the word spy was uttered several times, but Tem vouched for Li, and Dron too, and no one could deny that they needed the food and weapons she'd brought.

"I'll be honest," Li said, eyeing all the men, Lekko especially. They looked haggard and hungry. "I wasn't expecting a welcome party, but it's nice to know I'll have company in exile." Then she explained what happened in Bells with Herria's takeover and the failed assassination. "So what's the plan?" she said, turning to Neen. "When do we start the liberation?"

All eyes were on Neen. She had been waiting her entire life for a challenge, for something big. All that restlessness growing up, all that yearning to go beyond the limits of her world — now was the time to do something about it.

So then why did Neen feel so inadequate to the task? Why did she hesitate? Neen knew everyone was waiting. But what could she say?

She felt Tem's hand slip into hers. She smiled. His grip was firm, but his hand was soft. It was warm and large, wrapping itself around her thin fingers and holding tight. She could feel his steadiness flow into her. She had been waiting for something big to happen, and now it had.

"It's already started," she said, squeezing Tem's hand. "Now we just have to finish it. Together."

CHAPTER ONE - THE FEMALE UPRISING

BOOK TWO **in the Female Saga**

IT WAS TOO EARLY for sunlight to filter through the firehouse window, but Neen didn't need sunlight. Not yet. Her work wouldn't begin for at least an hour—when her comrades would awaken and start the day's chores, the daily tasks of survival that had sustained them these past few months.

It was too early for thinking about survival. As Neen sat nestled in the crook of one of the station's upstairs windows—they were lucky most of the windows in this building were still intact—she looked out over the town. It was still shrouded in darkness, and at the dim outline of the mountains encircling their quiet valley. Everything was still asleep, or so it seemed, in this pre-dawn moment.

The town was mostly a collection of ruins: crumpled roofs over decrepit houses, refuse and decay scattered where once there had been civilization. But a few buildings still remained, like the firehouse, the library, and a smattering of public places that had been built with reinforced steel and concrete. It was a town of ghosts, a reminder of a time and place from before the revolutions, when men had held power and women had to navigate a precarious path between being the scapegoats for all of society's ills or human-shaped objects meant purely for male gratification.

But the town that spread out before Neen, even in ruins, didn't seem like a place where women were enslaved, or men ruled with an iron fist. It was a place with homes and gathering spaces and shops and communities. A lot like the world in which she had grown up, if perhaps more antiquated in its architecture. Had the old world really been so different from the new one?

There was one difference Neen could see. There was no glass Dome in this town, no prison for housing all the males, no one-way glass for women to look through and see the males training for the honor of winning a chance to breed with a woman. In this ghost town, there were only ordinary buildings, ordinary houses, ordinary places where their ancestors had once lived and worked and played.

Of course, there were no more Domes in EVE either. Herria and her forces had seen to that. Neen could still see the smoke rising from the charred remains of the Benglion Dome, could still smell the acrid tang of burnt plastic and melted steel.

She and Tem had dared to witness the destruction from the edges of the wilderness beyond the official borders of the Benglion capital city, Bells. She remembered the tightness of his hand squeezed against hers as he watched the Dome smolder. They had both cried, raged, and felt hopeless. The men who didn't die in the riots or the final destruction of the Domes were at the mines now. As good as dead.

Neen pulled her knees closer to her chest and leaned her

cheek against the dusty, tarnished glass. She closed her eyes and waited for the sun to rise, for the light to filter past her eyelids and welcome her to the new day. She only had a few minutes left if her internal clock was right. A few more minutes to herself.

Neen craved these early morning hours. It was the one time in her day when she didn't have to deal with other people and their problems. Not that she begrudged people in the camp needing her help. She had wanted a mission, a chance to make a difference, and fate—as well as her old mentor Nekka—had given it to her. She was the leader everyone looked to for building this new life in the mountains. And she was good at it. She saw all the ways the leftover remains of the town could be put to use, helping them with shelter, warmth, and basic necessities. The other men and women in the camps had skills and talents, but Neen was the only Triverser in the group so far, the only one with the training and intelligence to engineer their survival. She loved being useful. Doing the work wasn't a problem.

The first rays of the sun crept over the mountain peaks. Neen shifted a little, her arms still wrapped around her knees.

What was the problem? She wondered.

She could hardly say it out loud, even though she felt it deep within her bones.

"Neen." Tem's voice was deep and steady, a voice that sounded almost like dawn itself.

She opened her eyes and saw him standing in the shadows of the doorway, the emptiness of the abandoned room between them. The only thing left in that upstairs room was some debris from the flaking concrete walls and several layers of dust on the floor. Neen's footprints had kicked up a path through the dust, evidence of her many trips to the window for solitude. The ceiling had been left unfinished, a network of pipes and air vents that made loud voices echo, and despite being camped out in this small town for several months, nobody had bothered yet to clean this room or find a use for it. Maybe everyone knew this was Neen's private place. Tem knew, anyway.

Neen smiled as he came over and sat down beside her.

"You know my habits," she said, letting him hold her hand gently. But did he know how she felt? It was her own fault if he didn't. Neen knew she needed to open up to Tem, but the gap between what she knew was right and what she could manage to do was ever-widening.

"Maybe," said Tem, "but I don't quite understand them. You come here every morning—" He stopped himself. "It's not my place to pry. I'm sorry."

"No," Neen replied, "it's okay." She put her head on his shoulder. "I just need time to think. These early morning hours, they help me work things out."

Tem nodded slightly. "There's a lot to think about."

"There is."

"Maybe talking about it would help."

She could hear the pleading in his voice even though he tried to hide it. He wanted her to let him in, to make him privy to her innermost thoughts, but something held her back. Neen wasn't used to intimacy. Friendships, for her, had always been pushed to the background. Her studies and training at the Institute in High City came first.

When she thought about it, Ems had been her only friend, even in childhood. And with Ems, Neen barely had to open up. Ems's hyper-advanced sensory abilities let her know Neen's feelings often before Neen herself had a chance to feel them. With Tem, it was different. With him, she'd have to share her thoughts and fears, and desires, but she didn't know how.

"What were you thinking about today?" Tem asked, softly.

The sun was entirely above the horizon now, the entire lower part of the sky illuminated by its golden light. The details of the mountains came into clearer focus, their slopes covered with the dark greens and browns of fir and spruce, their peaks capped by blue-white snow. Bells, High City, Herria, and all the turmoil of the last few months seemed a world away.

But it wasn't, not really. It still surprised Neen that Herria hadn't sent someone into the mountains to find them and crush them. Every day without incident made Neen's heart beat faster, the tension and anxiety climbing higher and higher as she waited and wondered why Herria hadn't yet attacked.

"I was thinking about the Domes," she said at last.

"Me too."

"And all the men sent to the mines."

Tem nodded. "We have to make a plan—"

Neen dropped his hand and stood up. She moved away from the window and into the shadows on the other side of the room. "There's no plan, Tem. What could we possibly do? You saw the flattened Dome in Bells. It was rubble. Obliterated. What hope do we have against that? Before this is over, every woman in EVE will be part of Herria's super-powered All-Clan. I've tried to find a way, but there's nothing we can do."

She hated saying all this to him—hated even thinking it—but there was no use denying reality. She had learned that lesson the hard way when she first walked into the High City

Dome and saw what her fellow women really did to the males inside.

"Neen, this isn't like you—"

She bit her tongue and didn't respond. What did he know? They had only been together in these mountains for a couple of months. They were practically strangers.

That's because of you, Neen. You've been keeping him at arm's length.

"It's very much like me," she replied. "I can analyze every angle and strategize every possible plan, and I can see that no matter what we do, we'll never be able to face off against Herria's army. The only thing left for us is to live off the grid and hope we can escape Herria's notice."

"How long will that last? Just waiting around for our own annihilation?"

Bitterness. Anger. Neen hated hearing those things in Tem's voice. "That's not what I meant—"

The sunrise was mocking her. All that beautiful golden light bathing them both, and here she was fighting with him.

Tem sighed and stepped toward her. She stepped toward him too. The morning had barely begun, and already she was exhausted.

He took her hands in his own and smiled. "I'm sorry. I barged in here without invitation and started making demands—"

"No, it's me. I'm not used to all this."

"None of us are."

"That still doesn't make it okay—"

"Neen." He pulled her towards him. His body was warm, his arms steady and strong. She let herself sink into him and feel the soft up-and-down rhythm in his chest as he breathed.

Then her face lifted toward his, and she leaned in to kiss

him. His beard had grown longer since they'd been in the mountains, and while it was soft against her skin, his mustache sometimes tickled her nose. Still, his lips felt good against her own.

"Ahem." Someone coughed awkwardly from the doorway.

Neen pulled back from Tem and looked. It was Dron.

"Sorry, I just—" He looked up to the unfinished ceiling as if there were a particularly interesting speck of rust to observe. "I don't think I can go trapping today."

Tem nodded. "I understand."

"Ems?" Neen asked.

Dron's eyes had shifted to a fascinating particle of dust at his feet. He nodded ever-so-slightly.

"Should I come talk to her?"

Dron shook his head. "I can manage."

"I'll come. Let me do my rounds first, and then I'll visit. Bring you both some tea."

Dron accepted this, nodding to both Neen and Tem before sliding back out of the room.

"Maybe I should skip trapping for today," Tem offered.

"Not a chance. We need every morsel you can catch. I can handle Ems and the others."

"I know you can, that's not what I meant—"

"I know what you meant." Neen smiled and kissed him again. "And I'm grateful. I know I've been a little bleak lately, but you keep me sane."

"A pocket of sanity in this messed up world?"

Neen nodded and drifted her fingers through his beard. "Maybe you should come with me next time."

"Come with you?"

"Here, to my private loft."

"What about your alone time?"

"I'm trying to come out of my shell. Make new friends."

Tem drew closer again, wrapping his arms around her. "Am I a new friend?"

"Something like that..."

The sun was fully in the sky now. Hues of daffodil yellow illuminated the valley, bringing to life all the rocks, pines, and underbrush that led down into their little ruined town. When Neen looked out the window again, she saw people emerging from their shelters to begin the day's work. As beautiful as the morning was, she hated to leave this dusty place and go out into the dewy air. Tem's arms were so warm, so solid.

"I'd better go," he said. "If Dron's not coming, I'll have to cover twice as much ground to check the traps."

"Right. Yes. Better go." Neen buried her feelings. "We've all got work to do."

❖

Neen made her way from the firehouse to the town library, down streets of crumbled pavement where nature had broken through the rubble and reclaimed the surface. In every crack and cranny, dandelions and clover and thistle flourished. It made Neen want to go off into the foothills of the mountains and find more wildflowers, to listen for birdsong and let the breeze blow through her honey-brown hair. It reminded her of childhood.

Whenever it was time for the children in her cohort to begin afternoon play, Neen would drift off to be alone. Her caregivers probably kept a close eye on her—they always kept a close eye on everyone—but to eight-year-old Neen, these wanderings made her feel like she was the only one in the world. Just her and the daisies and chicory. No one else to judge her or stifle her or tell her what to do.

In the distance, she could always hear the laughter of the

other girls and the songs they would sometimes sing as part of their games, but she pretended these sounds were just a strange species of bird or the wind whistling through the tall grass.

There was a part of herself that wanted to play with the others, but she never knew how to join in. When she spoke, she seemed to say the wrong thing. Or when she tried to add something to the game, the other girls whined that she was ruining it.

Better to be alone. That way, she couldn't be hurt.

It was hard not to think of her lonely childhood these days when so many people now looked to her for leadership.

This is what you wanted. She reminded herself. And directing people and developing systems for their survival was Neen's strength. No one else in the camp could organize their resources and engineer their tools the way Neen could.

And being a leader meant keeping others at arm's length. It meant not getting too close. Something Neen excelled at.

Only now, it was different. Now she had someone she wanted to get close to, and she was making a mess of it.

"Morning!" A blonde Benglion woman named Windar pushed open the heavy double doors of the library and emerged into the street just as Neen was drawing near. "Gonna take a group into that neighborhood down the hill and see what we can find. Should be good for a day's work!"

"Perfect," Neen replied. "Don't forget we need more copper wire for the traps."

Windar saluted Neen and then skipped off to find her comrades.

Copper wires, metal and plastic pipes, wood, batteries, any pieces of glass they could find, and whatever other random scraps that were salvageable from the ruins of the town were gathered every day by work crews and brought to Neen in the ground floor of the firehouse for inspection and sorting. She was like the quartermaster in an army, evaluating the detritus her workers brought her and assigning a use for everything. If they were going to survive out here in the mountains, they had to gather what they could from the surrounding area to help with shelter, warmth, food, and protection. They couldn't afford to leave any stone unturned.

Most crews went to work scavenging through the town, while a few others went into the wilderness to hunt, trap, and gather. Li took a special unit to scout the area and look for signs of intrusion. Or refugees.

They had a lot of refugees lately, women who escaped from the Benglion capital. Mostly Benglions, of course, but there were a few from other clans. They had come either as a way to escape getting the All-Clans injections or because they'd already gotten the injections and were suffering the consequences. These women came telling stories—stories of forced injections, special police rounding up protestors, thrice daily propaganda reports extolling the virtues of being All-Clan and downplaying the dangerous side effects of Herria's serum.

Some were wary of all the men in the camp, and in the earliest days, when Li found one or two women wandering around through the pine forests and brought them to Neen, they questioned the presence of the *males* and demanded to be let go, to fend for themselves in the wilderness. Neen and Li had refused to acquiesce, mostly for security reasons. Women wandering around the mountains were a liability. Of course, Neen didn't tell them that. Instead, she explained that their chances of survival alone in the mountains were slim. She showed them what she, Li, and the others had built in the town, and she reminded them that the ideals of EVE, the ideals of sisterhood and togetherness, were still alive in their little camp. It was just that now this togetherness included men.

It took a long time and a lot of luck, but eventually, these women's fear and hatred for the men dissipated. When they saw that their image of the *males* was based on propaganda and fear and that the reality was different, they opened up to living and working alongside Tem, Dron, Lekko, and the others.

Still, tensions sometimes ran high. Old habits and hatred died hard. That's why Neen only let men and women work together if the women were comfortable with it. If any woman objected, that woman wouldn't have to work alongside a man in her daily duties. A few still kept to themselves or stayed with an all-woman work group, but most were okay with the situation. Now, Neen was finding that men and women were pairing off and doing work in groups of two. She never questioned the arrangements, but she worried. All it would take was one of the pair to make an accusation, and their precarious little experiment might fall apart.

Neen was just about to push open the heavy oak doors of the library when a scream echoed from within. She ran inside and looked for its source. The foyer was aglow with orange light from the library's fireplace, and a couple of women were tending it and preparing food for breakfast. Their colony had converted the library's reading room into a common room for the group, a place to cook, eat, and sleep. Neen locked eyes with the two women by the fire, their faces anxious.

They all knew what the scream meant.

"Come on," Neen told the women as she dashed to the library's second floor.

The upstairs level of the building was a mixture of darkness and light, the looming stacks of books casting shadows over the room's interior while the large windows all around the perimeter let in copious amounts of morning sunshine. Members of the colony often came up here to eat their meals, and Neen raced between the stacks to the opposite end of the room where a Benglion woman was writhing on the ground and screaming, kicking her eating utensils in all directions. Another woman stood, panicked nearby, trying to get ahold of her companion and secure her.

"Grab her arms! Quick!" Neen knew they needed to ensure the writhing woman didn't swing her arms or kick, or else she might knock the tincture out of Neen's hands. Reaching into her pocket, Neen pulled out a small vial of amber liquid and got ready to administer it.

The other woman—a Trabador named Tollis struggled to hold her companion, but the women from downstairs came to her aid. Eventually, the three of them clamped the Benglion woman's arms and legs down and shifted her up so Neen could administer the sedative.

This was always the most challenging part. When the mania was at its highest, it was almost impossible to make one of these women drink the tincture. Neen had to act fast. No hesitation.

The woman was screaming. Her mouth twisted in an ugly snarl.

Neen opened the vial, gripped the raging woman by the chin, and poured the amber liquid down her throat. As swift as she could, she clamped the woman's mouth shut. Luckily, no bites this time.

It didn't take long for the sedative to work. The woman's head drooped, and her screams quieted. Eventually, she was in a twilight state, half-conscious but subdued. Tollis and the other women let go of her and stood up. Neen did too. The four of them all looked at each other, exhaustion, resignation, and grief coloring their faces.

"I'll take her to the cells," Tollis said. As a Trabador, bred for manual labor, she had the strength to carry the woman.

"We'll help," said the other two women.

Neen nodded. What more could they do? When the mania struck like this, the only safe option was one of the cells. This was the second time this week they had to lock up someone. And now Neen had no more of the poppy tincture. Another thing to have her foragers look for today.

It wasn't the most abundant flower in these mountains, but Neen had researched in the library to find out which native plants might be used to make a sedative strong enough to cool the mania these women suffered from. When she discovered there was a little orange poppy that could grow in this climate and that it worked as a pain reliever and sedative, she knew they needed to find it.

It wasn't hard to make the tincture, but the process took time. Neen had started fermenting alcohol almost as soon as they'd decided to settle in the town. They needed something to use for disinfectant, and Neen figured alcohol was their best bet. Much of the alcohol in town had lost its potency after three hundred years, so they gathered what they could from the stores, homes, and restaurants they found in town, and then Neen set out to ferment her own.

Tem and Dron were sent on missions to find beehives, wild sugar beets, berries, tree sap—anything Neen could use for sugar to ferment. They had fresh water from the stream that ran through the valley, and Neen knew that yeast was present in the air, so once she made her sugar water solution, she left the containers open to let the yeast in. Soon they had a few liters of strong alcohol. Taking some of that, she mixed it with the delicate orange poppies—flower petals, stems, roots, and all—and let the concoction sit for several weeks. When the process was finished, she had created a sedative that could calm nerves and make someone drowsy with only a few drops. In larger quantities, it could knock someone out.

Just what they needed to subdue the women suffering from the side effects of the All-Clans serum.

Only now, they needed more. Neen had just used the last of it to knock out this raging Benglion. The woman was new to the camp, only a few days in, but it was clear when she first arrived that Herria's serum was having adverse effects on her. She constantly complained of headaches and often stayed on the library's second floor to sit in the darkness between the bookshelves.

Neen felt bad that she couldn't remember the woman's name. But now—locked in the cells—it was a long shot that the woman would ever recover and become a functional member of the colony. Once any of these refugee women reached the mania state, it was hard to control them. They were ticking time bombs, and Neen didn't want anyone near them when the bombs went off.

She looked at the mess on the floor, the plates and food scattered everywhere, the sunlight streaming in from the window panes that spanned the outer walls of the building. One section of glass had several hairline cracks, and another was broken completely, and all Neen could do was sag her shoulders and think of how they might go about repairing it. So much to do just to survive. At least the woman hadn't broken the window in her mania. A small mercy.

Breakfast would have to wait. Neen followed the other

women out of the library and into the main street. What they called "the cells" were a handful of holding cells in the local police station. After this latest incident, it was probably best if Neen went and checked on everything before she did her usual rounds.

It wasn't far from the library, but as she neared the crumbling facade of the police building, Neen's pace began to slow. Her stomach clenched as she thought about all the women locked inside. And one in particular.

The police building was like the firehouse. Concrete blocks, structurally sound, but rust and ruin taking their toll on everything inside. The cells were in the back, and Neen could hear the slow footsteps of Tollis and the other women as they carried their comrade to her cell. The hallway was dark and narrow. Paint had peeled off the cinderblock walls long ago. Grim. Neen hated coming here, hated what this place was for and what it meant. But she'd said she'd come, so she did.

"Damn." It just dawned on her that she'd forgotten the tea. Up ahead, the women were dragging the Benglion through the doorway to the cells. There was no door anymore. It had rotted away. Neen could hear the clank of the cell door opening, the muffled echo snaking down the hallway toward her.

She sucked in a deep breath without thinking, particles of mold and dust making her gag. It was getting harder and harder each time to walk these steps. But she had to. Whether it was guilt or duty or sorrow driving her on, she had to.

The hall seemed to stretch and constrict at the same time. It was just the darkness. The only light came from two high, thin windows near the ceiling in the office room behind her. There was just enough light to illuminate the hallway and a bit of the opening to the cell room. Just enough light to see faint shapes in the darkness. The women in the cells preferred it dark. The pressure in their heads and behind their eyes was lessened by the darkness.

She turned the corner into the cell room. The three women were laying the Benglion woman down in the last cell at the far end of the rectangular room. Six cells. All lined against the same wall. The steel bars had once been painted a metallic blue, but the paint had flaked away, and rust had begun to eat into the surface. Still, they were intact. Still strong enough to hold.

They were lucky the keys still worked too. They were brittle, which meant Neen didn't like to lock or unlock the cells too often, but they did what was needed.

All the cells were filled now. Neen stood in the doorway and watched as Tollis took the key and locked the Benglion woman away.

It was for the best. That's what they told themselves.

Neen nodded to the women as they trudged out. There was no denying the defeated feeling that drifted between them as they passed by her and went out.

Dron was sitting on the near side, his back against the cold concrete wall. A bit of the concrete had started to crumble, and the aluminum sink mounted on the wall next to him hung down as the wall around it had started to give way. He was looking across the room to the cell opposite. The first cell. He didn't react or seem to notice when Neen stepped tentatively toward its bars.

"Ems?" Neen tried to sound gentle, friendly. But anxiousness made her voice come out wrong. She half-swallowed Ems's name in a garbled, scratchy croak.

Inside, the cell was dark, almost too dark to see. There wasn't enough light from the hallway to reach it. But there was something in the corner, a small, almost child-like shape.

"Ems," Neen tried again. "How are you today?"

No answer.

"If you think you're ready, maybe you come out and get some sunshine."

Dron had told Neen a few weeks ago that Ems was practicing new techniques for relaxing her rage. And it was true; she hadn't had an outburst in days. Neen had just visited a couple of days ago, and Ems never lost control. But that was a couple of days ago. Today, Ems was like a ghost, hidden away in the dark recesses of her cell.

"She told me her mind is starting to break," Dron said, his voice quiet and pained. "I told her we wouldn't let that happen."

"We won't. I'll figure out something." Neen bit her lip as she remembered they were now out of the sedative and would need to make more. But how long could they continue drugging Ems and the others to keep them calm? The poppy tincture wasn't a remedy. It was only masking the actual disease.

Neen could feel the fury bubbling up from her chest into her throat.

Herria. The All-Clans serum. It was destroying her best friend—the only real friend she'd ever had—and she didn't know how to cure it. She could have raged at that moment, too, pulled the bars off the cell, and smashed them into dust.

"Ems, you're stronger than the serum," Neen said, wrapping her fingers around the cold, rough bars, pulling herself as close as she could to the cell. "I know you can hold it at bay. Just give me more time, and I'll find a cure."

Neen clung to a desperate hope, but it was all she had.

From out of the darkness, a soft, ragged voice spoke. "You

can say the words, Neen. But I know the truth. I can see it in your mind."

"I will find a way."

"It's a comforting lie." There was a subtle glee in Ems's voice as if she was enjoying reaching into Neen's mind and reading her thoughts.

Neen tried to close off her mind, but nothing could really stop Ems from getting in and seeing what she wanted.

"Ems." Dron came over. He sounded more like himself now. More playful, though the worry still lingered. "Let's go back to the meadow again. The butterflies. The smell of wild rosemary."

"And wet pine needles." Ems's voice was brighter. She shifted her body, moved closer to the bars.

Neen could see her outline more clearly. The soft white curls of her hair looked matted and gray in the shadows. Her round face was barely there, like the reflection of a ghost.

"Yeah, the wet pine needles," Dron said, coming to stand beside Neen. "I know that smell now too. What else do you remember?"

They were talking about Ems's childhood. Neen could see it clearly, too. She remembered those meadows, how she used to chase the butterflies when she was little. Their caregivers believed it was important for the young girls to get fresh air and lots of exercise, so they took them on outings into patches of wilderness around Teska. The air tasted good, and it was nice to run, but what Neen really loved was trying to catch the butterflies. They fascinated her. She wanted to catch each one and study it, get to know all she could. Her desire to know and connect seemed much easier with butterflies than with the other girls in her cohort.

But as fast as she ran, she could never catch one. Instead, she had to lie very still in the tall grass and wait for one to land. The first to do so was a small white one, which flitted about crazily until it settled on her grass-stained knee.

Ems had been there that day. She had whispered into Neen's ear, so quiet and calm that the butterfly was never disturbed, saying, "It's good luck, you know. One of the other girls told me. A white butterfly in spring."

Neen wondered now if the girl had told Ems, or if Ems had seen into the girl's mind. It didn't matter at the time, though. Neen had felt connected to the earth, to the butterfly, and to Ems, her only friend. Her own white butterfly.

Now she stood facing her best friend, a set of steel bars between them.

"I remember pressing my fingers into the dirt and feeling the wetness of the soil," Ems continued. "I felt like I was touching the earth's skin."

"Kinda soft when it's wet like that," Dron added.

"Yes, soft. It grew warmer as I kept my hand there."

"I'm gonna try that. Maybe today. Just lay out in the sun and rest my hands on the ground. You wanna come?"

Dron was so gentle with her. Neen knew this was Ems's method of controlling her rage. These talks with Dron, these exercises in memory. Sifting back into happier times.

She stepped aside, letting them have their time together.

Slowly, she moved down the row of cells. Most of the women inside were sedated or asleep. In the last cell, the Benglion woman was in a twilight state, mumbling to herself but otherwise calm. Neen listened closely to decipher her words.

"No... no... not now... give me time... I'm not ready... I don't want it... Please..." There was so much fear in her voice, so much helplessness.

It was hard to watch a tall, muscular Benglion woman—

genetically enhanced to be fearless and bold—whimpering like a frightened child. Neen knew what memory the woman was reliving. The serum. The forced injections. Herria's attempt at a master race of women.

It had to stop. It had to be cured. They didn't know exactly what would happen in the end to these women who were having mental breakdowns from the serum, but Ems had said her mind was breaking. Neen worried that it was all too true. At some point... a breaking point... And then?

No.

No, she wouldn't let it come to that. She'd find a way. She had to. It wasn't a comforting lie. Neen would make it happen. Somehow.

The sun outside was getting hotter the higher it climbed toward its zenith. The early morning pale yellows were gone now, and everything, from the ruins to the surrounding forests and mountains, was as vivid as a palette of fresh paint. Neen stood with her eyes closed and her face toward the sun just to let it soak into her skin. She needed it after the darkness of the cells.

The irony of what they were doing to the women affected by the All-Clans serum wasn't lost on her. But isn't this what humans always do when they feel threatened? Lock up the dangerous ones.

There was movement along the main road into town. Three figures jogging down from the mountain pass. Neen squinted to see them, her stomach tightening like it always did when she saw people coming from the wilderness. She never knew if this would be the moment their colony was finally discovered.

One of the figures waved a hand while the larger one beside her shook his head. They were drawing closer, and Neen knew them. The tightening in her stomach lessened.

"Li!" She waved back. Lekko was with her, his chiseled body like a piece of granite that had sprung legs and come to life. In these hotter summer days, he'd taken to walking around without a shirt on, putting his muscles on even greater display. It annoyed Neen, but she didn't say anything. Li thought it was hilarious and told him maybe she'd walk around without a shirt, too, if she got hot.

There was another woman with them; her jumpsuit was Benglion colored. As they strode down the main street, getting closer to Neen, she could see clearly that the woman was limping and pale. She was tall, as all Benglions were, but she had the look of someone who'd just gotten over a long illness. There was a thinness to her frame that suggested long bouts of hunger. Her hair was brown. Not quite the honeyed shade of Neen's, but close and just as long.

"We found her passed out in a little cove by one of the streams," Li said as they met Neen in the street. "Been on the run for over four weeks." Li sounded impressed.

"Name's Zumie," the woman said, holding out her hands for the traditional greeting for the women of EVE.

Neen returned her gesture, and the two women clasped hands. These new women always did the traditional greeting, and Neen never disabused them of the practice, but it felt odd to her, a vestige of an old life that they could never return to. Still, Zumie seemed friendly enough, if obviously exhausted and in need of food. The woman pretended otherwise, standing stiff and at attention like she was being sized up by her commanding officer, but Neen was no lieutenant.

"There's breakfast in the library," she told Zumie. "Lekko can show you."

Lekko grunted at this, but he didn't argue. Neen sometimes thought he played up his gruff attitude as a way to keep the women at bay. Li, on the other hand, was the one woman who could get him to smile. A rapport and respect had built up between Li and Lekko these past few months, making the integration between men and women a lot easier for Neen to manage.

"Don't talk her ear off, okay, Lekko?" Li joked. "Poor Zumie might want to get a word in or two."

Lekko grunted again, but there was a hint of a smile on his lips directed at Li.

"Scintillating conversation," Li said, winking.

When they were gone, Li's grinning face dropped, and she turned a sober expression in Neen's direction. "We have to talk."

Neen never liked hearing those words, but not liking them didn't make the situation go away.

"About Zumie?"

"No. She's fine. Managed to keep herself alive with barely anything but the clothes on her back. A survivor. That's what we need."

"Injections?"

"None. She got out before her number was called. Had no idea we even existed out here, just ran for the mountains and hoped for the best."

"That's good. I used the last of the sedative earlier on that other new arrival."

Li winced. "You can make more, right?"

"I can, but it takes time."

"Lekko and I can go out today and forage for those flowers."

"Thanks."

"We'll be alright. Just gotta hold on."

Neen nodded. "So if we're not talking about Zumie, what are we talking about?"

Li looked around to see if anyone was near. They stood in the middle of the town's main street, the sagging and crumbling storefronts all around them listening in, but nobody else.

"I found this." Li reached into her pack and pulled out a broken wrist screen, like the kind all the women of EVE wore for communication. The screen was cracked, and the soft wristband was caked in dried mud.

"I'm guessing that's not Zumie's."

"Good guess."

Neen took the broken device from Li and looked it over. "Doesn't seem operational. No chance it's surveilling us."

"Not the screen, no."

"But this screen didn't end up out here by accident."

"Screens usually don't. They're usually attached to someone."

Neen and Li locked eyes. The hot sun didn't feel good on Neen's skin now. Now it felt like a glaring eye, an oppressive force.

"Where'd you find it?" Neen asked.

"At the bottom of a cliff, about two miles south of here. One of the zones Lekko and I have started mapping. New territory."

"Could be a friendly. Like Zumie and the others."

"Could be."

Neither one said what they were thinking. They didn't have to. The thought was always on their minds. One day, any day, they could be discovered. After all, what was stopping Herria? She had all the cards to play.

"Maybe it's nothing," Neen said, more to herself than Li.

"Or maybe it's not."

Neen sighed. "Or maybe it's not."

"I got a feeling, Neen. I can't shake it. Lately, when I've

gone out scouting, I can feel eyes watching me. Keeping tabs. Waiting."

"Waiting for what?"

"I don't know," Li answered. "But I don't want to find out."

ABOUT THE AUTHOR

Hello there, I'm Melanie.

By day, I'm diving into the world of molecular cell biology with a Ph.D., and by night, I'm an author.

When I'm not in the lab or typing away, I'm on the sports field – volleyball, handball, tennis, soccer, you name it, I play it. My family and I love exploring the world: fun fact, I met my husband during a trip around the world, in Bolivia to be specific.

Off the clock, I like to relax with my good friend, popcorn, and indulging in my favorites: chocolate, space, family and coffee. Please come along for the ride in my stories.

Thanks for being part of it!

ACKNOWLEDGMENTS

Thank you to my amazing husband, Ran, for supporting me with this crazy project, and my children Emma, Tommy, and Mia for putting up with me while I write at night.

Thanks to Grandpa Yossi for being there for my children.

Thank you, Mams, my mother Ina for always being there for me. *Always.*

And Rina and Larry, I wish you were here. I love you.

Made in the USA
Coppell, TX
18 May 2026

77778027R00184